DATE			

THE DONS
AND MR. DICKENS

THE
DONS
  AND
MR. DICKENS

The Strange Case of the Oxford Christmas Plot

A Secret Victorian Journal,
Attributed to Wilkie Collins

Discovered and Edited by
WILLIAM J. PALMER

St. Martin's Minotaur
New York

www.minotaurbooks.com

Library of Congress Cataloging-in-Publication Data

Palmer, William J.
    The dons and Mr. Dickens : the strange case of the Oxford Christmas plot : a secret Victorian journal, attributed to Wilkie Collins / discovered and edited by William J. Palmer.—1st St. Martin's minotaur ed.
        p.   cm.
    ISBN 0-312-26576-X
    1. Collins, Wilkie, 1824–1889—Fiction. 2. Dickens, Charles, 1812–1870—Fiction. 3. Oxford (England)— Fiction. 4. College teachers—Fiction. 5. Novelists— Fiction. I. Title: Dons and Mister Dickens. II. Title.

PS3566.A547 D6 2000
823'.8—dc21

00-040520

First Edition: November 2000

10 9 8 7 6 5 4 3 2 1

For Christy. Are you happy now?

EDITOR'S NOTE

The origins and provenance of these "Secret Victorian Journals" of Wilkie Collins have been clearly described in the editor's prefaces to the three earlier volumes in this series. This editor, however, once again wishes to express his deepest appreciation to Mr. Allerdyce Clive, the Special Collections Curator of the library of the University of North Anglia, for his professional assistance and his support of completely open editorial access to these manuscripts.

Collins's first commonplace book, published under the commercial title *The Detective and Mr. Dickens,* was composed almost immediately after Dickens's funeral in 1870. The other journals, all of which reside in the Sir William Warrington Collection (Sir William having been the personal solicitor of Wilkie Collins), were composed between 1870 and Collins's death in 1889. All are handwritten. They seem to have provided Collins with a vehicle for memory of his mentor and closest friend, Charles Dickens. Although composed in the 1870s and 1880s, these journals narrate events that actually took place in the 1850s when Collins was but a young aspiring novelist still learning his art from the greatest writer of the age.

The three previously published journals each described a specific case of detection undertaken by Dickens and his detective friend, Inspector William Field of the Metropolitan Protectives, London's first professional police force. Two of those volumes also explored a sensitive subtext, that of Dickens's growing love for and involvement with Miss Ellen Ternan, a young actress who would become Dickens's mistress for the last seventeen years of his life. Miss Ternan plays a prominent part in this latest journal as well. Also, the previously published journals introduced a rogues' gallery of friends, colleagues, and criminals with whom Dickens and Field consistently interacted.

The Detective and Mr. Dickens, the first published journal, which recounted the case of the theatre district murders that the Victorian tabloids christened "The Macbeth Murders," introduced Serjeant Rogers, Field's loyal second in command; Irish Meg Sheehey, a street prostitute and one of Field's prized informers; and Tally Ho Thompson, a reformed highwayman and professional thief-turned-actor who nonetheless cannot seem to resist the continued practice of the tricks of his former trades.

In *The Highwayman and Mr. Dickens,* Irish Meg had become Wilkie Collins's kept mistress and Tally Ho Thompson became the central suspect in a murder case which the Grub Street tabloids christened "The Medusa Murders." Also in this second journal, the personages of Sleepy Rob the cabman, and Captain Hawkins and his loyal Serjeant, Bert Moody (and Bert's obscene parrot), were introduced.

In *The Hoydens and Mr. Dickens,* which involved the affair of "The Feminist Phantom," as the newspapers of the time called it, the reader was introduced to Angela Burdett-Coutts, heiress to and manager of Coutts Bank, and one of the most powerful women in Victorian England. That third memoir chronicles the solving of a murder within the burgeoning Victorian feminist movement.

What is different about these commonplace books in terms of literary history is that they are not written in the usual abbreviated diary form that characterizes the vast majority of the private journals of the eighteenth and nineteenth centuries. Rather, Collins chose to compose his private journals in a novelistic style (complete with chapter-like divisions, narrative structures, and realistic dialogue) parallel to that of his novel manuscripts. These "secret journals," as Collins has called them in earlier prefaces, were clearly never meant for publication until long after their participants were dead, if ever. And Collins was fully cognizant of the fact that the absence of any publishing ambitions for the journals freed him to compose them with little or no regard for the repressive inhibitions which so limited both the style and subject matter of Victorian fiction.

As did the first three Collins commonplace books, this memoir begins with a brief preface set in the time of composition (the 1870s) rather than the time of the actual narrated events (1853). Typically, the opening meditation focuses upon the impetus that catalyzed his memories of the particular case and set him to writing once again. As he consistently reiterates, these private journals are about the evocative power of memory. They are Wilkie Collins's way of bringing back to life his closest friend and the most powerful influence upon his career. This series of personal factual mini-novels dramatizes that great man's biography as no biographer ever could.

THE DONS
AND MR. DICKENS

"PREFATORIES"

(November 1, 1871)

It is All Saints Day as I sit down once again to begin filling another little leather book from Lett's Apothecary and Sundries. What more fitting day to take the time to remember one's closest friend so prematurely gone? What more fitting day to remember one of the great (and good) men of our strange dark age? None of us was a saint then, but we were gentlemen all, and trying to do the right thing.

I remember a conversation we once had about how somebody had to stand up for the right. I can see it as if it were only yesterday, the four of us—Field and Rogers, Dickens and myself—in the Lord Gordon Arms. I think, if memory serves, that this particular evening occurred just after the unsatisfactory resolution of the first "Dr. Palmer the Poisoner" affair.[1] I remember that the whole conversation be-

---

[1]Dr. William Palmer was suspected of poisoning his wife and her maid in the case of "The Medusa Murders," which is detailed in Collins's second journal (published as *The Highwayman and Mr. Dickens*). But that case was never resolved and Dr. Palmer went free for lack of evidence. However, here Collins refers to the "first" Dr. Palmer affair, seeming to imply that

gan with Field expressing his frustration at the outcome of that case.

"Don't seem worth the effort goin' after rich gentlemen like Ashbee[2] and that Dr. Palmer, does it?" Field complained. "We brought neither of 'em to the dock."

"Then why do you do it?" Dickens asked.

"Because I won't be just a policeman of the poor." Field's voice was serious, almost sad. "But these rich scofflaws prey upon the poor and the innocent, kill their own wives, for God's sake!"

I know this was an especially tender subject for Field because he had lost his own beloved wife to consumption some years before.

"They are bad laws that protects the rich and only punishes the poor"—he thumped decisively on the table with his thick forefinger—"and that ain't right. Our slippery Dr. Palmer should be on his way to the gallows!"

"But what can be done?" Dickens tried to console him. "There was no evidence to be found, no witnesses left alive."

"Aye. No one knows that better than me." Field had that set look of relentless pursuit in his eye that we had seen many times before. "This time 'ee escapes, but 'ee shall never escape me. Someday 'ee will murder again and William Field will be waiting there to take 'im up."

"But it seems so unjust," Dickens opined, "as if God has just disappeared from our world."

"Ah, but you must learn, Dickens," and Inspector Field's gruff voice had calmed to an almost philosophical resignation, "that my world, the streets, is not the world of your novels. In my world, God truly is gone and all the villains

---

this particular villain and Field met again. They certainly did, since Field arrested Palmer for poisoning his fourth wife in 1855 (see the final footnote on the last page of *The Highwayman and Mr. Dickens*).

[2]Lord Henry Ashbee, the villain of the very first case upon which Dickens and Collins accompanied Inspector Field, that of "The Macbeth Murders," published as *The Detective and Mr. Dickens*.

do not get punished and all the crimes do not get solved and all the women are not angels and all their lovers are not always faithful. It is a world where everything does not get tied up neatly with a ribbon on the last page," and he chuckled at the cleverness of his thought.

"Yet even you," Dickens's voice was quiet, "in your determination to pursue this Palmer, express a sense of an ending, a clear need for resolution."

"You can't always end things right," Rogers broke in.

"The only sense of an ending I 'ave is death," Field laughed as he rose to go, "and it's one I don't want written for many more chapters."

That evening, as Dickens and I walked home through the gaslit city smoking our cigars, he could not let the subject rest. It had gotten under his collar and was chafing his sense of justice.

"Wilkie, we have been on duty with Inspector Field on two cases where a rich and powerful villain has escaped unpunished. Can the rich get away with anything? Have the poor no rights? They starve in our cities. We send them off to fight our wars and die on foreign fields. But our rich get away with murder."

"But Field has not given up." I tried to interject a positive point into what I sensed for Dickens was becoming almost a statement of his own social despair.

"No, Wilkie, but I feel sorry for Inspector Field. He is a fair man at the mercy of the courts and a country that is still unfair."

That evening was one of those rare moments when we Victorian gentlemen actually unburdened ourselves. Ours is such a reticent age. We always seem to be narrating ourselves from a safe distance. In a way, it was that sort of recognition of the unjust reality of our world that lay at the very heart of the Oxford affair.

This particular episode in Charles's and my relationship with Inspector Field is, perhaps, the one I remember most fondly. In those years, when I was but an apprentice novelist, it was a rare time that I ever commanded the stage over either Dickens or Field. But in this instance, I was the one who knew the territory, who could read the text of the world. Oxford was very familiar to me, for I had resided there with little respect and no distinction at Brasenose for two years before coming up to London.

A MURDER IN LIMEHOUSE HOLE

%

(November 25, 1853 — Evening)

I t had been a regular *Bleak House* day all day in London.
Implacable November weather, indeed! Dickens had described it "inimitably" only eighteen months earlier in
the opening of his great novel of the city. I remember all
of that day vividly, not just the shocking events of the evening. As I look out my window here in 1871, I can almost
see back to 1853 and the day on which the Oxford affair
began.

The entire city of London was smothered in a heavy blanket of fog. Just stepping outside one's doorway was dangerous. It was a dirty and diseased metropolis. It seemed that
London could not stop growing in those days, that the people would not stop coming, that the houses would not stop
falling down, that the poor and the sick would not stop
begging and dying in the streets, that the dust would not
stop accumulating in the doorways and alleys, that the
smoke would not stop blackening the buildings, that the
criminals would not stop preying upon the innocent and
unsuspecting, that the rush of Victorian commerce would
stop for no one and threatened to carry us all away.

London that long-ago November was indeed an oppressive place, but this particular affair of detection in which Dickens and I once again would go "on duty with Inspector Field"[3] would be the first "case" which actually forced Field to expand his sphere of detective influence outside the city.

That particular implacable November day, Dickens and I had barricaded ourselves in the *Household Words* offices on Wellington Street. For once in his life, Dickens seemed to be on top of the game. He actually seemed happy, not his customary restless self. Catherine and the children had chosen to remain at Broadstairs until mid-December in hopes that the sea air would be more beneficial to her faltering health than the pestilential mists of London. The new passenger trains that seemed to be going so many places did not yet travel to Broadstairs. So, pleading the hardship of winter travel, Dickens went to the family only every other week's end. But the real reason for his happiness was that his distance from his domestic hearth gave him more time to spend with his beloved Ellen, more time to lavish upon that May–December relationship, which those who knew him (besides myself and Irish Meg, who already knew for certain) such as Angela Burdett-Coutts, Wills, Thackeray, Forster, Macready, were beginning to suspect had gone beyond the benevolent interest of an older patron or guardian for his young ward.

On that particular implacable November day of which I write, Ellen Ternan had just closed in Macready's *The Taming of the Shrew,* in which she had played three small parts. But she was an established member of the company and was just waiting for the getting up of the next offering, which was rumoured to be a Sheridan comedy.

That is not to say that Charles's instinctive restlessness was completely subdued. He still took his frequent night walks,

[3]Collins's placing of this phrase in quotation marks signals a direct reference to a series of four articles under that title written by Charles Dickens, which appeared in *Household Words* in August to October of 1850.

only he did not as often ask me to accompany him, and, I only speculate, his evening walks frequently had a precise destination (the backstage door at Covent Garden), and he did not always return home, to the *Household Words* offices that is, until the following morning. Indeed, one morning I actually arrived at the offices a bit early, at eight instead of my usual time, and met Dickens at the doorstep, just coming in. He made some hurried excuse that he had just gone out for some air, but the state of his clothes when he removed his greatcoat indoors gave a different evidence. (Who knows? Maybe I was somewhat of a detective after all.)

As for me, I was bored, even somewhat confused. Irish Meg had been at work in her clerk's job at Coutts Bank for almost eleven months and each day seemed a new carnival for her in the bustling theatre of commerce. What bothered me, I suppose, is that she seemed so pleased with herself in her new life and so little concerned with me and the life we had shared together for so long.

On that day in question, however, Dickens and I had truly battened down the hatches at the *Household Words* office when Inspector Field, his pull-toy Serjeant Rogers, and our latest case came a-knocking. It was probably about five in the afternoon because dusk was already taking the city into custody when I descended the stairs from Dickens's second-storey office–cum–living quarters to open the door upon Field and Rogers.

"Wilkie, is 'ee 'ere?" Field demanded. "I think the two of you can be of 'elp to us on this 'un," he explained as I ushered them in and up the stairs.

"Field, what is it?" Dickens met us at the top.

All of our editorial work was forgotten, the dinner which we had not yet ordered was forgotten, the brutality of the weather was forgotten, perhaps even his Ellen was momentarily forgotten, because from the excited look on Charles's face as he extended his welcoming hand to Field, it was clear that he sensed we were about to embark on another case of detection.

"We 'ave a murder in Lime'ouse 'Ole," Field went straight to the point.

Rogers and I exchanged glances: his, as usual, tight-lipped and grim; mine, as usual, fraught with alarm.

"Chinaman?" Dickens shot right back at him.

"No, and that is why I've come for your 'elp, the two of you," and he nodded in my direction as a way of including me whether I desired to be included or not.

"If it is not a Chinaman dead in Limehouse Hole," Dickens pursued his line of inquiry, "then who is it?"

"A white man, not a yellow man," Serjeant Rogers solemnly pronounced.

"A rather well-dressed, full-bearded, bespectacled man, without a single paper of identification upon 'im," Field gave a full description. "I'd 'oped that you two might come and take a look at 'im. Per'aps you can see something that Rogers and I can't see."

"Yes, of course." Dickens was absolutely gleeful. "Wilkie, our coats."

But Field stopped him in mid-rush as he was scrambling for his waistcoat.

"We'll go in the Protectives' coach, Charles. I've got two constables guarding the corpse," and his voice took on a tone of warning, "but you've got to be careful down there. It is Chinatown, you know, and you never quite know what is going on. Stay in our shadows. If anything out of the common 'appens, let Rogers and me 'andle it."

"Fine. We understand perfectly, don't we, Wilkie?" And he nodded his head with an eager anticipation that I did not at all share.

"A gentleman murdered in Limehouse Hole," Dickens mused aloud as he climbed into the police coach whose horses stood like smoke-breathing dragons tethered to a gas lamp at the curbstone. "Rather unusual that, eh?"

"Oh yes, quite," Field answered as he too climbed in. "Gentlemen only go to Lime'ouse for one thing, and the

Chinee usually see to it that they stay safe so they can come back."

"The smoke?" Dickens asked.

"That's it," Field replied.

And with that, Rogers shut us into the coach, climbed up on the box, clicked his whip out over the pair's ears, and we were off.

THE TELLTALE CRAVAT

ॐ

(November 25, 1853—Evening)

Field's police coach carried us rapidly out of the West End. We struck out of Wellington Street and crossed the Strand, rolled along Fleet Street past the Royal Courts of Justice and down Ludgate Hill towards St. Paul's, but at the bottom of the hill Rogers swerved the horses sharply towards the river and we pulled up beneath the stone hulk of Blackfriars Bridge.

As we rode through the fog-choked city, Dickens pressed Field for more information about the murder.

"How was this gentleman killed?" Dickens began.

"Shot with a revolver, from in front, close in, we think. The bullet seems to 'ave gone clear through 'im."

"That is odd. Would a Chinaman use a pistol? Do Chinamen even own pistols?"

"You're absolutely right." Field grinned at Dickens's solemn deductive concentration. "The Chinee tend more toward sharp knives and throats slit from behind."

"Do you think it was a robbery?" Dickens plunged ahead with his detecting, undeterred by Field's amusement. "You said there was not a piece of identification upon the corpse."

"Nothing. Not a purse, nor even a stray card or scrap of foolscap."

"Were there signs of a scuffle, of violence before the shot was fired?" To my great surprise, that was my voice asking.

"None at all," Field answered. "That is what is so strange. It is as if someone just walked up and shot 'im, then cleaned out 'is pockets after. Most of London's strong-armers don't operate that way at all."

"It might well have been someone he knew." Dickens was not really addressing either Field or me, but rather just musing aloud. "Shot at close range from in front."

"Per'aps," Field affirmed Dickens's reasoning, "but in this beastly fog someone could be upon you before you even saw them."

It was on that pronouncement that our coach pulled up on the river embankment.

We disembarked at the head of a wide river stair, at the bottom of which waited a Thames River Police longboat with four burly constables at the oars. It obviously had been placed at Inspector Field's disposal by one of his counterparts on the River Police.

The fog hung over the river like a shroud as we pushed off from those wide stone stairs. As we picked up speed downriver under the rhythmic beating of the oars, the skeleton of the new iron railway bridge protruded out of the fog as if its limbs were hung on the city's enormous gibbet.

We landed at a tumbledown dock somewhere and quickly went ashore like buccaneers.

In three steps out of the boat we were swallowed up by the fog. Nonetheless, Field and Rogers were able to lead us through a succession of narrow streets between cobbled-together shacks and crumbling tenements directly to the corpse. It lay on its back in the middle of a dark alleyway with a blood-encrusted hole right through its heart. It looked as if it might simply be sleeping, but on closer inspection it was, indeed, quite dead. Every time I saw a corpse (and since becoming associated with Field we had seen quite a few), I could not help but think how its stillness, its coldness, attested to the terrible fragility of our lives.

Two of Field's constables presided over the body, and though the thick fog effectually veiled us from sight, one had a sense that eyes were upon us, watching, suspicious of these buccaneers from the river who had invaded their domain. But though the night was dark, in his sharp brown hat that shadowed his sharp detective's eyes, Field's gaze cut through that fog the way those new railways slice through the English countryside.

"There's our body, gentlemen." Field pointed straight ahead with his exceedingly sharp forefinger as we approached.

Field went to his knee beside the corpse, and Dickens immediately followed suit right on Field's shoulder as if he were some kind of perching tropical bird. Having little choice in the matter, I circled round and, much to my distaste, went to my own knee on the other side of the corpse opposite Dickens and Field. Serjeant Rogers was momentarily off talking to the constables who had been standing guard, so the three of us were alone with the unfortunate dead man.

We all stared down at the body. It seemed an ordinary enough corpse. The man was generously bearded, bespectacled, and very white in death. Once one sees that sickly white pallor for the first time, one never needs any other test to prove that a fellow human being has departed this life. This dead man was dressed in a staid, rather well-tailored dark blue suit and vest, a grey soft cambric shirt with a detachable white button collar, and a rather bright blue cravat. He was, indeed, a rather dapper corpse, as if he had gotten himself up in his best clothes to come out on this bitter night and be murdered.

"Why, he's an Oxford man!" I heard my own voice speaking out. "Christ Church. Not my college, but I'd know it anywhere."

Both Field and Dickens gaped at me in surprise at this confident revelation. But Inspector Field quickly collected himself. He seemed about to interrogate me when a curious thing happened.

A young, rather portly man materialized out of the fog and stood over us as we knelt by the corpse. This man was escorted by the ever efficient Serjeant Rogers.

"Sorry, sir, but 'ee insisted, sir," Rogers rushed his excuses in before this newcomer could explain himself and his interruption of our deliberation over the corpse. " 'Ee said 'ee was 'Ome Office, 'ee did."

" 'Ome Office?" Field looked up questioningly at this stout apparition in his quite official-looking dark suit, high beaver hat, and pointed umbrella.

"Yes. Holmes, Mycroft Holmes," the young man introduced himself, and extended his hand to Inspector Field, who in the meanwhile had risen to his feet to confront this intruder, "and I am, indeed, a member of the Home Office."

"Field," and he gave the young man's hand a shake. "William Field, Bow Street Station, Protectives," he identified himself and, ever utterly direct, posed the question that stood at attention in all of our minds: "What brings ye 'ere on this bitter night?"

This Holmes was indeed a rather young man, no more than twenty-three or -four, I think. He was a rotund, rosy personage, built upon the model of Humpty Dumpty, but he was very composed for such an ingenue and did not in the least flinch at Field's directness.

"One of my men was apprised of this unfortunate affair this afternoon by the River Police, much, I presume, in the same manner that you, Inspector Field, were called in," Mr. Holmes politely explained. "Since the Home Office presently has an interest in this Oriental section of our city, this rather untypical murder of a white man down here caught my attention."

"It did?" Field answered rather dully. I observed that the formidable Inspector, for one of the few times in my experience of him, seemed at sea and did not quite know how to proceed.

"Yes." Young Holmes, sensing Field's rising suspicions, immediately set out to reassure the policeman. "But I do not mean to intrude in any way upon your investigation of this terrible murder. I simply wish to observe, to share in any insight you might have into the affair."

"Might I ask why?" Dickens stepped in since Field still did not seem to have his wits about him in the face of this rather superior yet surpassingly polite young representative of the British Empire.

"And you are, sir?" Holmes turned equally politely to Dickens.

Dickens, in turn, was a bit taken aback at not being immediately recognized: "Why, Charles Dickens."

Now it was young Mr. Mycroft Holmes's turn to be surprised and unprepared, even slightly embarrassed.

"Charles Dickens, why, yes, of course. I certainly should have recognized you, sir, but I did not expect, you see, I mean, here, in Limehouse Hole..." young Holmes hemmed and hawed. "My great pleasure, Mr. Dickens, to make your acquaintance sir," our startled young public servant stammered to his end.

This whole exchange put a completely new complexion upon this rather unlikely meeting of three such separate minds in the fog. It certainly clarified for me why Field so carefully nurtured Dickens's friendship. Having someone as famous as Dickens at his side gave Inspector Field a credibility and power over anyone who might momentarily feel that he held the upper hand.

Young Holmes pumped Dickens's hand ardently, meanwhile mumbling all manner of compliments of the "I have read all of your books" sort. Dickens's presence seemed to have overthrown this young literary-minded government official's officious mastery of the situation. Dickens and Field exchanged a quick but significant look. Field gave Dickens a quick nod, which I interpreted as permission to proceed.

"I asked why you, and the Home Office, are so interested in this affair?" Dickens's question tugged young Mr. Holmes back to his official reserve, which had momentarily melted in the heat of his admiration for Dickens's art.

"I am sorry, gentlemen," young Holmes regained his formality by tugging down on the tips of his vest beneath his waistcoat and thus stiffening his whole posture, "but I am not yet at liberty to say what the Home Office's interest in Limehouse Hole is. All I can say is that it might, possibly, sometime in the future, involve matters of national security."

"So," and Field now had regained his power it seemed, "you wants to sit in on this murder case, and you wants me to tell you all I come to know about it, but you won't even tell me why?"

"Precisely," and young Holmes favored us all with a radiant smile.

"Bloody 'ell," Field cursed softly as he turned to Dickens and me, "sounds like we 'ave no choice at all in the matter."

Young Holmes did not say anything right away, just smiled benignly around at all of us, even Serjeant Rogers. "Please go on with your investigation," he finally prompted us, breaking the awkward silence. "I am sorry to intrude. I will only observe and listen, I assure you."

"Where were we?" Dickens was the first to go back down to his knee beside the corpse.

"Wilkie, you said 'ee was an Oxford man." Field also resumed his position at ground level.

"Yes," I answered eagerly, forgetting all about young Mr. Holmes's eavesdropping presence, "he's wearing a college necktie, a Christ Church cravat," and I went to my knee and extracted the cravat out from beneath the corpse's bloody vest. "See," and I showed it to Dickens and Field. "It is the Christ Church College emblem, the Tom Tower," and I pointed out with my finger the arrangement of little gold towers on the royal blue fabric.

"Wot's a Tom Tower?" Field asked.

"It is one of the gatehouse towers at Christ Church College, built by Sir Christopher Wren."

A blank look had invaded Dickens's face, for though he was one of the greatest men of letters of our age he was embarrassingly unschooled, had never been a university man, had left the regimen of formal education at the tender age of twelve years.

"It is Henry the Eighth's college," I was enjoying being the center of their attention. "We just call it 'the House.' It is one of the most prestigious and certainly the best endowed of all the new colleges at Oxford."

"New colleges?" From the look upon Dickens's face, he was asking out of genuine curiosity.

"Oh yes," I lectured on. "The oldest Oxford colleges—Trinity, Balliol, Magdalen—go all the way back to the twelfth century, when the French threw all of the English scholars out of the University of Paris."

" 'Ow do you know all of this?" Field interjected.

"I was at Oxford for almost two years before I came up to the city. Can't say I studied very much of anything while I was there, but I frequented a hard lot of public houses, and attended a goodly number of college parties, and went punting on sunny afternoons, and got to know a great many people."

"What do you mean, this Christ Church is one of the new colleges?" Dickens was still puzzled. "How many colleges are there, anyway?"

"Oh, dozens. Each college has its own quadrangle, its own dons, its own library. They are like little walled cities. I lived at Brasenose College. Ah, they were a group of revellers, known for it, in fact. Stout fellows all."

"Do you know this man, perchance?" Field interrupted my digressive excursion down the memory lane of my misbegotten youth. "Look closely at 'im," he commanded.

I did as I was so brusquely directed, but the man was dead and exceedingly white, and I am not sure if my eyes were

16

capable of actually seeing a living human being within that waxy corpse.

"No, I do not think so," I stammered. "He looks familiar, but I . . . in this light . . . him like that . . . I just do not know," and I stood up away from the corpse, shrugging my hands out to my sides. It was when I stood up that I noticed that our mysterious friend from the Home Office, young Holmes, was gone. "Where did he go?" I asked no one in particular.

" 'Ee's gone," Serjeant Rogers exclaimed vehemently as if some street criminal he had taken into custody had escaped. It was as if the man had just disappeared into the fog. Rogers had been standing right next to him as we worked at the body and still had not seen him go.

"That's an odd duck, that is," Field muttered.

"Good riddance to him, I would say," Dickens shrewdly said what he thought Inspector Field wanted to hear, I am sure.

"Nothing more we can do 'ere," Field put the top on it. "Let's get out of this damp. Rogers, clean up this mess," and he gestured negligently down at that poor dead soul; "we'll be at the Lord Gordon Arms."

THE LORD GORDON ARMS

(November 25, 1853—Late Evening)

Ever since we had made our acquaintance with Field more than three years before, the Lord Gordon Arms, a quite cozy public house sequestered in Maiden Lane just off the south end of Covent Garden market, within close walking distance of the Bow Street Police Station, had been our place of refuge from the beastly vagaries of the London weather. This night, the warm hearth and the sumptuously stuffed chairs around the Lord Gordon's stout oak tables provided an exceptionally welcome refuge. In other words, I was, as I am sure Dickens and Field were as well, chilled to the bone when we arrived. But in the Lord Gordon, Field was finally ready to talk, and Dickens, as ever, was all ears.

Yet, for once, much to my satisfaction, it was to me that Inspector Field wanted to talk, and to me that he addressed his remarks, without the slightest need for Charles's presence.

"Wilkie," he began, " 'ow can we find out who this dead Oxford bloke is?"

I thought on that a moment, and then a gas lamp went on in my brain.

"I know just the fellow," I exclaimed eagerly.

Field reacted with a stiff poke of his ferocious forefinger to the crow's foot at the side of his right eye. Dickens smiled in grim patience, waiting, I am positive, for his opening to enter the dialogue.

"And who might that be?" Field prompted.

"Old Dodo." I had to grin as I said it, and I thoroughly enjoyed the momentarily startled looks on their faces as I pronounced that eccentric name.

"Dodo?" Dickens sourly repeated, as if questioning the efficacy of ever asking an idiot like me a serious question about the science of detection.

"Oh yes, Old Dodo," I grinned with maddening relish.

"Who is 'ee?" Field barked. "And 'ow old is 'ee?"

"Oh, not old at all," I laughed, though Field's tone was a clear signal that I was to get on with it, "rather young, actually. Only now in his early twenties. Quite a prodigy really. Only seventeen years old when he first came up to Oxford. I was a fully corrupted twenty-four before I got there. One did not need to be a genius to see that he really was a genius."

"That is all well and good," Field prodded me, "but who is 'ee?"

"Dodgson. Charlie Dodgson. A strange bird, he is. That's why all of us, the Oxford literary fellows, called him Old Dodo."

"And why is 'ee our man?" Field sipped at his gin even as he was finishing his question, much more relaxed now that I was well underway.

"Because he's Christ Church, that's why," I answered as if it was the most obvious thing in the world. "He's a Teaching Fellow at the House. He will soon be a Don, I'll wager. Mathematics. He lives right in that very Tom Tower that is emblazoned on our dead man's cravat."

"And 'ow do you know this Dodgson?" Field pressed, with just the slightest hint in his voice of the skepticism that had momentarily flooded Dickens's face.

"Charlie Dodgson is really a good fellow," I assured them. "There was a whole group of us. We called ourselves the Ill Literates. All writers. Mostly poetry. Well, Charlie Dodgson was one of us. If you were as sharp a poet at Oxford as Charlie, it made no difference how old you were."

"I thought he was in Mathematics?" Dickens interrupted, trying to take a bit of my stage, I am sure.

"Yes, he is, but Charlie Dodgson is so brilliant that he can do anything. He writes poetry, he paints, he looks at the stars through a telescope in his window. But he is a regular fellow. He likes his pints. We would meet many a night in the taverns around Oxford to drink and laugh and talk about the latest books and read our latest poems. The King's Arms. The Turf behind New College. The Bulldog right across St. Aldate's from Dodo's rooms in the Tom Tower." I had been carried away like a punt on the Thames with the nostalgia of it all.

"Yes, well, 'ee seems like 'ee's our man," Field affirmed my enthusiasm.

"He seems like an absolute Leonardo." Even Dickens could not resist my excited nostalgia.[4]

"I am sure he will help us," I pushed my advantage. "If this murdered man is truly a Christ Church man, then Charlie Dodgson will know him."

"Wilkie, would you—I know this is awfully short notice—be able to accompany this corpse to Oxford on the railway tomorrow?" Field paused, thinking. "And, of course, you as well, Charles, if you can get away," he added as an afterthought.

"Of course, I would be happy to visit my old haunts," I answered immediately.

---

[4]Charles Dodgson truly was a prodigy. He matriculated at Christ Church, Oxford, in 1849 at the age of seventeen. He took up residence in the Tom Tower in 1851 and lived there the rest of his life as student, mathematics lecturer, sub-librarian, and ordained deacon. In 1853, he became the youngest lecturer in the history of the college, at the age of twenty-one.

You cannot imagine, dear reader, the satisfaction I felt at being declared the leader of this expedition. I was simply afraid that Dickens would not be able to go along as my valet. But Dickens was not about to pass up an opportunity to once again go on duty with Inspector Field.

"Of course, I can get away as well," Dickens answered rather glumly, lacking his usual enthusiasm, I am sure, because he was not, in this instance, the one in control.

"Dispatched to Oxford then, it is." Field raised his glass to his two willing irregulars. "Rogers, see that the body is in the railway car when the Oxford train departs tomorrow morning," he ordered his serjeant, who had come in out of the cold fog as we were speaking.

"What exactly do you want us to do there?" Dickens asked.

"Accompany the body to the Oxford Protectives' station. There was an Oxford constable down 'ere only a few weeks ago. Collar,[5] that fool, brought 'im around to observe our ways of doin' things. 'Ee seemed a good man. 'Ad a pommie name, though. Reginald, that was it. Reginald"—he thought on it a moment—"Morse, yes that's it, Morse. Use my name, and Collar's too if you must, but this Morse was very keen on detective work and I'm sure 'ee'll 'elp us out." Field paused a moment to think.

"And then we hunt up Wilkie's friend Dodgson, I presume." Dickens did not wait for Field to complete his thought.

"Yes, find 'im and take 'im to identify the body."

"And then?" I spoke up just to let them know that I was still there.

"And then we will 'ave to decide wot to do next," Field snapped.

---

[5]Inspector Collar, who first appeared in Dickens's and Collins's most recent adventure with Inspector Field (commercially titled *The Hoydens and Mr. Dickens*), was Field's counterpart at the St. James' Station in central London.

This time Dickens waited for Field to complete his thought.

"If your mathematical friend knows the dead man, where 'ee lives, can tell us something about 'is 'abits and 'aunts, then we will know 'ow to get on with it. If the fellow lived in Oxford and was just visitin' London, then maybe we'll 'ave to move our investigations up there. I'll 'ave to see wot you two find out."

"What do we do after we talk to Charlie?" I asked.

"Yes, what if young Dodgson does know the murdered man, what if the dead man is from Oxford, from Christ Church even?" I was always amazed at how quickly Dickens caught on to things.

Field took a deep, meditative draught from his mug of hot gin.

"Wotever 'appens. Whether all that proves true or not," Field plotted our course, "you two come back 'ere to London on the evenin' train, and I'll decide wot we do next. We will keep this murder as quiet as possible until you get back and we know wot we've got."

"Done." Dickens smiled as wide as a milk-gorged cat and turned eagerly to me. "Oh Wilkie, this is an unexpected adventure to brighten up the gloomiest time of the year."

I certainly could not disagree with him on that, and I must admit I was eagerly looking forward to this Oxford jaunt. I had been very happy there and I was sure that my young friend Dodgson would help us to identify this poor man with the bullet hole in his heart.

All of that settled, there was but a momentary lull in this discourse as the publican refortified our tumblers of hot gin. It was not long, however, until Dickens brought us back to another of the mysteries of that foggy evening.

"What do you suppose our friend Holmes of the Home Office who appeared out of nowhere tonight was after?" Charles posed the question for the general consideration of everyone at the table.

" 'Ee wos a queer duck, wosn't 'ee?" Rogers chimed in.

"Yes," Field speculated "and wot is the 'Ome Office doin' in Lime'ouse 'Ole? Those blokes in their frock coats and weskets never leave White'all. 'Ow did 'ee get wind of this?" Field wondered aloud. "And why did 'ee care?"

"He appeared and disappeared out of the fog like some kind of a portly phantom," Dickens chuckled.

"That 'ee did," Field grinned at the idea. "Perhaps 'ee is our murderer." We all had a good laugh at that possibility.

We finished our drinks in a rather subdued languor, as if the strain of the night and all our plotting had drained our strength.

"It is time to go," Field finally declared, emptying his tumbler of gin. "We 'ave got more work to do on this tonight," and he nodded to his faithful Rogers, "and you two must get up at dawn to catch the railway to Oxford."

I was more than grateful to see an end to this long and complicated evening. I hoped that Irish Meg was waiting up for me when I arrived at home in Soho Square. But I was not too confident of her. Since she had taken to honest work in Miss Burdett-Coutts's bank, she had been much less ardent in her attentions towards me.

I bid goodnight to Dickens beneath the gas lamp under the windows of his Wellington Street offices.

"I shall collect you at your rooms tomorrow morning at eight, Wilkie," he directed me, ever the leader, unable to take any other position in the regiment. "I think we will take Sleepy Rob with us to Oxford. We will need dependable transportation."

OXFORD

༄

(November 26, 1853 — Morning)

Dickens called for me in Soho promptly at eight of the clock the next morning. Irish Meg had already departed for Coutts Bank, never thinking twice about my going off to Oxford on a case of detection for Inspector Field. Instead of worrying about any possible danger to my person, all she said was "Hittle do you good, Wilkie, to get out of this beastly city for a spell." Me thus dispatched, she tripped off like a schoolgirl to her work.

What was attempting to pass itself off as the sun was gingerly poking at the thick fog when Dickens arrived to collect me in Sleepy Rob's new growler. As he sat at the curbstone high up on his gleaming new coach, I could not help but think how Sleepy Rob had moved up in the world. In recent months, Rob had almost become Dickens's personal coachman to the point that Charles had initiated an elaborate flag system in the bay window of the *Household Words* offices for the sole purpose of summoning him and his horse. A red paper flag set on the window ledge meant "Stop Immediately. I need your conveyance." A yellow flag meant "Report Here Early Tomorrow Morning." A blue flag meant

"Report Here at Five This Afternoon." Their little semaphore system seemed to work fairly well, to the point that the steady income which the connection had generated had allowed Sleepy Rob to exchange his rather tattered and worn hansom for a quite handsome new growler, entirely enclosed, which could carry four passengers quite comfortably. It proved the ideal conveyance, I soon found out, for this particular trip. Dickens somehow knew that coaches could be transported on the new steam trains, and that was why he had summoned Sleepy Rob to transport us to Oxford.

Dickens had seen to it that Sleepy Rob's growler was sumptuously laid out for our railway journey. Each of the plush overstuffed benches inside was fitted out with a heavy travel blanket to keep our legs and feet warm. Dickens had even provided a covered basket of foodstuffs to serve as our breakfast once the train got underway.

Dickens stuck his head out of the growler's side window and hailed me with the happy air of a man who had just been liberated from the prison of his workaday life: "Hallo, Wilkie, a foggy morn it is, but we're off to solve a murder."

I scrambled into the coach and wrapped myself snug in a heavy wool blanket, for my teeth were already set a'chattering.

"Yes, foggy and cold," I observed. "I hope we can keep ourselves from freezing on the train."

"Oh, no danger of that," Dickens assured me as he tapped the roof twice with his stick as a signal to Rob to go. "I have got wine and cheese and bread and fine cigars to warm us on our journey. It is an adventure, Wilkie," and he laughed uproariously at the prospect.

Sleepy Rob drove at his usual cautious pace to Victoria Station. When we arrived, he pulled even more cautiously down a rather steep cobblestoned embankment and drove right up onto the platform next to the waiting train. The steam engine stood like a racehorse in the gate. Behind it, in tow, stood five linked cars as well as the coaltender mounted behind the engine. The first two cars were enclosed passenger coaches. Behind these passenger coaches sat the Queen's Mail coach, also fully enclosed with one heavy wooden sliding door at its centre point, and Queen Victoria's emblem, a large gold crown, painted on its side. The final two cars were simply the flat wooden beds of farm carts mounted on the heavy iron railway wheels. These, I rather belatedly realized, were for the transport of land coaches. Sleepy Rob's new growler was actually to be our stateroom for our train voyage to Oxford. Each of these flatbed railway cars, it seemed, could hold two land coaches, since one large stage was already being loaded onto the foremost car. Being an utter neophyte to railway travel, having actually been on a train only once before in my life, and that in not the best of circumstances,[6] I had not fully appreciated Dickens's elaborate preparations for this trip.

Inspector Field and Serjeant Rogers were already waiting for us on the platform. As we pulled up, I glimpsed their final superintending of the loading of a stark wooden coffin containing the body of our unknown murder victim into the Queen's baggage car. Field greeted us with a growl of "Mornin', gents" as he breathed steam and clapped his gloved hands across his chest and onto his shoulders to ward off the cold.

Sleepy Rob was already down off his seat and unhitching his faithful business partner from the leads. As Rob led his horse away to the station livery, I realized that the horse would stay in London and we would be hiring a horse at the railway station in Oxford to pull us around that city.

As Dickens and I disembarked from our coach, I overheard the ever irascible Rogers growling from Field's coat-

[6]Here Wilkie can only be referring to his and Dickens's dangerous chase, over the tops of the cars of the Dover Mail, in pursuit of Angela Burdett-Coutts and her kidnapper in their previous case of "The Feminist Phantom" (published as *The Hoydens and Mr. Dickens*).

tails, "bloody freezin' this morning is. I'll be gettin' the chaise," and he stalked off.

" 'Ee's right, you know," Field grinned at his faithful bull-dog's departing back. "It is too cold to be standin' 'ere talkin' for long."

"Yes, it is," Dickens, who already was hugging himself against the cold, readily agreed. "Why don't we step inside to the *Salle d'attente* while Rob is loading our coach."

Field quite eagerly agreed to Dickens's suggestion and we all stepped inside where a hot fire was burning in a small iron boiler. We had not really expected to see Field this morning, since the night before he had given orders to Serjeant Rogers about the conveyance of the murder victim's body to Oxford. But apparently he had decided to come along and oversee the departure himself, and when we arrived inside and were warming ourselves by the small fire, we found out why. He had some final instruction in the art of detection to bestow upon us before we went about his business.

"If you are lucky enough to identify this corpse right off when you get to Oxford," he began, "then find out as much about the man as you can."

"Of course we will," Dickens assured him.

"You know the sort of thing then," Field pressed on undaunted, " 'is work, 'is friends, 'is haunts, the way 'ee thinks if you can get any sort of 'ook into that."

"Of course, of course," Dickens made a face at him, "you know Wilkie and I have done this job for you before a few times."

"Yes, I know, but no 'arm in remindin' you is all I'm sayin'." Field always seemed obligated to give us a speech like this. "There's Rogers," he broke off our briefing. "I'm off. Good huntin', coves!" and he was out the door and gone.

Preparing our travel accommodation for the railway journey to Oxford was truly a feat of engineering, but Sleepy Rob was up to the task. A rough trestle composed of two narrow planks was laid against the edge of the flatbed of the railway car. Upon closer inspection, we observed that those planks were fastened down with four heavy bolts that fit into holes in the flatcar's bed. This makeshift ramp traversed the four feet or so from the platform up to the bed of the car. When Dickens and I emerged from the station waiting room, Sleepy Rob was overseeing four burly men who seemed to be present on the Victoria Station scene solely for the purpose of lifting and loading large and cumbersome objects onto the trains. With dispatch, these worthies pushed our coach up onto the railway car and positioned it for the journey. That done, Rob dismissed them with tuppence all around and set about securing his precious new growler for the trip. Within minutes, all chocked and chained, we were ready to go.

While Rob was doing all of this, Dickens and I had lit up cigars.

"Oxford must be a quite popular place," Dickens observed as we looked around, for it seemed that the train was full of people and two coaches were mounted on both flatcars.

Finally, the whistle on the steam engine shrieked. Immediately, we were waved aboard by a blue-uniformed trainman swinging an unlit lantern. We climbed aboard and sat in the open doors of the growler, smoking and waiting to depart. But we did not sit in the open air for long.

The train pulled slowly out of Victoria—"getting up steam," I think is what those better versed in the lingo of this new railway age call it—and burrowed its way through North London in its sunken causeway beneath the level of the streets and houses like a smoking steel worm slithering through the earth.

It gradually picked up speed as it left the city. Red cinders and hot ash belched out of the smokestack and swirled back around our heads. It was a wonder this fiery rain did not catch our beavers on fire. We partially closed the shutters on the growler's windows, leaving them open a crack so we could look out at the passing scenery. Sleepy Rob had taken refuge from the cold wind and the cinders and come inside with us, but before we had left the environs of London he was curled up asleep under a blanket on the upholstered bench opposite Dickens and me. As for us, we were perfectly content with our cigars, our goblets of Anjou wine, and our occasional glimpses out at the passing sights.

Leaving London, picking up speed, fire and smoke bursting in clouds from its stack, our metal monster plunged through the grey English countryside. Like some latter-day mechanical dragon, our train raced through the Vale of the White Horse and turned west towards Oxford. Opening the window shutter but a crack, and watching the barren wintry landscape race by, Dickens indulged me with a bit of melancholy meditation.

"Oh, Wilkie, the stagecoach days of Pickwick are forever gone," he mused.

"What do you mean?" I humoured him, knowing full well that I was in for a lecture on the perils of progress and the threats of the Industrial Revolution.

"Just consider how different it all is. Our horse left behind. Our coach become a railway car. It's a new world and we've got to deal with it. Ten years ago, it was a day's ride to Oxford. Today, we will be there well before lunch." He fell silent for a moment.

I waited, having no idea where this meditation was bound.

"But it is better, you know," he finally said, though I am not convinced that he really meant it. "People can move from place to place with such speed."

"And goods, food, wood, and coal." I tried to catch up the spirit of his musing.

"Yes, that's true," he grinned wryly at me, "and we can take a day trip to find our out-of-town murderer."

On that ironic note, Dickens settled back to sip his wine and puff on his cigar as we thundered along towards Oxford.

I had not glimpsed those glorious spires in more than three years.[7] As we neared Oxford, I braved the wind and the cinders, removed my high hat, stuck my head out of the window, and gloried in the view of my old University town across the river and the fields. There was no sunlight gleaming off those fabled spires, for it was a slate grey November day, but my eyes drank it in as our train slowed and pulled into the Oxford station.

As the passengers poured from the train, the tiny station suddenly became quite a hurly-burly scene.

Our unloading was done with dispatch. Rob cashiered two young tramps (who might have been shabby pay students) and they rolled the growler down off the railway car, then fetched the murdered man's coffin from the mail car and tied it with ropes to the roof of the cab. That accomplished, Rob went off to hire a horse, giving Dickens and me a chance to look around.

The railway station was set off from the town across what would have been green fields had it been summertime. That day in November, however, that stretch of open park was ugly, fallow and brown. The distance between the railway and the town was traversed by a narrow dirt road along which lines of people were moving. While the majority of these people on this road were on foot or riding in hansom cabs, some were pedaling bicycles. In fact, as Dickens and I stood gawking, we realized that there were quite a few bicycles. At hitching posts where horses used to be tied, bicycles were now tethered. Some were leaned against the building. People getting off the train seemed to be collecting them and pedaling off for the short ride into the city.

To the east along that narrow dirt road was an equally narrow stone bridge that made a low arch over the river Thames. Where, in London, the Thames was wide and dirty

[7]Oxford is fondly referred to in all the guidebooks as "the City of Dreaming Spires" in acknowledgment of its impressive skyline of church and college chapel spires set in the sunlight of the Cumner Hills.

and deep, flowing with a lethal urgency towards the sea, up here the Thames was but a meandering stream no more than two boats wide flowing lazily between grassy banks. Soon Rob had our horses hitched and we set off along that very road and over that very bridge towards the town.

"Livery man 'ee said the police station is at the bottom of St. Aldate's just before the Folly Bridge, Mr. Collins, sir," Rob shouted down from the box. "Can you direct me there, sir?"

"Indeed I can," I shouted triumphantly, feeling somewhat like a seasoned explorer ushering two tenderfoots into the bush.

"I'll bet you can," Dickens chuckled. "Probably spent some time there, I'd wager, consequences of some of your student escapades?"

"I'll have you know," I took up his mocking tone, "I've never spent a moment in the Oxford jail. Our chaps always ran much too fast for the constables to catch us."

We had opened the coach's shutters as soon as we got it off the train, and as we entered the city, there was a great deal to catch our attention. It was half ten in the morning and the narrow cobblestoned streets were thick with people both on foot and on wheels. Workmen were unloading goods from handcarts. Students on bicycles, their black academic robes trailing out behind them, coasted past us on both sides. Bumpkins were carrying crates of vegetables and meats into the marketplace.

"That's the Haymarket, the next one," I shouted up to Rob, "turn right there. St. Aldate's is at the top of the hill by the Carfax Tower, the tall square tower."

"I sees it, sir," Rob clucked either to me or to his horse.

"My Lord, Wilkie, will you look at that," Dickens pointed.

I turned to see a man's cream-trousered legs rotating by our window as if suspended in mid-air.

"What is it?" I stuck my head out the window to see.

"Extraordinary!" Dickens, whose head was out the opposite window, exclaimed.

It was a cyclist on a huge high bicycle, riding along above the throng. His back wheel was tiny but his front wheel was enormous, in circumference reaching at least eight feet above the ground. He sat perched atop that huge wheel lumbering along like an Indian Rajah atop an elephant. We learned later that this particular type of bicycle was called a "penny farthing."

I looked about me as we proceeded up the Haymarket hill and realized that we were drawing quite a few stares from the passersby.

"Everyone is looking at us, Charles," I informed him. "They're stopping and staring. It is that coffin on the roof."

"Oh, Wilkie, don't be so stuffy," Dickens scoffed at my undue concern for public opinion. "How else are we going to put a name on Field's corpse? He knows, and you know, how at sea Field would be with all of these University poms. Who cares what the common people think?"

Put that way, I guess I shouldn't have cared, but I must admit that I did. I did not enjoy being stared at as if I was some attraction in a raree show.

We crested the Carfax, and turned down into St. Aldate's.

"There is Christ Church," I pointed the walls of the college out to Dickens. "It is Henry the Eighth's college, High Anglican. That's the Tom Tower," I pointed excitedly, "where Old Dodo, I mean Dodgson, lives."

"Straight on," I called up to Sleepy Rob as we rumbled down towards Folly Bridge. I rather enjoyed giving other people orders rather than just being the one receiving them all the time.

The police station was right where we were told it would be. We left Sleepy Rob with the cab and the corpse, and went inside to reconnoitre.

"Good day," Dickens addressed a fat, mutton-chopped police serjeant behind a wide desk, who was worrying over a number of little piles of stacked papers spread out before him like chips on a gaming table.

"Good day to you, sir," the man looked up, somewhat annoyed, from his paperwork. But when he saw two full-fledged London gentlemen standing before him, his look changed to surprise, then to curiosity, then to interrogation, which is exactly how he decided to proceed. "What would it be then, gentlemen? You don't look as if you are from Oxford."

"We are not, sir." Dickens gave him his most radiant smile and handed him one of the small white calling cards which he infrequently used to make sure that people recognized him. "We are just up from London and we have a bit of a problem."

"Problem?" The desk serjeant screwed up his face as if someone was twisting the top of his head with a pair of forceps, and painfully decoded the card as if it were lined with Egyptian hieroglyphics. Whatever translation he accomplished, it made no impression whatsoever. He did not recognize Dickens's name at all. Obviously not a reader! I found it somewhat amusing.

"Do you have a constable named Morse here?" Dickens asked.

"Young Reggie, you mean? Why, what sort of a problem could young Reggie be? 'Ee's a fine young constable." The desk serjeant immediately went on the defensive to protect one of his own.

"No. No," Dickens laughed. "Young Morse is not the problem at all. We were referred to him by Chief Inspector William Field of the Metropolitan Protectives of London."

"Chief Inspector?" The desk serjeant seemed duly impressed.

I was somewhat impressed myself, never having heard the word "Chief" appended to friend Field's title before. I gave Dickens a questioning look.

He tipped me a wink when the serjeant was not looking.

"Referred?" The desk serjeant seemed committed to offering only these single-word questions.

33

"Yes," Dickens smiled benignly. "Chief Inspector Field suggested we contact Constable Morse to assist us on a matter of murder."

"Murder!" Dickens's ambush achieved its desired effect. The man leapt up out of his chair. "Murder, you say?"

"Yes," Dickens remained as calm as if they were discussing butterflies, "we have the corpse right outside the door in our cab."

"Murder . . . in Oxford?"

"No, no," Dickens reassured him. "The man was murdered in London."

"Man murdered . . . corpse outside." What had been a rather burly and officious public servant was reduced in mere moments to a babbling idiot, utterly overcome by the weight of surprises that had dropped so precipitously upon him. He sank back down into his chair.

"Murder?" Our serjeant repeated for the third time.

"Yes, that is it," Dickens calmed him. "A murder was committed in London, but we have reason to believe that the murdered man is a citizen of Oxford."

"You do?"

"Yes."

"Of course," the serjeant was still quite puzzled by it all, "of course you do."

Finally, the serjeant rapped his desk with his knuckles and stood back up: "A matter of murder! Beglory! That young Reggie surely is a go-getter, that he is. Now"—and he paused to think exactly what his course of action would be—"you gentlemen wait 'ere and I'll send someone to scare young Reggie up."

"Excellent!" Dickens favoured him with a radiant smile.

Our thick serjeant went away into the bowels of the building, and Dickens and I took seats on a wooden bench against a bare wall. The Oxford Police Station was nothing if not functional.

"I hope our young Reggie is a bit quicker than this Oxford policeman," Dickens whispered to me in the course of our wait.

Our doltish serjeant finally returned empty-handed.

"Reggie Morse is not on duty today," he explained with an excess of boring formality. "I've sent someone to fetch him. It will be a time."

"Yes. Very good." Dickens continued to flatter this idiot. "Might we bring the murder victim in out of the street and establish the corpse somewhere where it might be identified if and when that time comes?"

"Right. Probably should 'ave done that before," the man headed for the door. "The surgeon's room. The surgeon's room. That's the place. We'll put 'im in there. 'Asn't been used in two years, though. Pretty dusty," the man spoke over his shoulder as we proceeded out to Sleepy Rob's cab.

"That is perfectly all right," Dickens gaily assured our major domo, then turned to me and whispered, "I don't think our dead man will mind the dust."

The surgeon's room of the Oxford Station was every bit as spartan and functional as the front reception. It was a tiny, narrow room, furnished with nothing more than a bare wooden dissecting table and two gas lamps mounted on the walls. Sleepy Rob and our serjeant carried the coffin in and deposited it on the surgeon's table. That done, none of us felt the need to linger.

Back in the front reception, Dickens informed the desk serjeant that we were going out to find another man whom we hoped might help us to identify the body and that we would immediately return with him. We hoped, by that time, young Constable Morse would have put in an appearance.

Though this was a tremendous weight of information for our desk serjeant to carry, he seemed to bear up under it pretty well. Thus, we took our leave and Rob drove us back up St. Aldate's to the gate of Christ Church College of the University of Oxford.

OLD DODO

༄

(November 26, 1853 — Midday)

As we passed through the tunnel beneath the Tom Tower which was the entrance to the Christ Church quadrangle, a tall, severe-faced man in a bowler hat dressed all in heavy winter tweed and sporting around his neck the identical bright blue cravat that graced the neck of our nameless corpse hailed us from a small side room in the stone wall. "Gentlemun, gud mornin'," he halted us with a Scottish burr whose rough edges had been anglicized to the point that we could actually understand him. "Wud kin we do for you gentlemuns this mornin'?"

Every Oxford quadrangle[8] had one of these thugs guarding the gate, the porter, who screened all who presumed to enter the confines of the college. These annoying gatekeep-

---

[8]All of the Oxford colleges are built on the quadrangle system: four massive stone walls or buildings enclosing the college courtyard. Each wall served a college function. One housed the library, one the chapel, one the sleeping rooms, one the lecture halls. This fortresslike arrangement dated back to the twelfth and thirteenth centuries when the townspeople would regularly attack the students who had invaded their provincial market town.

ers are, I suppose, a throwback to the medieval days of the Town-Gown riots, when the peasant townsmen would storm the student domiciles with scythes and pitchforks looking for blood.

"Good morning," Dickens greeted this Scotsman jovially and handed over another of his calling cards, evidently undeterred by the singular lack of effect his previous gambit had worked upon the decidedly unliterary policeman. "We are just up from London this morning on the train to talk with, ah . . . Wilkie?"

"Mr. Charles Dodgson, please," I answered promptly on cue, as if I were Dickens's puppet.

"Yes, Mr. Dodgson, who is a tutor of Mathematics here, I believe," Dickens explained it all as the porter read his calling card.

"Charles Dickens, Novelist. Gude Laird awmighty! Wif un may wuz raidin' the new *Blake 'Ouse* unly yestiddy." Obviously, this time Dickens's calling card had produced the proper effect.

"Why yes, how nice, you have read my work." Dickens fell quite comfortably into his humble recognized author role. "I hope you and your wife enjoyed it?"

"Oh yes, sir," our fawning porter confided, "not hay fortnight goes by the wife doesna bring 'ome one o' yer liddle green mags."[9]

"Yes. Splendid." Dickens was smiling and pumping the man's hand. Charles loved to bask in the admiration of his reading public.

"Might we go up to Mr. Dodgson's rooms," I interrupted their little game of mutual admiration. "He is an old friend and I know where it is."

"Of coarse, of coarse, toike thet stairsteps oer theer," and he pointed us towards a narrow portal in the massive stone

[9]All of Dickens's novels were sold serially in monthly numbers bound in green paper covers.

wall. " 'Ee's in, I'm sairtin'. Hi 'aven't sane 'im cum hout this mairn."

But this tweedy Cerberus was not going to let his prize go so easily, not without investing Dickens with some invaluable local knowledge. "That young Dodgson," the porter still held Dickens's hand in his grip, " 'ee's a gude un, ye ken. Mathamatics, a noombers squiggler, ye ken. Very smairt and a gude Christian man, 'ee saimes. Lives at the top o' this very gate tower, raight hup those steps," and he left go of Dickens's hand to point. " 'Ee'll be the next Don, we all thaink, the youngest one aever."

As quickly as Dickens could disentangle himself, we fled through that indicated doorway and climbed the narrow, winding stone steps up into Tom Tower. About every fifteen steps, a corridor with heavy wooden walls would open out of the stone stairwell. We passed by three of these before we reached the top, where I knew Dodgson's room to be. It had no number or plate or identification of any kind on the door, only a delicate iron knocker in the figure of a geometrician's compass. I tapped this eccentric knocker three times against its anvil and it emitted a barely audible scratching sound.

Nonetheless, in a short moment, the dark wooden door swung inwardly open and my old University friend stood before us, still in his sleeping clothes though it was getting on towards noon. I think he recognized me right off upon opening the door, even though it had been almost three years; but Dickens gave him pause.

"Dodo," I greeted him with a smile, "do you remember your old literary chum?"

"Of c-c-course, Wilkie," my salutation drew his attention away from his puzzling over the lurking presence of Dickens behind me, "I c-c-could never forget you. C-c-come in. C-c-come in, please. Ah, those were such c-c-carefree t-t-times."

The first thing anyone noticed about Charles Dodgson was his stammer. However, wonder of wonders, he did not seem to notice it at all. He spoke in a soft, quiet voice, the voice of a contemplative man, a thinker. He seemed genuinely pleased to see me in his somewhat distracted way. He ushered us politely in, but I sensed he was quite curious to find out who the tall bearded man accompanying me was . . . and why?

"Dodo, this is my friend Charles Dickens."

That brought him up utterly short and sent him into a rather comical stammer as he tried to collect his wits in light of the morning's second and even larger surprise.

"Why, why, why . . ." He tried to take it all in, his eyes darting back and forth from me to Dickens and Dickens to me. "why, Wilkie, your literary c-c-connection certainly has risen a bit since your days here in Oxford."

"Mr. Dodgson, I am very pleased to meet you." Charles extended his hand for a shake. "Wilkie has told me all about you."

"Of c-c-course, he has," Dodgson replied in that quiet scholar's voice of his, "but the question is 'why?' " and he laughed, somewhat awkwardly I thought, at his own little self-effacing joke.

And Dickens laughed. This exchange of surprised introductions had halted us in the foyer of his rooms. Realizing this, Dodgson ushered us into his inner sanctum.

Dodgson's rooms were then, and in my memory always had been, the very curious habitat of a rare and rather strange bird. The walls of his main sitting room were half-straight, dark medieval oak, and half curved, out of stone, conforming to the circular tower's convex outer wall. The ceiling was high and beamed, constructed of that same solid dark oak. The room itself was unbelievably cluttered. Not only was it overflowing with books lining shelves all the way to the ceiling, piled in precarious columns as high as a man on the floor, and strewn all over the furniture, but it contained all sorts of curious mechanical devices of iron and wood and brass.

Despite all the dark wood, it was not a dark room. Set into the curvature of the stone outer wall were two huge leaded windows, which let in a goodly amount of daylight. In front of one of these windows, before a section of the leaded glass that could be tilted open upon the night sky, stood a large telescope which, I presume, Dodgson employed in his Copernican studies. He was a hobbyist at heart and ever since I had known him he had always been intent upon spending his time away from mathematics and the college in the pursuit of unusual intellectual avocations. Poetry had been one of them. It looked as if now he had turned his attentions to the stars.

Against one wall on a small table sat a wooden contraption composed of three mahogany boxes with small hinged doors in their sides and brass cylinders protruding from their fronts, stopped with glass stoppers that looked like eyes.

"What on earth is that, Charlie?" I asked him, my curiosity getting the better of me, as he cleared piles of books off his chairs so that we could sit down.

"It is c-c-called a magic lantern, Wilkie. There's a small g-g-gas lamp inside each box and optical lenses inside each of those brass pipes. You put pieces of different c-c-colored stained g-g-glass inside the boxes and rotate them in between the light and the lenses and it throws magical c-c-colours on a blank wall."

"I would like to see that some time." Dickens feigned interest in this silly thing, I am sure. "It must be beautiful."

"Oh it is, it is," Dodgson assured him. "I must g-g-get you some tea, some tea," he said in his distracted, yet flustered, quiet scholar's voice. With that, he bustled off into the inner rooms of his lair, leaving us alone to take in the other wonders cluttering up his sitting room.

In the very centre of the room, in what looked to be a place of honour right in front of a small plush settee, which, unlike every other piece of furniture in the room, did not have books piled up upon it, sat another curious machine. Mounted on a wooden tripod, it consisted of another wooden box, with a larger round glass lens inset like an eye in its front, and wearing a long piece of black cloth on its back like a woman's mourning dress.

"What do you suppose that is?" I whispered to Dickens.

"I haven't the slightest," he shrugged back to me.

Before long, Dodgson came scurrying out of his kitchen carrying a tray full of cups and saucers and a teapot. He was truly a rabbity fusspot, scurrying around with the tea things trying to bring order to the book-strewn chaos of his rooms. To this day, my overwhelming impression of Charlie Dodgson is of his youth. He always looked so young, almost frail. He was strikingly handsome and slender, utterly clear-eyed beneath his brushed straight back, jet black hair. He seemed so young, and yet he was soon to be Christ Church's next Don, tutor to Queen Victoria's sons. At Dickens's question, he informed us that the gadget we had been puzzling over was his newest toy.

"It is a c-c-camera for the t-t-taking of t-t-tintype photographs," he instructed us. "I have been t-t-taking the likenesses, portraits if you will, of all of my friends and c-c-colleagues, anyone who visits here. I must have you and Mr. Dickens as my subjects before you leave, Wilkie."

"Of course, fascinating," Dickens said. "I would love to have my likeness taken, if for no other reason than to see how this unusual machine works."

"Oh, it is interesting," Dodo assured Charles with quiet animation. "Your likeness c-c-copied absolutely t-t-true t-t-to life with utter realism in only a matter of moments."

As they talked, I had wandered to a deal table at the side of the room beneath a high free-standing looking glass. Spread out on the table was a square thin varnished board, lined off in a grid of tiny squares. Piled on the board were dozens of small squares of wood, which appeared to be the exact dimensions of the gridded squares on the board. Each of these tiny wooden squares had a letter of the alphabet burned into it.

"What is this, Dodo?" I could not help but ask, distracting his and Dickens's attention away from the photographic machine in the centre of the room.

"Oh that," he laughed. "It is a little word g-g-game I invented for the amusement of Dean Liddell's children. They like to visit here. They c-c-call this place their Wonderland, because of all of the toys and books, I suppose. The game t-t-teaches them their alphabet. We call the game 'Jabber' because that is all we do as we play it."

We sipped at our tea.

I followed Dickens's eyes as they prowled the room.

Dodgson was studying us as well over the tilted edge of his teacup as we sipped, but he did not say anything or ask why we had intruded upon his shy, bachelor life. I finally stepped into the lull in our conversation.

"Dodo," I began, "we are here for a reason. We need your help. We are here on some criminal business from London."

"C-c-criminal?" he stammered softly, and his eyes went wide with alarm.

"Criminal is not really the proper word," Dickens took over. " 'Detectiving business' better describes why we are here, I should think."

"Detectiving?" Dodgson was still puzzled. For a man with a reputation as a master logician, we were having a great deal of trouble making him understand.

"Yes," Dickens explained patiently. "We were sent here by Inspector William Field of the Metropolitan Protectives to ask you to help us identify a man who was murdered in London last evening."

"Murdered. Oh g-g-good Lord," and Dodgson's eyes just seemed to go wider and wider until the rest of his face faded away and all that was left were those two large saucers gaping at us.

"Yes, murdered," Dickens pressed doggedly on. "Wilkie identified the murder victim as an Oxford, ah, Christ Church, man by his neckpiece."

"He wore a Christ Church cravat, Dodo," I interjected. "I thought you might know him."

"I might well," Dodgson's eyes had subsided, and one could see the logician's fascination for the deductive world of the detective taking hold within him. "Yes, I would be happy t-t-to t-t-try, but how?"

"We brought the body with us on the train," Dickens explained.

"You did, how charming," Dodo said softly, as if he found the whole situation precious and amusing and unutterably bizarre.

"It is in the surgeon's room at the Oxford Police Station just down the road by the bridge," Dickens explained. "We were hoping you would come with us to identify it."

"Yes, yes, of c-c-course," he stammered. "It will only t-t-take me a moment to g-g-get properly dressed," and he scurried out of the room like a flushed rabbit diving into his hole.

Dodgson insisted that we walk down St. Aldate's to the police station, so we left Sleepy Rob sitting in his growler wrapped up in blankets in front of the Christ Church gate.

At the station, a rather thick-bodied, bright-eyed young man in a dark blue constable's tunic rushed forward to greet us.

"Reginald Morse, your honours. At your service, sirs." He was so eager he almost bowled us over in his rush.

We introduced ourselves all around as young Morse expressed his great admiration for Inspector Field, the Protectives, London ("a great, great city!"), Dickens's novels ("wonderful stories!"), Christ Church ("the pride of Oxford, sir!"), and anything else he could gush on about.

Still talking at the speed of a runaway carriage, young Morse ushered us down the hallway and into the surgeon's room. Actually, his eagerness was really quite charming. He was about the most positive young person that any of us had ever met, clearly a young man who had decided he was going places and was putting forth all of his effort to get there.

"I've taken the liberty, sirs, of opening the coffin and taking the murdered man's body out so we can all get a better look at him," he announced as we entered the tiny surgeon's closet. "I hope that is acceptable."

"Very good. Very good," Dickens affirmed his judgment. "Thank you."

Dodgson showed no timidity whatsoever in this affair. Upon entering the room, he walked right up to the corpse, which was lying on the flat dissecting table still in its bloody clothes, and looked right into its cold, white, death-frozen face. It took him but a short second to connect the face in death with what had been the face in life. Then he gave a tiny little gasp and stepped back.

"My G-G-God, it is Ackroyd!" he exclaimed in a whisper. "He's a C-C-Christ Church don."

"A don?" young Reggie found this news startling. "Well, now!"

"Yes, he is a historian," Dodgson explained quite seriously, "working, I think, on what was supposed t-t-to be a g-g-grand biography of Cromwell and the Revolution."

"Did you know him well?" Dickens asked.

"Not really," and Dodgson paused a moment. "In fact, I did not really like him very much. He ran with an odd crowd, t-t-too fast for me. Every now and then we would t-t-talk at high t-t-table, about a student we had in c-c-common, perhaps, or a university lecture that was c-c-coming up. That sort of thing. Quite t-t-trivial really. Mostly I saw him out with his drinking c-c-crowd. They haunt the back room at the Bulldog."

His breathless speech done, Dodgson suddenly began to totter as if he were about to fall over in a faint.

Dickens quickly stepped forward and grasped him by the shoulders to hold him up. With the help of young Morse, Dickens proceeded to steer Dodgson out of that stuffy, death-permeated room.

Outside in the corridor, Dodgson was apologetic. He professed himself unable to understand why this weakness in the face of death had suddenly overtaken him.

Dickens and I exchanged knowing looks. In our adventures since becoming colleagues of Inspector Field, we had seen more than our share of dead bodies and neither of us had quite grown accustomed to it. Death was certainly no holiday for the dead, but death was also unsettling, disorienting, terribly troubling for the living, and that was what I tried to assure Dodo of as we fled the police station.

"It is just that I have not eaten anything this morning," Dodgson insisted. "My stomach just was not fortified for that shock."

"Well," Dickens laughed, changing the whole morbid tenor of the scene, "we shall certainly remedy that. Where is this Bulldog that you mentioned? It must be a public house. Can we eat a pub lunch there?"

Old Dodo and I looked at one another and laughed.

"Oh yes," I said, "it is a public house indeed. We spent many a long evening there talking about our poems, didn't we, Dodo?"

"Indeed we did," Dodgson whispered, the colour starting to come back into his face.

"Then I propose that we repair to this fabled Bulldog and lunch on meat pies and English beer," Dickens suggested, "and then perhaps you can tell us a bit more about this Ackroyd chap. He sounds like an interesting fellow and we have to find out why he was shot down in the street. Where is this Bulldog anyway?"

Again Dodo and I exchanged a small laugh.

"Why, Charles, it is right across the street from Dodo's rooms. You can look right in its doorway from his front window."

"Well, splendid then," Dickens joined in the fun. "We can walk there. Will you join me?" he included young Constable Morse in the invitation.

That worthy said that he would be happy to join us, but

45

first he had to make arrangements to properly store the body until the family could be found and notified. It being winter, he did not see this as much of a problem. He said he would join us at the Bulldog as soon as he could tend to these details.

All that resolved, Dickens and I walked the still unsteady Dodgson up the street to the tavern.

"Charlie, me boy, you look a wee bit peaked!" The bulky Irish publican bustled over to greet us the moment we passed through the doors of the tavern. He helped Dodgson to the nearest open table. "And lor 'amighty, you got Mister Collins with you, whom we 'aven't seen for all these many years."

"Yes, indeed, Mike," Dodgson was nearly recovered, "it is Wilkie Collins back to visit us, and I am fine, just had a bit of a shock on an empty stomach. That is why we are here in dire need of some of your exceptional food."

"Well, London gentlemen," he had arrived at this conclusion by taking an inventory of Dickens and me from head to toe, "Dodo 'ere 'as brought you to the right place. But," and he paused, smiling, "I'll bet you'd first like a drop to warm you from the winter chill. What say you?"

There was no mistaking this Mike for an Englishman or a Scot. He was so Irish that four-leaf clovers might have been growing out of his ears. His hair was as reddish-orange as a sunset over the Irish Sea and his face was as fair and freckled as the coat of a young deer. He was short and wide, with the shoulders of a bear, the chest of an ape, and the forearms and wrists of a strangler. He never had any difficulty keeping order in his public house. The story goes that he had come over to England from his beloved Ireland some ten years before after some accident had befallen his family and caused him great grief. But I remember him as one of the best-humoured men in all of Oxford, his eyes always a'twinkle with a greeting and always glad to see you, no matter what. And he remembered me (and by name) after years of absence. Now that is a publican who knows his business!

"Michael," Dodgson seemed fully recovered, "draw me one of those beastly black Irish stouts that you are so inordinately proud of."

"Inordinately or not, whatever that means," Mike returned his raillery, "my Irish stout comes in barrels by boat straight from Dublin. In Dublin they say, 'stout for strength,' 'cause it's rich in the iron of the Irish mountains."

"Yes, and made by leprechauns or pookas or banshees, I'm sure," Dodo laughed.

"No, sir," Mike the publican growled, "by good Irish lads right in the heart of Dublin."

After that jolly exchange, Dickens and I had no choice but to order two more of the same just to sample the source of Mike's national pride. He left happy, as if he had just converted a pack of heathens to the Irish religion.

When he returned with our drinks, he remembered that Dodgson had experienced a shock and he inquired into it.

"One of your t-t-tapsters, Mike, David Ackroyd, the History Don. He is d-d-dead." Dodgson spoke the news a bit too loudly to the whole pub. I observed Dickens wince at the manner in which the ears of so many of the other drinkers seemed to go on point, listening for more information.

"I just saw his body."

"No!" Mike reacted. "Why, 'ee was just in 'ere Saturday last, in the back room with his usual crew."

"Yes, well, perhaps we should order our lunch," Dickens changed the subject rather abruptly, in an attempt, I am sure, to keep the pointed ears of the rest of the pub from hearing too much.

And so we did. Veal pies with carrots were the order of the day, and Dickens, ever vigilant, ordered two extra. One with a small bucket of beer to be carried across the street to Sleepy Rob's black growler, which he pointed out through the front window and which had not moved an inch since our arrival at Christ Church College. The other for our young Constable Morse when he should arrive.

" 'T'will only be a few moments for warming gents," Irish Mike assured us.

"Mike," Dickens was fully in control of the situation now and had detained the publican by a tug at his apron. He spoke in a low voice that no one beyond the boundaries of our table could hear. "When the food is ready, might you be able to join us for a short time? I would like to ask you a few questions about this man Ackroyd who has been murdered. I think that you can help us in this affair."

"Murdered!" the startled barman exclaimed in a whisper, looking questioningly at his friend Dodgson as if he had been betrayed. "You didn't tell me 'ee was murdered."

"Yes, he was, in London," Dodgson too had caught the necessity for whispering, "and Wilkie and Mr. Dickens are up here to investigate the murder."

"Mr. Dickens!" Irish Mike exclaimed again, each new revelation seeming to hit him harder than the last. "Not *the* Mr. Dickens," and Dodgson nodded solemnly. "You didn't tell me this was Mr. Dickens. I am honoured to have you in my establishment, sir."

Dickens assured him that the feeling was mutual and he assured Dickens that he would return as quickly as his warmers permitted with our food. In a conspiratorial whisper, he confided that he would be honoured to join us for what he quaintly termed "some murderous conversation."

The dark Irish stout was tasty, much stronger yet smoother than our English beer. I have ordered it ever since when I can find it in our country. I suppose one should not be surprised that the Irish would know how to make good beer.

THE MURDERED MAN

༞

(November 26, 1853 — Afternoon)

M ike the Irish publican was true to his word. In the space of no more than ten short minutes our solid wooden table was steaming with meat pies and our pints of Irish stout were in the process of being topped off in creamy foam. In the interim, young Constable Reggie Morse arrived as promised, and when Irish Mike returned with our pints and sat down with us, the cabal was complete.

"Tell us, Charles and Mike," Dickens began the interrogation, "what do you two know about this Ackroyd?"

"As I told you, he is, ah . . . was, a historian," Dodgson began thoughtfully. "He lived c-c-completely at the other side of the c-c-college in the Meadow Buildings, so I did not see a g-g-great deal of him. He held the undergraduates in c-c-complete c-c-contempt. They hated him. They c-c-called him 'batty Acky' behind his back. He was a respected historian, had published monographs on our own English history in the sixteenth and seventeenth century."

"I didn't like 'im much," Dodgson had paused for a draught of beer and Irish Mike took up the characterization. " 'Ee was a dark, scowly one, 'ee was."

"Very political," Mike and Dodgson had become like a single voice finishing each other's thoughts. "He ran with a fast c-c-crew. While Wilkie and I and a few others t-t-talked about literature, all they t-t-talked about were p-p-politics and how bad things were and how change had to c-c-come."

"Radicals, the lot," Irish Mike slapped the table demonstratively. "I never saw a more negative crew of rascals in my life. Radicals and Anarchists!"

"You say they, this group of political radicals, spent a great deal of time in here drinking?" Dickens waved a forkful of steaming veal at Dodgson as if to punctuate his question, but Irish Mike answered.

"Drinkin' and plottin' and even cursin' each other. Why no more than a fortnight ago, this Ackroyd and another one, sixteen-stone bloke with the walrus mustachios . . ." and he looked to Dodgson for a name.

"Stadler, a Chemistry D-D-Don." It took Dodgson only a moment's thought to come up with it.

". . . yes, Stadler, the two of 'em got into a real shouter with the others, stomped out mad as two foaming dogs."

"Political argument?" Dickens asked.

"I suppose," Irish Mike shrugged. "That's all I'd ever overhear them talkin' is politics when I'd drop off their drinks."

"Who were the others in this group besides this Stadler?" Dickens seemed perfectly at ease asking questions of these perfect strangers, and, wonder of wonders, they seemed perfectly content in answering him.

"Well, there is B-B-Barnet from Queen's," Dodgson began slowly to recover their names from his memory.

"Jack Bathgate and little Wherry Squonce from Balliol," Mike was gleeful, as if it were all a game of trumps.

"And Carroll from All Souls," Dodgson added.

When Mike was no longer forthcoming with any additional names, Dodgson leaned forward over the table with too evident curiosity: "Those are the m-m-main ones of that g-g-group. There may b-b-be a few more. Do you think that one of them is the m-m-murderer?"

Dickens drew in a deep breath.

Everyone at the table hung on his answer.

"I have no idea," he finally said, utterly deflating all of the anticipation which the question had occasioned. "It seems much too soon to be speculating on who might be the murderer when we have barely identified the murder victim."

Young Reggie Morse, who to this moment had not said a word, who had silently been all ears as he seemed to busy himself with his meat pie, suddenly entered the debate with a flourish.

"I think we should search his rooms," the young police-man blurted out.

All of us stared at him.

Dickens and I looked at each other. Dickens could not believe our good fortune or repress his excitement.

What a novel idea!

I think I saw some dismay mixed with exhilarated joy on Dickens's face (because, I am sure, he regretted that he had not thought of it first).

The meat pies sat utterly decimated on the field of battle. Our pints were all limping towards their dregs. It was time for a decision. Should we order another round and continue our discussion? Or should we break into the dead man's rooms?

"Inspector Morse . . ."

"Constable, sir . . ."

"Not for long," Dickens was already on his feet. "What a splendid idea! We shall go there straightaway. Perhaps we can find some clue that will tell us why he was murdered," and Dickens chuckled with glee, "or even better, by whom."

Dickens was so utterly transparent. He was glorying in the fact that he had taken over for Field as the Chief Inspector on this case and he was setting out to collect all the evidence on his own without any other detective of authority to challenge his deductive powers.

"Charles, do you know the man's room?" Dickens stood over us like a general marshalling his troops for battle.

"No, but I c-c-can find out from the p-p-porter at the Meadows B-B-Building." Dodgson snapped to attention.

"Excellent! Morse, how will we get into the rooms? Dare we break down the door?"

"There will be no need for that," the young constable answered. "My father is Oxford's finest locksmith. He has taught me the tricks of the trade since I was a boy of eight years. I am the disappointment of his life. He wanted me to go into the business with him, but I went for the police instead. I have a set of picks that will open any door in Oxford in the time it takes to whistle 'toor-a-loo.' "

"Oh doubly excellent!" Dickens could not believe his continued good fortune. "Then," and he beamed around the table at all of us, "we are off!"

In fact, Dickens was so happy with this turn of events that he paid the bill for all. I heard him say to our host, Irish Mike, as we took our leave, that he was sure we would be back to Oxford soon and to keep his eyes peeled and his ears tuned to the dealings of those political dons, the late Ackroyd's friends. I am certain that Dickens made it well worth Mike the publican's time to do as he bid.

Sleepy Rob leapt up in the growler as we emerged from the Bulldog. We crossed St. Aldate's, which was surprisingly busy with traffic, mainly of the bicycle sort, for the early afternoon. I am sure we looked as if we were primed to enter his cab.

No sooner did Sleepy Rob ask, like a house dog with a stick in his mouth and a game of fetch in his eyes, "Where'll it be now, gents?" than Dodgson assured us, "Oh, no need for the c-c-cab; we'll just walk across the meadow."

Sleepy Rob sank back onto the cushions of the cab as if he had been hit on the head with a barrel of beer. Indolent as he typically was, I think Rob was growing bored by just sitting around in this small town.

It was a pleasant enough march across the Christ Church meadows. Cows were grazing at the far end, a bend of the river glistened in the grey distance, and, though it was cold November, I could still remember sitting under the trees that formed a thick canopy over the Long Walk and reading Keats or Byron or even Dickens on sunny summer afternoons.

It took Dodgson only a moment to obtain the location of this Ackroyd's rooms from the porter. That done, we went up. At the dead man's door, Dodgson, Dickens, and I formed a shield around young Morse so as not to alarm any curious eyes as he worked at the lock. True to his word, young Morse could pick a lock as well as any London housebreaker. In short minutes, he straightened up, turned the ornate antique doorknob, stepped back, inviting us in with a palm-up gesture of his hand and a smiling "Gentlemen, please."

As we walked through the door into the dead man's rooms, each of us in turn stopped short in our tracks, running up against one another.

Someone had been there before us.

The door opened upon a parlour-library similar to Dodgson's arrangement in his rooms, but this parlour was an utter shambles. It looked as if a mad bull had been turned loose in the room. It had been ransacked from floor to ceiling, corner to corner, window seat to wainscotting, and cover to cover. Books were strewn about everywhere, many of their covers torn from their spines. Every drawer in every desk, table, secretary was rifled and tossed. Papers drifted across the wooden floor like snow on a winter field.

"My God!"

"Good Lord!"

All in unison we drew in our breaths in a low gasp of shock at the devastation.

Morse closed the door behind us, which momentarily threw the room into a deep darkness.

Quickly Morse lit a lucifer and found a gaslight on the near wall. In the flickering yellow light, the ruins of that room looked even more sinister. Morse went around lighting other lamps, and soon the room was flooded with light. But the other three of us had not moved. It was as if the shock of the violence that had been worked upon this room had frozen us.

Dickens was the first to thaw. He joined young Morse at the far side of the room.

"What do you think happened here?" Dickens asked.

"Someone else besides us knows 'ee's dead," young Morse answered, "perhaps the one who killed 'im, and 'ee came lookin' for somethin'."

"Yes, of course," Dickens solemnly agreed, "but who, and what was he looking for?"

Young Morse nodded in silent agreement. The two of them stood across the brightly lit room, their eyes darting here and there in search of some clue.

"If Field were here, Wilkie," and Dickens crossed back to me through the wreckage of the room, "he would say that the answers to those questions are here, in this room, if we can just see them. We must try to see this room through Field's eyes. We have traversed crime scenes with him before. Where would he bid us look? What would he tell us to look for?" Dickens was not really talking to me, nor was he talking aloud to himself. It was as if he were invoking some spirit of the detective that resides within all of us, some powers of observation that we all possess but we do not fully trust.

"Field would say, 'Look for what does not belong. For what should be there but is not. For what has been left behind by the murderer.'" Dickens was almost chanting this litany as he prowled the ruins of the room.

All of that is easy for Field to say, I thought, *but how can we possibly find anything in a mess like this?* Nevertheless, all four of us began moving slowly about the room pretending we were Inspector Field.

"By the way," Old Dodo finally broke the silence that had descended upon us, "who is this Field chap that we are sup-. posed to be emulating?"

That gave us all a good laugh, especially Dickens. I think it took the weight off our observation, helped us to see things that we might not have seen if the burden of being Field had not been lifted from us.

"Mr. Dodgson," young Morse asked, "do you know if Mr. Ackroyd smoked cigars?"

The young constable had dropped to one knee on the floor over what appeared to be a small pile of cigar ash. He proceeded to rummage amongst a pile of torn and dis-carded books. "Aha!" he exclaimed, and pulled the stub end of a gentleman's thin cigar out from beneath the pile.

"I c-c-cannot say for certain," Dodgson ruminated upon the question. "B-b-but I'll b-b-bet Mike would know."

Then young Morse did something I had many times seen Field do. He took a small envelope out of one of the pockets of his capacious coat and deposited the cigar stub into it.

"Look here," Dickens called to us from the dead man's desk, "this must have been a manuscript he was working on. Look, the pages are numbered." He hunted around on the floor near the desk, collecting papers that had been flung about. In this manner, he managed to reconstruct the pile of pages from back to front. He ended up holding the title page of the manuscript in his hand and reading it to us aloud: "Guy Fawkes and the Gunpowder Plot of 1605."

"Sixteenth- and seventeenth-century history was his b-b-bailiwick," Dodgson reminded us. "That must be a historical monograph in p-p-progress."

"It must not have been what the intruder was looking for," Dickens turned away from it, "because it seems to be all here."

"Heigh ho," Morse hailed us from yet another quarter of the room, "it's what's left of our dead friend's appointments book, it seems," and he held up a tattered piece of leather with the remains of torn pages hanging out of it.

"Do you think someone tore it up on purpose?" Dickens asked in all seriousness.

"They seem t-t-to have t-t-torn up almost all of the b-b-books in the room," Dodgson observed.

"But they tore those books at the spines," young Morse was thinking aloud, "tore their covers off. This one they tore all of the pages into pieces."

"So that no one would read his appointments for the day he died," Dickens joined in Morse's speculations, "or for the days leading up to his death."

"If I could find those torn pages and piece them back together," clearly young Morse had already decided upon his course of action.

"Like a p-p-picture p-p-puzzle," Dodgson was caught up in the detective enthusiasm.

"Exactly!" Dickens seconded the motion. "We must do it," Dickens encouraged our enterprising young constable, who was already on his hands and knees on the floor collecting bits and pieces of torn paper that seemed to match the paper of the appointments book, "it will be the first thing that Field will ask for."

The mere invocation of the impending presence of the great Inspector Field sharpened young Morse's resolve and made him redouble his efforts to reconstruct the evidence.

We all wandered about in those rooms for another thirty minutes, but no more promising clues leapt up to collar our attention. Finally, the afternoon getting on towards the departure time of our return train to London, Dickens broke off our investigations and tendered our good-byes.

He thanked Old Dodo profusely and implored him to continue as our Oxford and Christ Church liaison on the case. Dodgson assured him that he was at our service. Little did we imagine how helpful Dodgson's strange conglomeration of interests and talents would prove as this case unfolded.

Dickens then proceeded to put young Morse in charge of all of the evidence—the corpse, the rifled rooms and all their contents—until Field should make his appearance on the scene. The eager constable assured him that nothing would be disturbed until the great man himself deemed it necessary.

Finally, Dickens implored them both to keep utterly secret everything they knew about the case. He even asked Dodgson to visit Mike the publican that evening and swear him to secrecy.

Those details attended to as we walked back across the meadow to St. Aldate's and Tom Tower, we climbed back into the growler for our ride through the bustling town to the railway terminus. Sleepy Rob seemed in a growly, muttering mood, but we did not find out why until the coach was loaded onto the railway car and we were once again underway in a shower of ashes and sparks for our return journey to London. What a miracle, to travel forty miles and back in a single day and never leave the security of your private coach.

As we raced through the countryside in the gathering dusk, Sleepy Rob, at the prodding of Dickens, regaled us with his grousing dislike for Oxford and its inhabitants.

"What sorts o' poofters ride around on those silly two-wheeled curtain rods all day?" Rob began his tirade. "One o' those clumsy fools lost control coming down that cobblestone 'ill and ran full into the side 'o my new cab. Put a bloody long scrape in the paint, 'ee did. I cursed 'im almost all the way down the street to that bridge, but 'ee just wobbled off with 'is long black robes trailin' behind 'im like some Methodistical preacher. That was the first one that woke me up, then another one comes tappin' on the side o' my new cab with his walkin' stick. A real curious one, 'ee was. Seemed 'ee just wanted to talk about 'ow odd it was to see a shiny new London growler in such a small town as Oxford. I told 'im I was engaged. I wanted to tell 'im to go stuff 'is 'ead in a dunghill, but I didn't, and 'ee went away."

"What did he look like?" Dickens inquired, purely for the purpose of making conversation to pass the time of the train journey. At least that is what I supposed at the time.

" 'Ee was a fat little one, 'ee was," Sleepy Rob described the curious man, "with a bowler and a monocle on a ribbon and a shiny black walking stick."

THE PLOT AND THE PLAYWRIGHT

(November 26, 1853 — Evening)

e steamed into Victoria Railway Station at about half seven and galloped across London to the Bow Street Police Station. To Dickens's great delight, both Inspector Field and Serjeant Rogers were waiting for us in the bullpen. Ah, the bullpen! From its blazing hearth to its rocking chairs to its bottles of gin secreted in the storage cupboard to its metal cage attached to the back wall, it has served over the years as our meeting place, interrogation room, and the hatchery for all of our plots. This night it served as Dickens's lecture hall as he spun out in the novelist's most studied detail the story of our entertaining afternoon in the city of Oxford.

When Dickens was finished, Field had a number of immediate questions.

Is this Morse a good man?

Can Dodgson be trusted?

Did we warn them to keep their own counsel on these events?

Who do you think ransacked the rooms and why?

We answered in the affirmative all of his questions except

the last, for which we could only offer the sheerest speculation.

"The person who entered those rooms," Dickens tried to
explain, "seemed more concerned for covering things up,
throwing things about."

He went on to tell about the possible clues that young
Morse had found—the cigar, the torn "appointments" book.

" 'Ee collected all the torn pieces 'ee could find of this
book?" Field's bushy black eyebrows narrowed.

"Yes, young Morse did, and has promised to reconstruct
them for us." Dickens beamed.

"Excellent," Field congratulated us all.

"Morse promised that he would keep the dead man's
rooms exactly as they are, keep everyone off," Dickens assured him, "in case you wish to look at them yourself."

"Well, now," Inspector Field seemed satisfied as he turned
to Serjeant Rogers, "I see nothing for it but to go to Oxford.
Eh, Rogers, don't you think?"

"Yes, sir, of course," Rogers offered his usual toadying
answer.

"We shall all go back there"—Field leaned forward towards us with his elbows on his knees like an earnest con-
spirator—"but not together like a plague of locusts. If the
murderer is there and suspicious that someone is on 'is trail,
all of us descending in a crowd will drive 'im underground.
No, we will stay apart from one another except at specified
times in specified places."

"But he was murdered here in London," I spoke up, not
relishing the idea of being away from Irish Meg, "should we
not look for his murderer here?"

"We 'ave spoken to our people in Lime'ouse 'Ole and
many others, 'ave we not, Rogers?"

"Yes, sir," Serjeant Rogers gave his usual answer.

"And no one knows nothin', is that not right?"

"Yes, sir. Not our coves, nor the Chinamen who can speak
English."

"The man was well known in the quarter," Field elaborated as Rogers shook his head in affirmation. "We even found the opium 'ouse that 'ee frequented. But 'ee never caused any fuss, just smoked 'is pipes, dreamed 'is dreams, and left quietly as 'ee came. The Chinee never asked 'is name, simply took 'is coin."

"Had he been there the night of the murder?" Dickens asked.

"Yes, 'ee 'ad. 'Ee came at about half ten and stayed until the early morning hours."

"Alone?"

"Yes, this time."

"What do you mean?" Dickens had caught the sly invitation in Inspector Field's voice to pursue the deductive possibilities of this one detail.

" 'Ee was not always solitary in the smokin' of 'is pipes," Field went on. " 'Ee 'ad brought women with 'im before, and sometimes 'ee was accompanied by other men. Unfortunately, the Chinee could not remember what any of these others looked like."

"The women?" I asked with a raised eyebrow.

"Whores, probably," Field shrugged.

"He was murdered upon leaving the opium house, wasn't he?" Dickens voice quickened as he began to piece together what Field already knew. "The murderer was lying in wait for him, wasn't he? The murderer knew his goings and comings and was waiting in ambush. That's it, is it not?"

"Yes, I think so," the tiny grin around the corners of Field's mouth showed that he was amused at Dickens's intensity. "I think 'ee was murdered by someone 'ee knew, someone who knew that when 'ee came to London 'ee went to the opium 'ouse in Lime'ouse 'Ole, perhaps someone who 'ad actually accompanied 'im there."

"Then we must find out who this Ackroyd's opium companions are," Dickens declared, as if he were in charge of the case rather than Field.

"Yes," Field indulged him, "and in order to do that we must go to Oxford, but we must go discreetly."

"What do you mean by discreetly?"

"First of all, I mean separately," Field weighed his words. "Two gentlemen from London out on the town in Oxford, like you and Wilkie, would certainly be noticed. Good Lord, Charles, you would be noticed almost anywhere you go! You 'ave already been there once, 'ave been seen in the town," Field continued. "You can return without attracting too much attention."

"But you said that we were all going to Oxford." Dickens either was not following along too well or was getting impatient with Field's coyness.

"We are, only not together," Field answered mysteriously, tipping a wink in Serjeant Roger's direction, "and not just the four of us."

"What do you mean?" Dickens was all ears.

"You and Wilkie can go and stay with this Dodgson at the college, can you not?"

"Yes, he has said so," I assured Field.

"Rogers and I shall go to Oxford and take lodging," Field paused for effect, "but not as London detectives. We will be there to purchase beer. There is a famous brewery, isn't there? Or to buy a riverboat. Or . . . well . . . something."

"How about bicycles?" I suggested rather archly. "There were certainly plenty of those about."

Field looked at me as if I were some sort of blithering idiot. I am not certain that he even knew what a bicycle was, though he probably did since he seemed to know almost everything else.

"But I 'ave a further plan," Field confided. "I want someone else on the scene. I want open eyes very close to the action."

"What action? Who? What do you mean?" Dickens now took his turn at waxing idiotic.

Field just left Charles hanging, and turned unexpectedly to me: "What about this Irish publican of the, the . . ."

"The Bulldog," I supplied the name that he was groping for.

"Yes, what about 'im? Can 'ee be trusted? Will 'ee 'elp us?"

"Yes, he can be trusted," I answered his first question, then countered his second with my own: "Help us how?"

"You said that this Bulldog place is right across the way from Christ Church College?" Field was quietly interrogating me.

"Yes, it is," I answered. "You can look in its doorway from Dodgson's room."

"And you said that this murdered man's gang of political Dons 'angs out there, right?"

"Yes, according to Mike and Dodo, they do, yes," I answered.

"Good, then 'ere is my plan," and he leaned in close to us. "I wants to get up a little play, some street theatre, if you will, only it will be real, not on a stage."

We all leaned forward towards him, tightening the circle of our conspiracy. I felt like one of those silly witches in *Macbeth*.

"I want to put someone into this Bulldog place to spy for us, someone who will 'ave the run of the place, can eavesdrop on the customers, maybe even make friends with some of the people we wants to check up on, eh?"

"Mike the barman?" Dickens guessed. "You want him to spy on his own patrons?" he added with a note of rightful skepticism.

"No, not at all," Field quickly corrected. "I am sure 'ee is a good man, but that would be too much to ask. I just want 'im to 'ire a new server who can go amongst the customers, per'aps 'ear what they're talkin' about."

"A server," Dickens was thinking aloud again; "it would have to be a woman, then."

"Yes, to serve them pints and spy on the Christ Church people," Field paused as if weighing the wisdom of proceeding, "and perhaps entice one of them into 'er confidence so that 'ee might reveal their secrets."

"Entice?" Dickens repeated.

"Well," Field hesitated, "perhaps that was not quite the proper word. 'Tempt'? No, that is no better. Somehow enter their closed circle in order to expose their secrets. That is what I meant."

For some reason Dickens looked strangely at him: "Who did you have in mind to play this spy?"

"I first thought of Irish Meg," Field began, glancing across to register my reaction, "she 'as done this sort of thing for me before, she 'as. But then I thought better of it. She'd always been a spy among a lower class of people, the dodgers of the streets, and these are Oxford Dons we are tryin' to deceive 'ere."

The look of relief on my face must have been telling because Field threw off a tight little grin in my direction.

"What I need 'ere is a real actress." Field's voice rose at the excitement of it. It was he who was doing the acting turn and I suddenly realized that Dickens was his audience of one. "I need a professional actress who can make these Oxford blokes open up, who can get 'em in their cups and make 'em tell who killed this Ackroyd in Lime'ouse 'Ole."

"And who might that be?" Dickens's voice seemed almost resigned to the power of Field's will.

"Why, Miss Ternan, of course." Field laughed as if it had all been decided and the joke was on all of us for taking so long to figure it all out.

But Dickens chose not to acquiesce without a good grumble. "Now that is out of the question," he protested. "It is too dangerous. Why she is just a child, ahem," Dickens caught himself, "a young woman, I mean."

A stifled grin of amusement at Dickens's discomfiture twitched at the corners of Inspector Field's mouth, but was successfully subdued.

"I won't allow it," Dickens blustered on, "and I know Miss Ternan would never be foolish enough to consider such a proposal."

"Why I think she will be all ears," Field chided Dickens. "I know that she is presently between plays at Covent Garden and I shall pay 'er 'andsomely for 'er time and talent.

And besides, this is a capital chance for 'er to polish 'er acting skills in a starrin' role rather than those merely decorative parts she 'as been playing in the plays she 'as been in since returning to London. Why, I think Miss Ternan will jump at the opportunity."

"Oh come now, you cannot be serious," Dickens scoffed unconvincingly. "She is a professional actress. She would never stoop to this."

"To play such a part in the theatre of the real?" Field was almost taunting Dickens with his intuition into the motivations of that young woman's mind. "Do you think a real actress could ever pass it up? And especially Miss Ternan, after all she's been through. Why, it's that kind of turmoil in a life that makes 'em actresses in the first place, sends 'em into the world of make-believe. It's the bad childhoods and the brutal fathers and the unloving mothers and the lack of attention that puts 'em on the stage, pretending to be somebody else, 'igher, better, richer, more loved. Pass up this part? Not likely. No *real* actress could."

Field's animated soliloquy on actresses squashed all of Dickens's bluster. It made him realize that it was not his decision at all, but Ellen's, and that Field had some compelling arguments that might well overrule all of Dickens's possessiveness and fears for her safety. As for me, I was unutterably relieved that Irish Meg, who was so happy (and safe) in her work at Coutts Bank, was not going to be drawn back into Field's web.

Field waited a long moment upon Dickens's silence.

"I can ask 'er then, Charles?" He posed it in the quiet, serious voice of a close friend concerned for his comrade's permission, but he did not wait for an answer. "She is absolutely perfect for this role. You know it, and I know it, and she will see it right away."

"But it could be dangerous," Dickens protested weakly. He was defeated and he was beginning to realize it.

"Perhaps," Field was unperturbed, "but we shall keep a close eye upon 'er, and she will not be alone."

"What do you mean?" Dickens's whole demeanour had changed. No longer was he the alarmed protector of innocent womanhood. He had returned to his more familiar role of detective co-conspirator.

"Thompson will go into Oxford with 'er. 'Is orders will be to never let 'er out of 'is sight. We shall borrow 'im from Miss Burdett-Coutts and, who knows, 'ee may come in 'andier on this case than any of us can imagine."[10]

"Tally Ho Thompson!" Dickens was aghast.

"Yes." Field smiled benignly. "Who better? 'Ee will fit perfectly into the woodwork of this Irishman's pub. Who better to be a tapster? An Oxford workingman whose wife 'as driven 'im out to the pub? You know 'ow Thompson is. 'Ee can fit in anywhere. 'Ee can come and go at will. And 'ee will protect Miss Ternan with 'is life, you know 'ee will," and with that Field closed the subject. Dickens retreated, almost sullenly, into his own thoughts.

Field, obviously not wanting to leave it like that, made one more attempt to appease him: "Should I ask 'er, or would you rather?"

"No. No," Dickens looked at each of us in turn, realizing that he must abdicate whatever power he held over the young woman and let her decide for herself, "you ask her. I only fear that you are right and she will say yes."

"I have no doubt that she will if I can gauge 'er mettle at all." Field clapped the table with his closed fist. "She is a spirited young woman, beautiful, well-spoken, perfectly cast for this part."

The rest of our conversation that evening dwelt upon some of the other minor mysteries of the case that needed to be solved.

Why was Ackroyd murdered? And why in London?

[10]After the affair of "The Feminist Phantom" as recounted in *The Hoydens and Mr. Dickens*, Tally Ho Thompson became full-time bodyguard to Miss Angela Burdett-Coutts, the director of Coutts Bank, and one of the richest and most powerful women in Victorian England.

Obviously so he would not be identified so easily, so that it could be made to look like a street robbery.

Who ransacked his rooms and what were they or he looking for?

Speculation upon these matters kept us talking well past midnight. The gas lamps were blinking weakly through the heavy November fog when Dickens and I said good evening to Field and Serjeant Rogers at the door of the Bow Street Station and struck out on the short walk to Wellington Street. Predictably, Sleepy Rob's growler was tied up in front of the *Household Words* offices. Our personal cabman seemed to have this sixth sense that told him where to be when Dickens needed him, and he rarely disappointed. This night, however, when we roused him from his slumbers beneath the horse-blanket, it was to ferry me back to my rooms in Soho. Normally, I would walk, but it was such a bitter, dark night that I rejoiced to see Rob's cab waiting to take me home.

Imagine my great surprise when Dickens decided to ride along. He gave some lame excuse that he needed to take some more of the night air before retiring. It was only after I had been left at my doorstep and Rob's growler had clattered off that I realized what Dickens was really up to. He was going to seek out his Ellen. To warn her? To caution her against Field's plan? To press her to refuse? Irish Meg was fast asleep when I let myself into the flat, and as I lay awake beside her in our bed I was curious to learn what degree of success Dickens's nocturnal visit to his beloved mistress would bring.

Months later, in fact, after that whole Oxford affair was finally resolved, I asked Dickens if he had gone to Ellen that night to argue against Field's plan.

"I wish I had," he answered grimly. "I went to her house, had Rob pull up in the street right before her door, but, in the end, I did not go in. I wanted to warn her against it, to tell her my fears, describe her risks, but I did not do it."

"Why not?" My curiosity was aroused. "What did you do?"

"Nothing. I just sat there in the cab in the dark street and looked at her house, prayed that she would not do it, and if she did, which I knew she would, that she would not be hurt."

"What made you change your mind?" My interrogation was impertinent, for I really had no business asking these private questions, but my curiosity had quite run off from my sense of propriety.

"She did," Dickens did not hesitate to answer. I think he actually welcomed the opportunity to talk to someone about his unwieldy relationship with this fiercely independent young woman who was not even half his age. "She had made it quite clear that if I was ever going to be to her what I wanted to be, that if we were ever truly to be lovers, that I must stop treating her like a child, that I must treat her as an equal. She was adamant about that, and her rule applied to every aspect of our relationship, from the most public to the most private."

I was rendered almost speechless as he spun out this remarkable meditation with such alarming openness. It was the sort of confidence that rarely passed between two gentlemen. It was as if the drawbridge had been let down over the moat that protected our whole intensely private age and real life had been allowed to come in.

"Don't you see, Wilkie," he said it as if he were trying to understand it himself, "it had to be her choice. I could not tell her what to do, because my fears were those of a father, a protector, not a lover. She held all the power. I had to let her make her own choice in the matter. God help us," and he broke the tension with a shrug and a tiny inimitable bubble of laughter.

Ah, the fictions that we all weave around our lives. Dickens's personal novel was proving much more difficult in the composition than any of the published novels that he purveyed on a monthly basis.

THE REHEARSAL

(*November 27, 1853 — Morning*)

T he next morning, without hesitation, Ellen Ternan agreed to be Inspector Field's spy in Oxford. Dickens and I had accompanied Field and Serjeant Rogers to Miss Ternan's rooms, which were in a high, gabled house on Garrick Street just off St. Martin's Lane. They were pleasant enough lodgings, possessed of the advantages of being within an easy walk of Covent Garden Theatre, Ellen's place of employment with Macready's troupe, and being equally convenient to Dickens's offices and mid-week residence in Wellington Street.

"Oh, Inspector Field," Ellen Ternan answered in high seriousness when he made his case for her to take the leading role in his play, "I will play any role that you give to me. You have done so much for me in the past that there is little I could ever do to repay you. Oh, Charles," and she turned to Dickens, "this is so exciting. I shall go along on one of your detective jaunts. What a lark!"

As you might imagine, Dickens looked on with much less enthusiasm. I must credit him, though, with not interfering. Instead, he rolled up his sleeves to help Field prepare Ellen for her role as our agent in Oxford. Her preparation that morning was truly like a rehearsal for a play. First off, Field and Dickens (he was, after all, the reigning novelist of the age, and if anyone was going to give Ellen a fictional life, he decided that it was going to be him) gave her a name and a past life that she could take into Irish Mike's pub and trot out for the entertainment of the customers. We all thought that her new identity would be a theatrical one, with a name out of Shakespeare and an exotic past, but that was not Field's style at all.

"Your name will be Ellen," Field started off the rehearsal. "You won't 'ave any trouble answering to it. Ellen Byrne, let's say. Irish, so you'll fit in with Mike the Irish publican. Parents from Dublin, but you've never been. Grew up in London, a railway builder's daughter. The Bulldog is where you will work as a server, carrying pots of beer to the drunkards, the Dons, and the laughing students. They will all fall in love with you, and you will smile and tease."

She realized that it was Inspector Field's turn to be centre stage with Dickens feeding him his dialogue. He was like all of the stage managers she had known: demanding, yet offering her the chance to escape all of the confusion in her life. It was an attractive offer, but she knew, as every good actress does, that taking on a new life meant giving up the old, meant consenting to live by the playwright's script and the stage manager's rules. Oh yes, Ellen Ternan knew what Field was offering as he bombarded her with the facts of her new identity. If she did, however, she did not show it in any ostensible way. She listened as Field thundered around her as if he were Macready blustering away as King Lear.

Field pummelled her with questions about her life as this barmaid character: "Your father, 'ow was 'ee?"

"He wasn't. He was never there. Always working on the railway. On Sundays he'd be drunk."

"Ugly drunk?"

"No, he left us alone. Slept it off all afternoon. Went to work next morn."

"Where?"

"Wapping, on the railway line."

"And your mum?"

Ellen darted a quick glance at Dickens, then made a rather comical, sour face.

"Ah yes, Mummy." Ellen's voice was laden with sarcasm to the point that Field and Dickens and I all burst out laughing. Ellen's humorous quip was but one more indication of how far she had come from that terrible low point caused by her own mother's exploitation and abandonment of her.[11]

"Mummy," she went on. "She also worked out of doors, a washerwoman for a big house on Finsbury Square. She left me to care for my little brothers. A bad lot, those two tykes were. But they sent all three of us to the Ragged School. They did that. How's that sound?" and she broke character to get reassurance from Field and Dickens that she was playing her part in the right key.

"That's fine, wonderful," Field applauded.

"And 'ow did you become a barmaid, a public 'ouse serving girl?" Field prodded Ellen back into character.

"I don't know. How did I? You haven't given me that yet," she answered with a quiet shrug of her hands, her soft eyes moving from Field to Dickens and back to Field.

Field hesitated, looked to Dickens for aid.

Suddenly, Dickens's whole demeanour changed. The sullen worry which had hung over the proceedings from the moment Ellen had consented to take the role of spy suddenly lifted like a mist from a moor. By accident, Ellen and Field had bumbled upon the one role in this whole

[11]In Dickens's first case with Inspector Field (*The Detective and Mr. Dickens*), Ellen Ternan's perverse actress mother attempted to prostitute her daughter to three different men. It was this betrayal by her own parent that drove the sixteen-year-old Ellen to attempt suicide. In a later case (*The Hoydens and Mr. Dickens*), Mrs. Ternan reappeared as a participant in a blackmail plot against the fortune of Miss Angela Burdett-Coutts.

theatrical production that he could play better than anyone else, that of the creator of the fiction.

"Why, you left home for a boy," Dickens answered almost without thinking, "when you were only sixteen."

"And you are 'ow old now?" Field broke in gleefully.

"Nineteen, twenty next month."

"You loved him, but he was—no, became—a drunkard, got in with bad fellows," Dickens was wading knee-deep into his story. "He abandoned you and you had to find work. You went to work in a public house in London, the Lord Gordon Arms," and Dickens canted his head for Field's approval.

"Aha, very good." Field grinned. "They will vouch for 'er there if anyone takes the trouble to inquire. Yes, they will."

"But after two years there," Dickens gleefully spun out his story, "you needed to get out of London. Your mother had found you and was begging you to come home. You went to Victoria and took the first train out of the city. It landed you in Oxford. Irish Mike gave you work at the Bulldog."

Almost as if spent by the effort, Dickens subsided back into the cushions of the loveseat upon which he sat.

"The publicans of the Lord Gordon are James Potterson and 'is wife Abby." Field tapped the table with his formidable forefinger. "I will tell them to vouch for you if anyone asks."

"You are nineteen, almost twenty. You are an experienced London serving girl, despite your young age. You are quite friendly and smart despite your 'ard life and your ill luck at love." Field pounded these facts of their fiction at her as if he were nailing down a lid on her new identity.

"Wilkie," Field startled me, " 'ow should she dress? Where should she live? What victuallers should she fancy? Where can we meet 'er? 'Ow can we get messages to 'er?"

Clearly, Field was done pummelling her part into her for the moment and had turned to me for help in setting his scenario.

"Why, uh, dress? Uh, live?" I was trying to gather my wits.

"Yes." Field's violent forefinger raked at the side of his eye in impatience. "Do the Oxford servers dress differently from our London barmaids? Where would a pub girl live in Oxford? You know the place better than we."

I think Field must have meant it as a compliment, but the way he said it, so clipped and impatient, it came out something like "Get on with it, man, we haven't got all day!"

An expectant silence fell over the room as I tried to address one issue at a time. *How would Dickens do this?* I thought. *Conjure a character out of thin air?* I looked hard at Ellen, tried to envision her as a barmaid in the Bulldog.

"She'd show her neck," I said in an outburst of memory. "I've never seen a barmaid who didn't. A form-fitting blouse cut low beneath her neck."

"Scooped," Ellen nodded.

"Yes, scooped, but rather low, down to her, the tops of, well . . ."

"Yes, I see," and a tight little grin at my discomfiture took possession of Field's hitherto rather grim face.

But Dickens was not amused. I think he thought I was tarting his beloved Ellen up for the sake of the performance. He looked as if he was going to speak out angrily in protest, but Ellen Ternan never gave him the chance.

"Of course, a peasant blouse with small puff sleeves off the shoulder; perfect." Ellen seemed to be envisioning herself in costume as I had been attempting to do. "Over a long flowing skirt of grey cotton."

"And black leather boots that lace up the front in eyelets," I completed her costume.

"You seem to have been highly observant of the barmaids during your stay in Oxford, Wilkie." Dickens made a rather sour joke.

I was sorely tempted but I resisted. I almost blurted out what kinds of undergarments they wore as well, but I held my tongue, only because such gentlemen's raillery might have proved embarrassing to Ellen.

"And with your hair tied back, and colour on your lips

and cheeks and around your eyes," I added seriously for the sake of the illusion, but cocking one eye in Dickens's direction to register his dismay at each heightening of the commonness of his Ellen's fictional persona.

"My God!" Finally Dickens could stand it no longer. "You are going to make her look but one cut above a common street whore!"

Field was calm, almost amused. "But Charles," he said quietly, "that is exactly what a barmaid is."

Ellen laughed and smiled at Dickens. "He's right, you know. It must be believable or there 'is no use in doing it at all."

Dickens stared silently at us as if a cork had been stuck in his mouth.

"And where should she live?" Field tugged me back from my enjoyment of Dickens's momentary discomfort.

I thought on that and lit upon the perfect solution: "There are cheap boardinghouses on Blue Boar Street and Bear Lane just off St. Aldate's, directly behind Christ Church. The covered market is where she would buy her bread and eat her meals when she didn't take them in the pub. What do you mean by 'Where can we meet her?' " All this hard thinking was making me rather nervous.

"Once she is in place, working in the Bulldog for the Irishman, we will need a safe place where no one will observe us or disturb us as we speak, a place where she can safely go without anyone following her, somewhere none of the frequenters of the Bulldog would venture," Field answered.

"I see. Then it must be away from St. Aldate's and Christ Church and the Bulldog. Somewhere the Dons would never go."

I thought hard on it.

"What about St. Mary's Church on the High Street?" My voice sped up with excitement. "It is well away from Christ Church and the Bulldog, and anyone can go there to pray.

It has quiet corners where a conversation could go on un-noticed."

"And pray tell, how would you know?" Dickens mocked.

"Well, God knows I haven't spent a great deal of time there in prayer," I took his teasing with good humour, "but Dodgson and I used to go there for the choir and the pipe organ. It is the biggest in all of Oxford."

"Splendid, then," Field put his seal upon that plan. "Take a dark scarf that will cover your 'ead and face when you go to church. We'll 'ave Thompson, who will never be far from you, tip you a wink or pass you a note when we wish to speak with you in private and you can meet us in St. Mary's Church. Other than that, if you meet any of us anywhere in the city, you will not know us. Do you understand?" But he was looking at Dickens, not at Ellen, and his gaze was send-ing a message that Charles could not mistake.

Dickens acquiesced. He stared morosely first at Field, then at Ellen, but he did not object to the plan, to the enforced separation from his love that the plan occasioned. Sensing Dickens's acquiescence, Field grew more bold, pushing the plan in a direction that I am sure he knew would torment Charles.

"Well and good," Field nodded, tapping his formidable forefinger upon the arm of his chair, "but now let us get down to things a bit more personal."

"And that would be, pray tell?" Dickens had not com-pletely lost either his sarcastic voice or his protective con-cern for his mistress.

"That would be," Field proceeded carefully, "the manner that 'er charges in the pub will treat 'er."

"What do you mean?" Ellen asked with an innocence that would actually have been charming if it had not bespoken so much danger.

"I mean," Field turned on her, "that you will be a com-mon barmaid, a young, 'andsome woman, unmarried, and these men will treat you as such." That bluntly said, Field turned suddenly to me: "I don't suppose, Wilkie, that these Oxford Dons behave any differently than do your usual run of London rakehells and blades in our city pubs, do they?"

"No, no, they do not," I stammered. "Serving girls in Oxford are every one fair game just as they are for gentlemen on the town in London. Why, in fact, Oxford Dons, because they are all lifelong bachelors and locked up in the dark halls of their colleges all day, are perhaps an even more lustful and drunken lot when they are out on the town of an evening."

"There you 'ave it!" Field slapped the arm of his chair decisively. "You are goin' to 'ave to fight them off every evenin', Miss Ternan. You are goin' to 'ave to laugh and smile and wink and tease, and that will just inflame them the more. They will want to take you 'ome with them, or to an 'otel."

"An Oxford Don would never take a woman back to his rooms," I corrected Field. "The whole college would know about it by morning. It just isn't done."

"So, where would 'ee take 'er, then?" Field asked, more out of simple curiosity than as a furtherance of Ellen's spying education.

"Well . . ." I thought about it, "perhaps to an upper room in the pub hired for that purpose, or, as you said, to a disreputable hotel, or, if it were summer, they would go walking by the river, or," I suddenly remembered, "to the boathouses. I've heard some Dons have keys to the boathouses."

"Aha! Beware the boathouses!" Dickens growled in exasperation. "Really!"

"Miss Ternan," Field grew suddenly serious, "I brought this up as a warning to you. These men's raillery will seem innocent at first, but some of them, especially in their cups, will want to go farther. You must take care. You must be friendly with them, stand their bawdy jokes and rude advances, but do not be mistaken, you are there only to observe, to listen and remember what you 'ear, to gain whatever information you can about their dealings with this Ackroyd, our dead Don. It is the information we want. Nothing is more valuable than information these days."

I do not know if this speech was meant so much for Ellen as for Dickens, to placate his fears for her safety. I must say though that it did seem strange to hear Field giving his "only observe" speech to someone other than Dickens and myself. That speech was always how he sent us off in the past to gather information for his investigations.

"Yes, I understand," Ellen Ternan answered Field's warning speech. "I have dealt with these types of men before, in the theatre."

"And you shall always 'ave Thompson close at 'and if anything 'appens that you cannot 'andle," Field assured her (and Dickens).

"But what if I am not in trouble, and yet he thinks that I am or it appears that I am?" Ellen asked.

"You are really going to be quite good at this," Field signalled his approval of her spy's foresight. "That is a brilliant question."

Dickens shifted nervously in his chair, not comfortable at all with his mistress's brilliance at this whole unsavoury business.

"I will instruct Thompson," Field proceeded, "to never let you from 'is sight except in those most obvious of times when no 'arm can come, when you are bolted into your room for the night or when you are busy working in a crowded public 'ouse. But you must develop some signal for Thompson to pounce, a danger sign that cries out 'elp and brings 'im on the run."

"But what shall that be?"

"Somethin' out of the ordinary, I would think, somethin' 'ee would pick up on right away." Field was more thinking aloud than directly answering her question.

There was a restive moment of silence as we all thought on it.

"A cigar!" Dickens burst out. "Light up a cigar, as so many of the hoydenish women are doing these days. That will catch that scapegrace Thompson's eye."

"Yes, a cracking good idea," Field agreed.

"You'll carry some small gentleman's cigars, and if you find yourself in any trouble that you cannot get out of alone, just light one up and Thompson will know to step in."

"As long as I don't have to smoke the whole thing," Ellen laughed. "That would be worse than the fate Tally Ho is rescuing me from."

We all laughed, but I sensed that Dickens's gaiety was a bit strained. Is it not ironic how ultimately we become the victims of our own fictions? You might say that Ellen Ternan was a character in a novel that Dickens had been writing for almost three years, ever since he met her backstage at Covent Garden and fell in love at first sight. Now we all were rewriting her character for this new fiction that we were creating. My whole goal in life in those days was to write a novel, create fiction out of thin air as Dickens did every day, and that was exactly what we were doing. And that was what made Dickens so nervous about this whole affair. Unlike his novels, he could not control the outcome, write a happy ending.

"That's it, then," Field's proclamation startled me out of my reverie, "the day after tomorrow, you and Thompson leave for Oxford, Miss Ternan, and the rest of us shall not be far behind. Wilkie, send an urgent message to your chum Dodgson and direct 'im to make the proper arrangements with this Irish publican. Rogers, contact this Morse and tell him that we are coming and what we will need."

All his orders barked around our small circle of plotters like the true Serjeant-Major that he was, Field turned back to Ellen, his voice much quieter: "Remember, you are only there to gather information. Find out who Ackroyd's opium companions were, what those men talk about and think about, 'ow they spend their time when they are not being Dons. The smallest thing may be the most important. But"—

and Field turned with a mischievous grin towards Dickens—
"as it was so eloquently put a minute ago, 'Beware the boathouses!' "

Even Dickens could not help smiling at that.

SETTING THE STAGE

୬

(November 27–29, 1853)

With our leading actress in place and her supporting cast given their parts, we left Ellen Ternan's house that sharp November morning ready to get up our play. It had been determined that Rogers would collect Ellen in the police coach that afternoon and transport her to the Lord Gordon Arms to go shopping with Mrs. Abby Potterson, the wife of the publican, for clothes appropriate for an Oxford tavern server. Messages were sent to both Dodgson and young Morse, instructing them to scout accommodations and generally prepare for the arrival of our theatre troupe. Her wardrobe complete, Ellen and Tally Ho Thompson would depart London for Oxford on the evening train.

When they arrived in that city, they would disembark the train separately. Thompson would make his way to the town and contact young Morse at the police station, while Miss Ternan would make her way to Christ Church and inquire of the porter for a message (from Dodgson) that would direct her to her lodgings. The next day, she would take up her employment at the Bulldog and Thompson would take up, once again, his not unfamiliar life of loitering. We hoped that only Mike the Irish publican would suspect that she was anything other than what she appeared. Inspector Field and Serjeant Rogers expected to make their entrance into Oxford the following day, and take up their lodgings in the town.

As for Dickens and me, we were unable to join them until the weekend because we both had commitments to fulfill before we could take the train down. But as those days passed and first his Ellen and then the others left town, I could see that Charles was agitated, champing to be near his love, to watch over her. He was committed to a charity dinner on Friday, the success of which was utterly dependent upon his speaking, thus we could not leave until the morning train on Saturday. Sleepy Rob was alerted, and a message was sent to Mrs. Dickens at Broadstairs proclaiming that her husband would not be able to join her and the children for the weekend, due to pressing business out of the city.

On Thursday and Friday, Dickens prowled the *Household Words* offices like a caged panther. He would work on his novel for a few minutes, then move to the mag's editing table, then come back to my cubicle to bother me.

"This is all a terrible idea, Wilkie," he finally blurted out on about his fourth or fifth circling of the premises. "What if something should happen to her? What if one of them realizes that she is a spy and kills her as they did that Ackroyd in Limehouse Hole? I will never be able to live with myself."

I wanted to just tell him outright that he should quit deceiving himself, that he really had no say in the matter at all, and that his beloved Ellen had no interest whatsoever in his rather comical image of himself as St. George, her protector. Somehow, he was simply not capable of seeing the rather rude fox-in-the-henhouse interpretation affixed to his relationship with the young Miss Ternan. But I had neither the heart nor the stomach for telling him the truth.

The charity dinner on Friday night took place at the London Tavern, a popular place for these affairs due to its huge, open commons room, which could accommodate scores of spectators as well as a number of dining tables and a podium for speaking. The evening was to benefit the Guild of Literature and Art, which collected funds to help both serious struggling artists and older destitute artists who have fallen sick. "In order to benefit from this one," Dickens would joke, "you have to either be so bad you can't sell your work or so sick you can't do your work."

It should have been a lovely affair, and it was (for the revelers who witnessed the proceedings). But for Dickens and me, it was just something to be gotten through before we could get on with the case.

I had heard Dickens give this speech perhaps a dozen times before. He was masterful in its presentation; after all, he had spent his whole life as an actor and entertainer. It was light and funny and serious all at once, and well worth listening to; but as he spoke, I found my mind wandering into other taverns and more private rooms.

I saw Ellen Ternan in the pub moving slowly around a table filled with heavy, tweed-coated men, collecting empty pints, serving full ones, moving slowly, listening intently, missing nothing.

I saw my Meggy coming out of the great stone bank and on the steps meeting a man in a dark greatcoat and a high beaver hat. Placing her hand in the crook of his arm, she walked off with him into the cavernous expanse of Trafalgar Square.

Perhaps it was the drink? I had consumed three pints of English ale. I do not know, but my thoughts filled with panic. I saw Ellen being dragged by her hair down a dark Oxford alleyway, thick twelfth-century stone walls rising on each side. I imagined her being beaten in the shadows by some dark phantom in a black cape. And I saw my Meggy naked in bed with some fat-backed bald man, her legs clasped hard around his pounding hips, her hands gripping tight the posts of the headboard.

"Every person deserves the freedom to live his life," Dickens was shouting to the crowd, "and that is what this fund supports for those artists in London whose lives have fallen upon hard times. We have all known hard times, haven't we? So please give what you can to help our fellow artists through their hard times."

Dickens's voice brought me back to reality and out of my fevered dreams. Upon returning to the table, he immediately bent down to one of those ubiquitous subscription cards and started writing intently.

"I thought you already made your subscription, Charles," I joked.

"Oh no, Wilkie, that's not it at all," he replied, never looking up. "It is 'hard times.' A good title for these times, don't you think, Wilkie? I just thought of it as I was speaking. 'Hard Times.' Perfect. It may well be the title of my next novel, Wilkie. It may well be." He smiled gaily, folded the notecard, and placed it in his waistcoat pocket.

Walking home through the London streets, Dickens was more animated than usual. I had seen him this way before. It was the anticipation of the chase.

"Finally, tomorrow, we are off to Oxford, Wilkie." He was excited.

And I really did try to share his enthusiasm, but I must admit that I felt the same misgivings that I felt each time we embarked on a new adventure with Inspector Field. Dickens, who had no fear at all, always felt that we were off into a world of intrigue, adventure, and romance, something out of Sir Walter Scott, for God's sake. As for me, I never seemed able to get over the fact that we were entering a realm of murder, violence, corruption, and deceit. Dickens thrived on these cases. They scared the living daylights out of me.

A GOOD IRISH LASS

(November 30, 1853 — Morning)

We left for Oxford on the Saturday morning train in Sleepy Rob's growler. The trip was swift and uneventful except for the hot cinders, which once again forced us to close up the windows of the coach and miss the passing scenery of the countryside. But it was a dreary, cloudy day and we spent most of the journey enclosed within our own thoughts. Dickens had brought along copy from *Household Words* to be read and edited, and he worked on that as the train sped us towards our destination.

Rob left his growler in the livery barn at the Oxford railway station. Its shiny black presence had been deemed by Inspector Field as too conspicuous for the streets of Oxford. Rob was to be on call at any hour to liberate the growler from its dungeon at the railway station and transport us if the need arose. Dickens offered to get Rob a room in a boardinghouse near Christ Church, but that worthy insisted upon sleeping in his cab with the horses in the livery.

"Never mind, guv," Sleepy Rob insisted. "I'm more comfortable with the straw and the 'orses than I would be with some tribe o' gorps in some boardin' hestablishment."

On that note, leaving Rob in the stable, Dickens and I walked into the town. It took us about ten minutes to reach the Haymarket where it meets the High Street. As we climbed the cobblestoned incline of the Haymarket, I broke our trudging silence and demanded of Dickens our destination.

"Oh, Wilkie, I know that Field would erupt if he knew, but I simply must see her. Good God, it has been three days!"

That question answered, we proceeded straight on over the top and down St. Aldate's into the front door of the Bulldog. Ellen was serving, but since the luncheon crowd had not yet arrived, she was loitering beside the tap talking with Irish Mike and some of his regular morning tapsters, all of whom seemed quite taken with her. I must admit, she looked quite fetching in her blue and white peasant blouse with its rather low neckline and her long hair pulled back into a large puffball over her neck.

Dickens spotted her as soon as we got in the door, but he acted his part well and never let on. He went to one of the small tables against the wall and deposited himself on the cushioned bench facing the tavern. But then he did a curious thing. Getting up right away, as if he didn't like his seat, he came around and took the straight-backed chair before I could sit down in it. Humouring him, I took the seat against the wall as he sat with his back to the room. It took me a moment to realize why he had done it. It was so that he could talk to her without being observed by the others in the room.

Unfortunately, Dickens was destined for disappointment. His Ellen picked up her tray as soon as we sat down and was going to come right over to serve us, but Irish Mike stopped her and came rushing over to serve us himself. He was only being the old friend and diligent publican, but I could see Dickens's dismay at being cut off from close proximity to his love.

"Wilkie, my boy, and"—lowering his voice—"Mister Dickens, faith an' it's good to see ya back in here again."

"Hello, Mike," I greeted him.

"Yes, Mike, it is good to be back in Oxford," Dickens answered somewhat sharply, "but it has been a long trip on the train and Wilkie and I are very thirsty. Why don't you send the barmaid over and we shall order some drinks."

"Oh, no need for that," Irish Mike insisted, "it'll be stout again, won't it? Ye liked it well enough last time." And not waiting for an answer, he blithely shouted, "Lass, two pints o' the dark for these gents."

It seemed to take an eternity for Ellen Ternan to draw those two pints of Irish stout. But finally she arrived with the foaming glasses, and Dickens got his chance to look her in the face. Since Mike knew only that she was Field's spy and not that she was also Dickens's mistress, it was necessary for the two of them to keep up their act. Ellen did it much better than Dickens. When she arrived with the pints, he looked up at her like some moony country bumpkin.

"Gentlemen, two pints." Ellen was all business as she delivered our glasses to the table.

"This is our new server, gents." Irish Mike turned his back to the rest of the pub and tipped us a broad wink. "Her name is Elly—a good Irish lass, she is."

"Thank you, Elly," Dickens said in a near whisper, hardly able to speak as he looked longingly up at her.

"Yes, thank you, Elly." Irish Mike dismissed her and Dickens's face fell with an almost audible thud. Even Irish Mike could not help but notice Dickens's reaction. "Yes, she is a pretty young thing, isn't she?" he misinterpreted.

Fortunately, we did not have to make small talk with Irish Mike for very long as the Bulldog rather quickly filled up with the luncheon mob eager for their meat pies and hard-boiled eggs, their mashed potatoes with peas. Neither Ellen nor Mike had any more time to talk, so Dickens and I fin-

ished our pints and got up to leave. As we were walking out
the front door, Dickens turned to take one last look at his
beloved Ellen and I also glanced back to follow the tableau.
At that moment, I bumped flush into a workman coming
through the door, and the impact spun both of us around.

"Sorry, guv," the man mumbled as he brushed past me.

"Oh, my fault, sorry," I graciously apologized in the direction of the man's back as he moved away from me towards the tap. But that back looked familiar, and I had
heard that particular voice before. It took me but a short
second to place it. *O my God!* I thought. My right hand leapt
in panic to the watch pocket of my waistcoat. Yes, it was
Thompson, and my gold repeater was gone.

THE TELESCOPE

❧

(November 30, 1853 — Afternoon)

S tunned, still poking at my watch pocket in disbelief, I
followed Dickens out into the street.

"That scoundrel has stolen my watch again," I
fumed. "I'm going back in to get it." Not thinking, I turned
and started for the door.

Dickens yanked me back by my greatcoat like a head-
master collaring an errant schoolboy. "You can't do that,
Wilkie." It was all he could do to keep from laughing. "You
will give it all away. Never mind for now. You know that
Thompson will give it back. It is just a joke he enjoys playing
on you. Take it in good humour."

Dickens may have found it funny. Thompson may have
thought it a great joke. But I did not see any humour in it
at all. The idea of Tally Ho Thompson sitting in that pub
fingering my gold repeater and laughing to himself made
me furious. It was, however, abundantly clear that there was
nothing I could do. Still fuming, I followed Dickens down
St. Aldate's and into the Oxford Police Station in search of
our conspiratorial familiars.

The heavy constable with the unkempt muttonchops

spreading across his face like Scottish gorse was sitting at his desk bothering over a pile of papers as if they were ancient hieroglyphics. This time, however, he recognized us immediately and jumped up with rather astounding dispatch for one so large and bulbous. "Young Reggie is expectin' you gents," he informed us even as he was scuttling off to find that Oxford worthy. In mere moments, young Constable Morse appeared, greeted us by name, and ushered us down the corridor, saying, "We 'ave been waiting to fill you in. We 'ave set up back 'ere."

And set up indeed they had. Inspector Field and Serjeant Rogers were waiting in the small surgery room where we had laid out our stiff friend Ackroyd only four days before. Young Morse had arranged for the corpse to be preserved in a nearby icehouse. Field had commandeered the room to serve as his base of operations for this Oxford investigation. The surgery table upon which the corpse had been laid was now pushed against the wall and had become Field's worktable, all cluttered with scraps of paper, dirty teacups, and various evidence specimens of the case. Leaning against the wall atop that table and all written upon in chalk was a large, black, square slate. Young Morse had evidently somehow cashiered some distressed wooden chairs, which comprised the rest of the furnishings of the room.

Without the pleasantry of any sort of greeting, Field, upon our entrance, looked up from his contemplation of the accumulated clues and growled, "We expected you somewhat earlier."

"We stopped at the Bulldog on the way," Dickens confessed. "I was just curious to see that all was going well with Ellen."

A cloud began to form on Field's brow.

"Oh, all is going quite well," I groused. "Thompson has already stolen my gold watch."

Field, who had been about to scold Dickens and me for breaking his rules, looked at Rogers.

Rogers looked at Field.

Suddenly they both broke into knowing laughter and Field took a sixpence from his pocket and handed it over to Rogers in obvious payment of a bet.

" 'Ee said 'ee'd do it first day you wos in town," Rogers gloated, flipping the coin tauntingly in the air, "and 'ee wos as good as 'is word, 'ee wos."

Dickens breathed freely in relief that he had escaped Field's reprimand, and all I could do was glower darkly at the two of them who were having so much fun at my expense.

When the hilarity subsided, Morse and Field spent the next hour telling us what they had discovered in the two days since the investigation had been moved to Oxford. In fact, most of their narrative was comprised of information that young Morse had been gathering since that first day when we had delivered the corpse to him. It seems he had been virtually living in the dead man's rifled rooms, reconstructing order out of chaos, piecing together a scenario of what had happened there, and why.

"Constable Morse is quite the detective," Field openly praised his young protégé, as Rogers sourly looked on. " 'Ee 'as done a deal of work on 'is own while waitin' for us to arrive. Tell them, Morse. 'Ee's all but took up residence in the dead Don's rooms."

"Yes, the rooms," young Morse began. "Since we broke in that day, I 'ave spent some time there. In fact, I 'ave been sleepin' there."

"Tell them why," Field interjected like a proud father placing his son atop the piano to perform (as Dickens once told me his father used to do).

"For several reasons," young Morse carried on.

Serjeant Rogers looked as if he wanted to stuff a large cork down the young policeman's throat.

"For one thing, I wanted to ensure that whoever tossed the rooms did not return and disturb them further. I also 'oped to be there if anyone tried to get in, because he would most likely be our culprit. For another thing, I wanted to search the parlour room more closely and work with the things that 'ad been tossed, not bein' disturbed or 'avin to carry it all back to the station and then 'avin' Inspector Field want to look at it back 'ere in the room where it was first found and where it rightly belonged."

Stopping for breath, young Morse gave Field a chance to nod his approval.

Serjeant Rogers tossed his head in disgust as if he wished that young Morse had been murdered in his sleep in the dead man's rooms.

"Bein' there, right in the room, really 'elped, I think," Morse was in dead earnest, "because I'd just sit there in the room with the gas lamps on and try to see where the things on the floor 'ad been before they was thrown on the floor. I'd close my eyes and try to see things fallin' off the desk and off the shelves and off the bookcases."

"Could you see the one who wos doin' it?" Rogers muttered sarcastically.

"Yes, I could," Morse replied, deadly serious, "in a manner of speakin'. I could see 'im movin' about the room, and where 'ee went and what 'ee did. 'Ee came in all excited, knockin' the books off the bookcases and the trinkets off the knick-knack shelves, but then 'ee settled down and tossed the desk because things from the desk, stationery, paperweights, were on top of the books and the broken glass of the plates and figurines. 'Ee must 'ave found what 'ee was seekin' because then I think 'ee sat down in Ackroyd's armchair and lit 'is cigar. I think 'ee was readin' Ackroyd's little black appointments book, which 'ee found in the middle drawer of the desk because the side drawers were not tossed at all. When 'ee got done readin' it, 'ee tore it up, and threw the scraps on the floor in front of the chair then put his cigar out by grinding it into the rug with his boot."

"Pity you could not see his face," Dickens chuckled. "You seem to have seen everything else."

"It is, indeed, an interestin' way of remaking the scene of a crime or whatever 'appened in that room," Field complimented the young constable yet again. "A way of readin' the room that we could all learn from," and Field shot a quick glance at Serjeant Rogers, whose lips were stretched tight with jealousy.

"I wish I *could* 'ave seen 'is face," young Morse replied to Dickens eagerly. "That would certainly make our job much easier, wouldn't it, Inspector?" he asked, turning back to Field.

"The mind and imagination can take us a long way in the solvin' of a murder," Field agreed, "but finally it only ends when you can look the murderer in the eye and 'ee somehow shows you that 'ee is the one. Then you 'ave got 'im. When I caught up with the famous Mister Manning in Scotland, 'ee took one look at me and knew it was all up. 'Ee broke down like a spaved 'orse."[12]

"But what it seems Constable Morse's ruminations have accomplished," Dickens led us out of the realm of detective philosophy, "is to emphasize the importance of the remains of our friend Ackroyd's appointments book."

"Exactly!" Field thumped his forefinger down on his makeshift worktable. "And Morse 'as done a smashing job with that one, too."

Rogers scowled darkly.

We all turned to Morse.

"I put it all back together," he began, actually a bit embarrassed by all the attention he was receiving, "and it's all there, except for one page. 'Ee dated each page before 'ee wrote down who 'ee was meetin' that day," Morse explained, "but November 24, the day before 'ee was murdered, isn't there. I put all the other torn-up pages back together, but November 24 is gone."

[12]John Manning, husband of Maria Manning, was hung with his wife at a public hanging in London in 1850. It was at this hanging that Dickens and Collins first made the acquaintance of William Field. The scene is described in Collins's first commonplace book, titled *The Detective and Mr. Dickens*.

Dickens and I looked at each other, not immediately realizing what that meant.

"Whoever tossed the room, probably whoever killed Ackroyd," Field spoke softly, "took that page away with 'im."

"Because 'is, the killer's own name, was on it," Rogers declared brightly.

"Exactly." Field tapped the table again for punctuation.

"And perhaps even why 'ee and Ackroyd were meetin'," Morse added. "Ackroyd frequently made a short note in the book concerning what business was to be transacted."

"Tell them about this Stadler," Field prompted.

"The little book was not a total loss because that page was missin'. Or at least I 'ope that is the case. The missin' page, November 24, was a Thursday, so I looked at the notations for the other Thursdays that month and for October as well. Not every Thursday, but most Thursdays, and Tuesdays as well it seems, Ackroyd was meeting with Stadler, the Chemistry Don, in the late afternoon, four, half four. There were a few short notations: 'Build,' 'Work, Pub,' 'Work on project.' There is a good chance that Ackroyd and Stadler worked together on something that Thursday afternoon before they went to the Bulldog and got in their big argument with the others." And, for a moment, young Morse rested his case, as the Old Bailey lawyers would put it.

"Fine. 'Ee seems to 'ave reserved Tuesdays and Thursdays for workin' on some project with this Stadler," Field summed up, "but what would bring together a History Don and a Chemistry Don?" He looked around to see if we had an answer. None forthcoming, he nodded back to young Morse, who continued.

"I also interviewed the college porter. 'Ee showed me the gatebook. 'Ee writes down everyone who comes into college and who they are visitin', but since Stadler is a Christ Church Don, 'ee would just be waved through. I looked at the notations for the twenty-fourth and no one came a-vistin' Ackroyd. I asked about the twenty-sixth as well, the day the room was probably tossed, and nobody came in for Ackroyd that day, either."

"So the porter was really no help?" Dickens asked. I sensed that he was starting to become bored by this meticulous policeman's narrative.

"Oh no, not at all," young Morse shook his head. "The porter's answers told us much about Ackroyd, 'is 'abits, 'is comin's and goin's. The porter remembered that Ackroyd went out early in the afternoon that Thursday, but came back carryin' a bag of goods, greens or meats, food for 'is rooms, the man thought, but then 'ee remembered that Ackroyd did not walk in the direction of 'is rooms. But 'ee did not know where 'ee went."

"Per'aps 'ee went to this Stadler's rooms with 'is bag of whatever," Field added. "It was Thursday afternoon."

"I also asked him who Ackroyd's frequent visitors were, and this added to our list." Young Morse returned to our interchange with the porter.

"List?" Dickens looked to Field.

"We 'ave made a list of all the people who knew Ackroyd or spent any significant amount of time with 'im."

"Hit's not a very long list," Rogers remarked wryly.

"Yes," Field nodded to his serjeant. "Ackroyd did not 'ave many friends."

"The porter said that very few people ever visited Ackroyd in 'is rooms. We mostly made our list from Irish Mike telling us who 'ee drank with in the pub. The porter merely verified those names."

"Who is on this list?" Dickens posed the logical next question.

"It is 'ere, on the slate." Field pointed to a column of names written down one side of the black slate in white chalk.

We all turned our attention to it. Beside each name was noted that person's college affiliation and academic discipline.

"Ackroyd, David—Christ Church—History" headed the list. I do not know whether it was because his name began with an "A" or because he was the focus of the investigation, but his was the first name. Tactlessly, or brutishly, or perhaps just matter-of-factly, written next to his entry was the rather obvious word "DEAD." I remember wondering if that commentary upon its referent's present whereabouts implied that other similar annotations might be expected to go up next to some of the succeeding entries on the list. My restless mind pictured words like "wounded," "maimed," "lost," "drunken," "drowned," "hell," "heaven," "London" going up next to the other names on the list. Those names were:

Stadler, Horace—Christ Church—Chemistry
Crenshaw, William—Oriel—Biology
Norman, Gerard—Trinity—Chemistry
Bathgate, John—Balliol—Literature
Squonce, Wherry—Balliol—Literature
Watson, Martin—Brasenose—Physical Science
Carroll, Welsey—All Souls—Philosophy
Barnet, John—Queen's—Engineering Science
Hayman, Alan—Exeter—Physiology

Dickens and I stood pondering the list. The others waited expectantly as if they had already tried to predict what our reactions to it would be and had placed their bets.

"Mostly scientists," Dickens finally said. "That's rather curious, isn't it?"

"Not really," I answered. "Oxford is renowned for the physical sciences, probably more so than any other study, even religion."

"Fine, then," Dickens seemed to be trying to work this all out by talking aloud, "but what are a historian, a philosopher, and two literature Dons doing with all these scientists, and why was the historian killed?"

"We don't know," Field confessed. "Per'aps they all just ended up in the same pub. Per'aps something else 'olds them together. This is something that I 'ope Miss Ternan's listening can answer for us. Per'aps it's political, or 'as to do with the University?"

"Who sought out whom? That might be the way to understand this list." Dickens had been thinking hard on it and inserted the hitherto most sensible comment into the speculation. "Did the historian and the philosopher go out seeking the scientists? Who started this Bulldog drinking society? Per'aps Irish Mike can answer that one for us."

"I took the liberty of doing some preliminary interviews," young Morse piped up, "just to give Inspector Field some idea of the lay of the land, so to speak." The young policeman was apologizing for his resourcefulness. "Irish Mike tried to remember who the first regulars from that crowd 'ad been, and Stadler and Ackroyd were the ones that popped into his mind, the Christ Church Dons who lived closest to the Bulldog. Mister Dodgson said the same thing, that Ackroyd and Stadler had been goin' to the Bulldog ever since he could remember."

"What about the cigar you found in Ackroyd's rooms?" Field prompted his new young protégé once again.

"They all smokes cigars, sir. What gentleman doesn't these days? The young lady who is workin' at the Bulldog is alert for small cigars like the one I found, but they are pretty common, sir, and I would not depend on them as evidence of anything."

"In fact, Mister Morse, you could say that of all of this"—and Field, with a sweep of his hand, indicated the cluttered table and the full scrawled-over slate. "None of this is any evidence of anything. We really know little more about this murder than when we started."

Rogers perked up. Was his master going to put this young pretender in his place?

"Yes, sir, quite true," young Morse was unabashed, "but all of this 'as certainly directed us 'ow to proceed."

"And that would be?" A mischievous glint had come into Field's eye.

"Well, sir," and Morse hesitated just a moment, glancing around the circle of his auditors from Field to Dickens to myself. "Well, sir, you see," and he decided to forge ahead nonetheless, "I thinks we should pay close attention to this Stadler, the Chemistry Don, as well as try to find out what this whole group of Dons is up to, if it's more than just meetin' in the Bulldog to drink ale at night."

"Quite right." Field smiled benignly at the young man. "Quite true. I think Mr. Stadler might be a fitting target for you, Charles and Wilkie."

Both of us suddenly went on point, flushed from our state of complacent observation by the challenge that Field was pressing upon us.

"You can make up some story, can you not, Charles, that will get you an introduction to this Stadler through Wilkie's friend, Dodgson?" Field's stony gaze fell heavily upon us. "After all," he joked, with all the light and playful sarcasm of a Jonathan Swift, "you do occasionally make up stories, do you not?"

Dickens could only smile and bow silently to Field. Of course he would fabricate some story in order to talk to Stadler. Of course he would obey Field in any task that worthy assigned us. Of course Dickens would play the eager and willing Mephistopheles to Field's implacable Satan.[13]

That settled, Field turned back to young Morse. "There is one other aspect of this case that intrigues me, Morse," he began, "and that is the opium. I want you to go back to Ackroyd's rooms and search for any evidence of 'is drug use. The Chinaman in Lime'ouse 'Ole said that sometimes 'ee brought other men to partake of the evil smoke. Per'aps they were these dons, or some of 'is Oxford students.

---

[13]Collins seems to be getting carried away in this chapter with his literary allusions. His earlier sarcastic reference to the heavy-handed satirist Jonathan Swift is followed by this reference to the reigning devils in Christopher Marlowe's *Dr. Faustus.*

Per'aps there are drugs secreted in 'is rooms. Go over them from floor to ceiling and see what you find."

Morse accepted his commission brightly. I almost expected him to salute like some respectful young midshipman.

"And as for Serjeant Rogers and myself," Field drew to the end of his assignment chit, "I think we shall be policemen down from London trying to solve the murder of an Oxford don. I think we shall interview friend Ackroyd's colleagues one by one just to see what they 'ave to say about their good friend's death. It was only announced in the broadsheets this morning, you know," that last being for Dickens and me, the new arrivals in Oxford. "I think we shall stir things up with a little touch of real detective work while all this play-acting is going on around us." And with that summary pronouncement, Inspector Field made it abundantly clear that we were dismissed.

Dickens and I merely walked up St. Aldate's to Tom Tower and knocked on Charles Dodgson's door. Sleepy Rob had already delivered our luggage, two small grips each containing enough clothes for a short stay and our shaving kits. It was to be an almost military bivouac. Dodgson had been waiting expectantly for us to arrive and was all enthusiasm and curiosity as to the intricacies of the case. Old Dodo installed Charles and me in his guest bedroom. He had somehow dragged a small couch in from his parlour (its presence was not missed in the least from that cluttered room) to complement the single sleeping bed already occupying that guestroom. As soon as I saw the arrangement, I entertained no doubts as to who would be sleeping on that couch and who would be enjoying the comparative luxury of the bed.

But Dodo was proudest of his personal contribution to our detective intrigues. After showing us our room, he ushered us eagerly back to the parlour with its low windows opening out over the street below and led us to two chairs, which he had placed in front of the window looking out onto the street and directly behind his beautiful copper telescope.

"What d-d-do you think?" he asked expectantly.

"About what, Dodo?" I questioned his question.

"The t-t-telescope."

"It is, indeed, a very nice telescope."

"I know that, it's m-m-mine, you b-b-boob!"

"Then what?" I asked in exasperation.

As we were sparring, Dickens sat down in the straight-backed college chair with its little royal blue velvet tie-on pads, which was placed directly behind the telescope for the obvious purpose of viewing. Out of simple curiosity, he bent down and looked through the telescope. What he saw made him straighten directly up with a smile of delight on his face. "Why, Dodgson, it is perfect," Dickens gushed. "Perfect! Wilkie, here, have a look."

One usually expects a telescope to be pointed at the stars, but this one was pointed at the open door of the Bulldog tavern.

"Why, you can look right in the door, Wilkie." Dickens was carried away with his excitement as he literally grasped me by the shoulders and ushered me out of that chair so that he could regain his seat. "You can see halfway inside the place. Oh Dodgson, this is an inspired idea. Perfect for our spying on the tavern."

"I thought you would l-l-like it." Dodo nodded his head like some oversized caricature of the extinct bird whence his nickname was derived.

"Look, look, there is Ellen. She's sitting down on the steps with some man." Dickens fell silent, his gaze riveted to the eyepiece of the telescope, spying upon his mistress. "Why, he has rolled up a cigarette and given it to her." He spoke as if he were in awe of this revelation.

"Here, Charles, let me see." I startled him out of his strange reverie and he got up from the chair to let me sit and spy upon his Ellen.

It truly was a miraculous instrument, and upon first looking through it and seeing the clarity and the closeness of the people so far below in the street, I too was somewhat awed at its power. There was Miss Ternan, sitting on the steps, and a mustachioed gentleman in a flat townsman's hat standing over her, both smoking cigarettes and conversing in the freest, most unaware way. Looking through the telescope, I felt as if I was standing right next to them on the street. It could only be better if we could have heard what they were saying.

"I did not know that she smoked cigarettes." Dickens was once again pushing me out of the chair so that he could sit back down.

"Perhaps she doesn't," I speculated as I vacated my seat. "She's probably just doing it so that she can converse with that man."

"I have never seen her smoke a cigarette." Dickens couldn't get over it.

In the days that followed, that telescope trained on the front door of the Bulldog would become almost an obsession with Dickens. He would sit there for hours on end reporting on who went in and out of the front door of the establishment and who was sitting at the front tables under the windows just inside the front door. Actually, his grotesque novelist's descriptions of the patrons of the tavern were often really quite comical. I must acknowledge that Dodgson's idea for monitoring the comings and goings of the patrons of the tavern was a good one; but as I watched Dickens playing the spy, or perhaps more appropriate, the Peeping Tom, I began to think that what he was doing was unhealthy, perverse. He seemed caught up in his spying upon his young mistress, as if he wanted to know more about her life or even to catch her in some indiscretion.

AN EVENING IN THE BULLDOG

୧୬

(November 30, 1853 — Evening)

Dickens's fascination with Dodo's telescope as a tool for spying upon his Ellen entertained him throughout the afternoon. As for Dodo and me, we occupied ourselves with catching up on our histories of the two and a half years since we had seen one another. I, of course, did not tell him all the intimate secrets of my London life, and I am sure that he did not tell me all the details of his rise to imminent academic glory. What he did describe, however, was his migration towards God, based not only upon his theological studies but also upon his aesthetic consciousness of the godliness of art, which had been awakening in him even when we were young poets of Oxford years before. Dodo had always been drawn to Oxford's wealth of choirs and concerts of liturgical music. I remember him talking of how beauty manifests itself to all of the senses as God's messages to men. We whiled away the afternoon talking of these philosophical things as Dickens played with Dodo's telescope.

The Bulldog, of course, closed at three, but Ellen spent the afternoon cleaning and preparing for the evening's business. Twice she came and went through the front door on tavern errands. Each time Dickens would shout, "There she is!" and snap erect in his chair, swivelling the telescope slowly to follow her up the street until she turned a corner or moved out of the instrument's ken. The public house opened again at half past five and I was certain that it would not be long thereafter before Dickens would want to go there. But he surprised me.

"We shall not go to the Bulldog until some of our Radicals are in residence," he declared. "Perhaps even this Stadler will come and you can introduce me to him," Charles alerted Dodgson to his evening's responsibility.

That afternoon, Dickens had taken enough respite from his telescope spying to concoct his story for meeting Stadler. He was to be, indeed, Charles Dickens, down from London doing research for his next novel, which involved poisons and drugs. Since Stadler was one of the few chemists with whom Dodgson was acquainted, Dickens suggested that chemistry be an entrée to gain this introduction, perhaps even in the pub if the chance presented itself.

Six of the clock passed, and then seven. The only light that illuminated the street in front of the Bulldog came from the two gas lamps mounted on the facade of the building on each side of the door. We ate a lunch (even though it was the dinner hour) of bread, cheese, and wine right there in Dodgson's rooms because Dickens insisted upon maintaining his surveillance. His eye glued to the telescope, he gave us a running narrative of everyone who entered or left the Bulldog's premises.

"Aha, two tweedy gentlemen smoking cigars and wearing soft hats. Must be Dons."

"What makes you think that?" Dodgson taunted him.

"Middle-aged, forties, I'd say. It's the soft hats gives them away. Frenchified," Dickens answered, as if he were Field. "And they stride in with authority as if they own the town. As gentlemen or bankers do in London."

Time passed. We ate. Dickens kept watch.

"There's Thompson going in."

"Three hatless students on a spree."

"Mousy man in spectacles and a brown Mackintosh."

"More college chums."

"Two more students with a plump girl between them. All laughing."

"Fat couple. Just come from dinner. Both had large stuffed capon, I'll wager."

"Two plump widows dressed in black. Out for toping with the college boys?"

It was amazing and amusing how Dickens could bring to life complete strangers walking through a distant doorway. He gave them character and motive and a whole fictional life in a mere moment of observation and a quick line of commentary.

"What ho! Dodgson, come here quick. Is this he? Tall man, walrus mustaches, you said, did you not? Is this our Stadler? Come quick, he's lighting his cigar in the doorway."

Dodgson moved with surprising agility for an academic and slid into the chair even as Dickens was sliding out of it. His eye was to the telescope before Dickens's subject had savored his first puff and proceeded into the pub.

"That's him all right," Dodgson confirmed it. "With those must-t-t-achios, friend Stadler is rather hard t-t-to miss."

"Well then, gentlemen, our fox is in the field. Let us ride to him," Dickens declared gleefully.

Pulling on our waistcoats and greatcoats, for it was a bitter November night, battening our hats down hard on our heads, for the wind was whistling down the narrow streets with the speed and heedlessness of De Quincey's murderous coachman,[14] tugging on our gloves, we descended Tom Tower, crossed the street, and entered the front door of the Bulldog.

The tavern this Saturday night was roiling with revellers.

[14]An allusion to Thomas De Quincey's prose essay, *The English Mail Coach* (1849).

After all, the Christmas season was already upon us and the college term was almost up. The students' responsibilities, such as they were, were almost nonexistent and it was, indeed, a Saturday night in a University town.

The Bulldog was a narrow but quite deep tavern, divided into two almost equal drinking rooms, front and back, connected by a narrow walkway. This slim corridor ran between the tap on the left, which was always crowded with men standing and drinking, and the ancient stairway on the right, which both ascended to the pub's upper floors and descended to the basement.

The pub was crowded with standers and sitters, but at the very moment that Dickens, Dodgson, and I entered the front door, a group of students abandoned a table against the wall, and Dodgson, impressing me once again with an unacademic speed and agility, pounced upon it before anyone else in that crowded front room could claim it.

It was, indeed, quite a crowded public house. Irish Mike looked to be enjoying a very profitable evening. As we sat down, Ellen was standing at the tap waiting for Irish Mike to fill her tray with foaming pints. Thompson stood near Ellen's server's station at the tap, sipping on a pint of Mike's Irish Stout and talking to a mousy-looking man who had not yet removed his brown Mackintosh. Even as we sat down, this man in the Mackintosh raised his glass to Thompson as if to say "Cheers" and left the tap to take a stool against the wall by the doorway to the garden. I don't know why this utterly nondescript man caught my eye, but he did. All the rest of the evening he just sat on his stool like some clerk in a countinghouse, a character out of Dickens's own *Christmas Carol*. I remember thinking how sad it must be to be that alone in a public place.

Loud laughter emanated from the back room. No sooner had we sat down at the table than Dickens stood up. Dodgson had already turned to converse with a table full of students next to ours. They had addressed him respectfully as "Mr. Dodgson" as soon as we sat down.

"Come with me, Wilkie. You can help me fetch the drinks from the tap. Charles can stand guard over our table." Dickens fabricated a reason to move into nearer proximity of his precious Ellen.

But even as we traversed the crowded room toward the tap, Irish Mike placed the last brimming pint on Ellen's full tray and she turned to pick her way through the crowded corridor and deliver her drinks to the back room. As for me, my eyes were locked on Thompson. I hoped I was glaring forth my displeasure as powerfully as possible. He saw us coming and that maddening, self-satisfied, comical smirk of his took possession of the corners of his mouth. In utter disdain for all the proprieties, he reached into the pocket of his vest and proceeded to consult my gold repeater for the time. That accomplished, he arrogantly twirled the watch on its chain as we came abreast of him and replaced it in his pocket but an instant before I could lunge at him and snatch it out of his grasp.

As we stood at the tap, waiting for Irish Mike to serve us, Dickens nodded jovially at Thompson, who smirked back at him. I glared angrily at the two of them, co-conspirators in my humiliation.

"You're a saucy little minx, you are," a tipsy bit of raillery borne on the smoky air from the back room put Dickens's ears on point.

"Mister Dickens. Mister Collins. Good evenin'," Irish Mike greeted us at the tap, but Dickens, straining to overhear the conversation passing between his Ellen and the drinkers in the back room, never heard him.

I acknowledged Mike's greeting and ordered three pints of Irish brew.

"Allow me to introduce myself." Thompson stuck out his hand to me, engaging one of Dickens's ears while the other quite clearly stayed cocked towards the other room. "Terence Thompson, it is." Our light-fingered friend grinned jovially. "Terry to most folks. In town for the 'oliday season, I am, visitin' my sis, lookin' to buy some 'orses."

"Yes, quite," I muttered, taking his outstretched hand purely to keep up appearances. To my pleasant surprise, when I came away from this handshake I found my gold repeater magically transferred into my hand. Stunned, I still had the presence of mind to secrete it in my trouser pocket without opening my fist.

Irish Mike had poured our pints of stout and was letting them settle before topping them off. He was serving pints of English bitter to two other tapsters as Dickens and I waited for our drinks.

Dickens was rather obviously craning his neck to see what Ellen was about in the back room. Thompson was babbling on about how jolly Oxford was during the Christmas season. My eyes followed Dickens's gaze and I could see Ellen's dark hair as she served the pints around a large round table of men.

"Good work, lass," one of the men taunted her boisterously, his lewd voice carrying over the murmurings of the crowd. "What would you say to riding me a St. George?"[15]

Ellen, swirling around their table as she delivered her pints, simply ignored this obscene raillery and laughed as she pirouetted away with her empty tray held out before her like a shield.

All the colour went out of Dickens's face in an instant. That told me that he too had overheard the lewd comment.

"Wilkie, get the drinks when they are ready"—he hesitated—"please." He tried to make it sound as if it wasn't an order. But before Ellen had fought her way through the loiterer in the walkway, he fled back to our table, not wishing, I suppose, to have to face her in light of the insults he had just overheard her having to endure. Ellen, on the

[15] This lewd comment refers to that sexual position in which the woman sits on the man's lap facing away as the sexual act is performed. Its derivation, according to Partridge's *Dictionary of Slang*, is said to come from the phallic paintings of St. George sitting on his horse with his lance extended before him.

other hand, seemed not the least concerned with the whole incident. She saw me as she returned to the tap and blessed me with one of her most winning smiles. To anyone who might have been watching, it was simply a serving girl ingratiating herself to a gentleman who by his dress bore the promise of generosity.

It occurred to me that if Dickens actually thought he could, like St. George, shelter her from all sexual innuendo, then he was embracing the most fundamental hypocrisy of the almost universally hypocritical Victorian age. For a novelist whose whole career focused upon exposing Victorian hypocrisy, this sudden delicacy seemed rather out of character.

We drank our pints.

Ellen stayed quite busy serving the tables in both rooms.

Pouring one beer after another with only brief surcease to greet a new customer or to answer a question from an old, Irish Mike seemed indefatigable.

The man in the Mackintosh sat morosely by the door.

Then Stadler walked right by the Mackintosh man and out into the garden.

"There he goes," I alerted Dickens and Dodgson, whose backs were to that part of the pub.

"Who?" Dickens turned quickly to look.

"Stadler, the Don with the mustachios," I answered.

"He's just stepping out t-t-to have a p-p-pee," Dodgson assured us. "All the gentlemen d-d-do it."

"Yes, quite," Dickens accepted Dodgson's explanation. "Couldn't you cut him off when he comes back in? Bring him over to meet us? Eh?"

"Of course, I shall t-t-try," and Dodgson was up in an instant and moving towards the garden door in pursuit of his prey.

We looked on as Dodgson quite skillfully, a matter of timing it was, bumped into Stadler just inside the doorway as our walrus Don came back in rubbing his hands together from the cold. They exchanged pleasantries. Dodgson pointed out our table to him. Dickens and I sat drinking, studiously unaware. But to our disappointment, friend Stadler, our most likely candidate for Ackroyd's murder, did not return to the table with Dodgson.

"He has promised t-t-to join us later," Dodgson assured us upon his return. "He said he would b-b-bring his p-p-pint into the front room and join us for a moment when he t-t-tires of his c-c-companions."

An hour passed.

Ellen circulated through the pub delivering pints. Everyone seemed to like her. She brought us another round and smiled at Dickens as he paid. It was really quite comical watching him contain himself.

"Let us hope you tipped her well," I could not resist taunting him.

"You and Field and this whole business can be damned," he said as he raised his glass and smiled tight-lipped at Dodgson and me.

"Cheers." We raised our pints to him in unison.

The man in the brown Mackintosh stared like a stone statue.

Stadler finally stumbled back out of his lair in the back room, smoking a fat cigar and precariously balancing a half-full pint in his unsteady hand. He was obviously quite drunk. His cigar in no way resembled the thin cheroot we had found in Ackroyd's rooms.

"Ah, Stadler, how g-g-good of you." Dodgson rose hospitably to greet him. "These are the gentlemen I t-t-told you about, up from London they are, and hoping t-t-to p-p-pick your b-b-brains." He nodded at Dickens and me even as he was quite adeptly commandeering a wooden chair from his students' table next to ours and seating the Chemistry Don in it. "Charles D-D-Dickens," Dodo understandably, made the more prominent introduction, "and an old schoolmate of mine from our undergraduate days, Wilkie C-C-Collins of B-B-Brasenose."

"*The* Charles Dickens?" Stadler's attention steadied

despite his obviously tipsy state. "The novel writer that everyone is always talking about?"

"Yes, the same." Dickens smiled benignly.

"I've never read of any of your things," Stadler confessed, seeming actually rather proud of his neglect, "but among many of my colleagues you are quite the rage. Wait until I tell them I met you right here in Oxford," and he laughed too loudly, obviously enjoying the prospect of it.

"Yes, I am here to do some research for a new novel, a sensational murder story, and when Mr. Dodgson mentioned that you were a Chemistry Don, I hoped that you might be able to help me."

"Help you? How?" This Stadler was settling into his chair, sipping from his pint, puffing his cigar.

"Why, my fictional murderer is a poisoner. He kills off his wives for their money with poisons he cooks up in his private laboratory.[16] You being a Chemistry Don, I hoped you might recommend a good wife-killing poison, one easy to secrete in food or drink and hard to detect in its symptoms and effects."

Stadler laughed as though it was a hilarious joke on all of us.

Dickens waited patiently, smiling like a half-witted fool.

Dodgson and I wondered what Stadler found so funny.

"Don't know a damned thing about poisons," he finally said, explaining how thoroughly the joke was on us, and had another hearty laugh at our expense. "Couldn't recommend a good poison if I wanted to make away with my own wife, if I had one. All my work is in incendiaries, explosives. Sorry, old chap."

"Oh, that's quite all right." Dickens kept smiling like a silly sod even as he took a sip of his beer. "It was just an offchance. When Dodgson mentioned chemistry . . . well, you know. But explosives, now that sounds exciting."

---

[16]Dickens obviously is recycling the case of Dr. Palmer the poisoner.

"And a b-b-bit d-d-dicey, eh," Dodgson put in his words of encouragement.

"Oh, explosives can be dicey all right," Stadler quite easily donned the pretension of the professor, "if you don't know how to handle them."

As Stadler was speaking, Field and Rogers entered the pub by the front door and fought their way out of their greatcoats. I watched them walk by behind our explosive Don's back. Though they were disguised quite appropriately in respectable merchant-class clothes, wool coats and trousers, button collars and grave cravats, they still looked like policemen to me, bulldogs on leash! I imagined that everyone else in the pub saw through them in the same way. But nobody seemed to notice, and they quietly purchased their pints and found themselves two stools along the wall across the room from the Mackintosh man.

Ellen noticed them. I saw her head turn quickly at the tap when she heard Field's voice ordering.

"What kinds of explosives?" Unheeding, Dickens was engrossed in his conversation with Stadler. "Do you make them? Actually set them off?"

"Oh yes, of course," Stadler bragged pompously, "but mostly I try to find new ways to use them, or new combinations of explosives to do more efficient things. Soon, I hope, we'll actually be using controlled explosives down in the collieries to help extract coal."

"My God, wouldn't that be terribly dangerous?"

"Not with the right explosive used under properly controlled conditions." Stadler was quite sure of himself for a man intoxicated with both his own expertise and copious amounts of beer. As he spoke, he waved for Ellen to bring him another pint.

"Fascinating," Dickens encouraged.

"It really is." Stadler, his glass empty, leaned in over the table to Dickens as if he were Victor Frankenstein out of that Gothic tale imparting the secret of life. "I have been studying exactly that," he thumped the table, "the instability of explosive compounds. I have been corresponding with a young Swedish chemist who is living in St. Petersburg. Alfred Nobel is his name. He is combining a new explosive he calls nitroglycerine with ordinary black gunpowder and the results are extraordinary. The outcome could be the most powerful explosive known to man; but it is dangerously unstable. And that is where I come in," and he slapped the table once more as he collapsed back in his chair at the very moment that Ellen sat his fresh pint down on the table before him.

"Fascinating," Dickens repeated. "Nitroglycerine, you say? Here, allow me," and he paid his Ellen for the man's pint.

"Cheers." Stadler raised his glass to Dickens before taking a deep draught.

We all waited for him to drink. An expectant silence fell over our table. I could not tell whether Dickens was just waiting for Stadler to go on or if he had been momentarily distracted by Ellen's closeness.

Finally, Stadler spoke in that wistful philosophic vein that great minds and maudlin drunkards sometimes take.

"You know, instability is fascinating," he began, in what would have been a very thoughtful Oxford professorial tone if it hadn't been punctuated by a large hiccup. "I live with instability. The chaos of the microscopic world. But everything is chaos." And he turned to Dodgson. "Did you know that Ackroyd has been murdered in London?"

"Yes, I read it. T-t-terrible thing." Dodgson encouraged him to go on.

"Terrible. Terrible." Stadler wandered drunkenly. "Not poisoned, but shot with gunpowder, they say. Instability"—he directed his jumbled train of association at Dickens.

"I am sorry, but I know nothing about it," Dickens feigned ignorance.

Suddenly, Stadler stood up, grasping his half-drained pint in one hand and scissoring his cigar in the other. "I must get back to my friends," he declared through yet another explosive hiccup. "All that plotting going on without me, you know," and he laughed at what he evidently thought was a tidy joke.

Dickens stood also, thanking him for his company.

"Honour to meet you, sir." He shook Dickens's hand genuinely if rather shakily, and with a nod to Dodgson and none to me, he turned to leave. But after one step, he turned back as if he had forgotten something. "Sorry I couldn't poison your wife for you," he leered at Dickens, who gaped back in amazement.

"Perhaps I'll have to blow her up rather than poison her," Dickens recovered, "with nitroglycerine."

"Yes, quite right, nitroglycerine," Stadler guffawed as he left to rejoin his fellow Dons in the back room.

"Seems like a nice enough chap," Dickens remarked with heavy sarcasm.

"D-d-drunk as a lord." Dodgson could not hide his disdain.

"A dead . . . no, murdered . . . historian who was studying the Gunpowder Plot, and now a chemist experimenting with explosives. For a place called Christ Church, you seem to have a rather violent faculty," Dickens quipped.

Dodgson almost spit forth the beer he was in the act of swallowing.

"He did not seem the least bit uncomfortable discussing his friend Ackroyd's death," I observed. "He actually seemed rather saddened by it."

"That was b-b-because he was in his c-c-cups," Dodgson speculated.

"Or because he did it," Dickens countered. "Perhaps Stadler is not as drunk as we think. Perhaps even in his cups he is still a very good actor."

At that moment, we were interrupted by Ellen Ternan's voice: "Are you chaps ready for another round?" She had placed her hand on Dickens's hunched shoulders, and at her touch and the surprise of her voice speaking so close by, he sat bolt upright as if he had been struck by lightning.

If anyone was watching our table he would certainly have found his spasm queer.

"Yes, p-p-please," Dodgson answered. "My t-t-turn."

"Good." Ellen smiled, and then, lowering her voice, "we will meet in the church at midnight. I have told Tally Ho to tell Field," and she tripped off between the tables towards the tap.

"Good," Dickens said. "We need to know what she has seen."

The rest of the evening in the pub passed uneventfully. After a while, I saw Field and Rogers leave their position against the far wall and make their way into the rear room. I presumed they were positioning themselves to eavesdrop on Stadler and his fellow Dons.

Dickens was the one who made the decision.

"Enough for one night," he declared, standing up from his empty pint. It was ten of the clock, still an hour from closing, when we left the pub. Dickens proposed a return to Dodgson's rooms to freshen up before we set out for the church to meet his Ellen.

From the beer and the stress of the evening's small subterfuges, I was really rather fatigued and quite in danger of dropping off as soon as I sat down on Dodo's loveseat.

As soon as we entered the rooms, Dickens went straight to the telescope. Remarking my drowsiness, Dodo scurried off to brew some coffee.

I dozed.

Dickens spied.

Dodo returned with steaming mugs.

Time passed.

"The pub is starting to empty out," Dickens alerted us.

We joined him at the window. The people in the street below looked like Lilliputians as they poured out of the narrow doors of the tavern.

"There go Field and Rogers," Dickens was like a narrator leading us through the text of the evening from his point of vantage at the telescope. "The Dons are leaving *en masse*. Stadler is crossing the street right towards us alone."

"He is g-g-going t-t-to his rooms in c-c-college," Dodo was sure. "He will enter through the T-T-Tom T-T-Tower g-g-gate and c-c-cross the quadrangle t-t-to the c-c-cloister passage."

"The others are dispersing in all directions."

It was almost half past eleven when the revellers stopped staggering out of the public house.

"Shall we g-g-go?" Dodgson asked. "Inspector Field has p-p-probably g-g-gone straight there."

"No. Wait." There was no room for objection in Dickens's voice. He did not explain, but his eye stayed riveted to the telescope, and I knew that he was waiting for his Ellen to emerge from the pub.

Long minutes passed.

The street below was dark and deserted with only the dim glow of the Bulldog's gas lamps for illumination. Suddenly, those lamps blinked out. For Dodo and me, the street below was a dim grey haze. For Dickens, it must have been clearer.

"There is Ellen coming out," he announced. "She is alone."

"Well, then, let us g-g-go." Dodgson started for his greatcoat.

"Wait!" There was alarm in Dickens's voice. "What's this?"

"What's what?" I squinted to see down into the gloom.

"There's a man . . . out of that mews next to the pub. He is following her up the street."

"Is it T-T-Thompson?" Dodgson also was bent to the windowpane, trying to penetrate the darkness of the street below.

"I don't think so. Not tall enough. My God! He is after her! Where *is* Thompson?" And Dickens leapt up from his seat, grasped his greatcoat in passing from the back of a chair near the door, and rushed out.

NIGHT SOUNDS

༉

(November 30, 1853 — Midnight)

Dickens plunged down the spiralling stone stairs of
Tom Tower, pulling his greatcoat on as he went.
Dodgson and I followed, but by the time we had
struggled down the stairs and out through the small door
inset in the towering wooden gate, he was already running
up the street. We ran after him, afraid that he would lose
himself in the unfamiliar streets and alleys of nighttime Oxford.

But our fears were unfounded. As we reached the first
turning, Blue Boar Street going sharply and narrowly to the
right with the blackened stone steps of Oxford's medieval
town hall on the far corner and the high black stone wall
of Christ Church running all along its near side, Dickens
was waiting for us, standing stock still in the middle of the
cobblestone street.

He was listening.

He raised his hand in a command for us to stop and be
quiet.

We obeyed.

This silent waiting and listening was his only recourse. He

had plunged heedlessly after his Ellen and the man he had concluded was stalking her. But when he reached the street, she and the stalking phantom were gone. We listened. Nothing for long moments. Dickens waited like a coiled animal, ready to spring. We were searching for some sound, anything, a footstep.

Suddenly a woman's scream, in the darkness of Blue Boar Street, sharp then muffled, broke the silence. Then a man's voice shouting something unintelligible.

My head swivelled to the sounds in the distant dark. When I turned back, Dickens was already gone, plunging into the black well of Blue Boar Street. Dodgson and I ran after him down that dark tunnel, stone buildings careening by on our left, the great dark wall of Christ Church looming on our right.

We seemed to run on forever until the street turned precipitously to the right, sloped sharply downward, and perceptibly narrowed. I learned later that Blue Boar Street turned into a narrow alley called Bear Lane. Whatever its name, it was little more than a dark mews barely wide enough for a single horse and cart to pass through. Just inside this black hole of an alley we found Ellen Ternan.

She was on her knees on the cobblestones ministering to the fallen figure of a man. Dickens ran up to them and went to one knee beside his beloved.

"Ellen, are you hurt?" He ignored the wounded man, who proved to be Thompson.

"Yes, yes, I'm fine. Tally Ho drove them off."

"Them?"

"Yes. Two of 'em. Get after 'em." Tally Ho Thompson's voice was laden with pain, but also angry and impatient. "Get after 'em, I say. That way. Through that passage there. The one was after the other." He was pointing the way from his back on the stones through a narrow passage in the high stone college wall.

"Two of them?" I repeated stupidly, looking first in the direction he was pointing and then at Dodgson.

"Get after them, Wilkie." Dickens quite graciously volunteered me for this hazardous duty. "See if you can catch up to them, but don't engage them. See if you can see where they go."

"Two of them?" I repeated.

"Yes. For God's sakes, Wilkie, go! You will lose them."

Not understanding, totally unwilling, utterly terrified, I took off running into that infernal passageway that the fallen Thompson had pointed out. For some strange illogical reason utterly unbefitting a mathematician, Dodgson followed.

Even as I was plunging into the blackness of that passage, I was asking myself: "Why isn't Dickens doing this? Why am I being sent and he is staying?" But I did it nonetheless. Thank the Lord that Dodgson followed, for I had no more idea of where I was or where I was going than does a blind man in a maze.

A short run brought us to a heavy door that stood ajar. It had either been open already or had been somehow opened by the men we were pursuing. We passed through it and emerged onto the frozen grass of a small quadrangle.

"It is P-P-Peckwater Quad," Dodgson informed me. "There," and he pointed through the darkness. "A man running, around the c-c-corner of the library."

Dodgson was a better man than I because I could not see a thing across that gloomy quadrangle. Yet I took off running in that direction with Dodgson lumbering along behind me. He may have had sharper eyes than I (for my shortsightedness was legendary in those days), but he was cursed with an academic's lungs. When I reached the far side of the quad, I had to pull up and wait for him because he had become winded about halfway across.

"Which way now?" I asked as he drew up, gasping.

"There," he pointed, "around there I think. G-g-go ahead. I'll c-c-come along as soon as I c-c-catch my b-b-breath."

Wonderful, I thought, *now I am alone with two strong-armers in some maze of a college on the darkest night of the year.* But I ran around the corner of the library nonetheless and came into a grassy area with the high steeple of Christ Church Chapel towering over me.

I heard running footsteps on stone receding in the distance but could see no one. I stopped and listened to the night, Dickens's touch. Nothing.

Dodgson came up, around the corner of the building, still breathing in laboured gasps.

"Where have they gone?" I asked him, as if he had more privileged information than I.

"I d-d-don't see anyone," he answered. "They c-c-could be into the main quadrangle, but then they would have to g-g-go through the g-g-gatehouse to g-g-get out. Or they c-c-could g-g-go through the c-c-cloisters to the Meadow B-B-Buildings and into C-C-Christ Church meadows."

"They could be anywhere, then?"

"Yes," he agreed.

"This is futile." I gave up the chase and began choosing my words to explain my failure to Dickens.

We retraced our steps in the darkness and returned to Bear Lane, where Dickens and his Ellen had Tally Ho Thompson up and on his feet.

"We lost him—them—in the darkness," I explained lamely.

"They escaped into the c-c-college," Dodgson, fully recovered, speculated. "They either reside there, or they g-g-got out into the meadow on the other side."

Dickens did not seem too angry at our failure. All of his attention was focused on his Ellen, who seemed unmolested. Thompson, on the other hand, was limping gingerly around in a small circle testing his right leg.

Ellen was shaken but unhurt. Her voice quavered as she tried to tell us what had happened: "I was on my way to St. Mary's Church to meet all of you when this man's voice shouted at me from the darkness. Then a man rushed upon me! He was tearing at my clothes. He called me a slut. Oh, it all happened so fast. Then Tally Ho was fighting with the first man and another man came at the two of them. He knocked them both down. Then those two other men ran off. Then you came up."

"Second bloke knocked me off me pins," Thompson explained. "But 'ee knocked first bloke down too. Then the two of 'em ran off, they did. It was strange, like second bloke drove the first bloke off."

"Can you walk?" Dickens inquired.

"Yes, but pretty rough." Thompson had regained his smirking equanimity. "If I was a 'orse, I'd shoot me."

"Field is waiting for us at the church," Dickens plotted our next move. "Let us go there and see if we can figure out what happened here."

Following Dodgson's lead, we traversed Bear Lane to a narrow passage that took us through to the High Street. St. Mary's was just down the hill on the other side from where he brought us out. In that chill November midnight, St. Mary's was a gloomy-looking place, its steeple piercing up into the cold sky as if trying to stab the stars. The Radcliffe Camera brooded behind the church like a giant toad squatting amidst all the towers reaching towards the sky.

When we entered the church, we disturbed a tramp sleeping in one of the back pews. He growled at us as we passed, turned over, and went back to sleep.

"TO SEE MORE CLEARLY"

❧

(December 1, 1853—After Midnight)

W hat a God-awful gloomy place," Thompson said as we walked down the central aisle of St. Mary's Church.

Dodgson frowned at that, but let it pass as Rogers and Field with young Constable Morse in tow stepped out from behind a thick stone pillar.

"Where 'ave you been?" Field's voice could barely hide his impatience. "And why are you together?" His angry forefinger raked at the corner of his right eye as if he wanted to poke it out. "I told you not to be seen together. God save me from amateurs!" He turned in exasperation to Rogers and young Morse. It made me want to retch to see the look of satisfaction bloom in Rogers's face as Field put us in our place.

"Yes. I know. I know," Dickens placated him. "But Miss Ternan has been attacked in the street and Tally Ho saved her. He has injured his leg."

Field turned to Ellen and to Thompson, his impatience turning to concern.

"Oh, I'm sound, guv. A bit of a gimp is all," Thompson

assured him, limping comically three steps up the aisle and back for his benefit.

"Wot 'appened?" Field turned to Dickens and Ellen Ternan. " 'Ere, sit down," and he ushered them into a nearby pew and seated himself looking backwards in the pew in front of them. The rest of us stood aimlessly about waiting to hear the full story. Dickens began:

"I was watching through Dodgson's telescope when Ellen came out of the Bulldog. A man followed her up the street. He must have been waiting for her."

Ellen Ternan looked sharply at Dickens as he made this revelation. She knew she was being watched, but not by him and not so closely. Dickens drew back from her look. He knew he was in for it, for not telling her that he was spying.

"I turned at Blue Boar Street, which is the way to my lodgings, in case anyone was watching me go," and she cast another sharp look of disapproval in Dickens's direction. "I did not see anyone following me, but it was dark."

She looked around at all of us and realized that she had our strict attention.

"I walked to the end of Blue Boar Street to Bear Lane, where I was going to take the passage through to the High Street," she went on, "but that is where the man shouted at me to stop." Ellen stopped her narrative as if obeying his order.

"Wot did 'ee say?" Field prompted her. "Where was 'ee? Was 'ee after you from behind? 'Ad 'ee been followin' you, do you think?"

"No. He was in the dark shadows by the college wall. I could not see him at all, I could only hear his voice. He stopped me with his voice. He frightened me so that I could not say anything. It was as if he was waiting for me there."

We looked at each other around the circle that had closed about Inspector Field and Ellen Ternan.

"If this man was followin' you," and Field shot a look at Dickens, who gave him a quick nod, "then 'ow did 'ee get in front of you to be lyin' in wait?"

"I do not know"—Ellen's hands, clasped tight in nervousness, came up to her lips as she spoke—"but he was waiting there in the dark for me."

"Wot did 'ee say to you?"

"He called me a slut. He shouted, very ugly, 'Come here, you little slut!' When I did not say anything, he said it again: 'Come into the meadow with me, you little slut,' he said. 'I'll pay, never you mind.' That is what he said," and Ellen looked at Inspector Field as if for an interpretation.

"It sounds as if 'ee thought you were a 'ore," Field, rather bluntly for Dickens's taste, obliged her. "Go on."

"Then I tried to run. But I did not know exactly where he was and he came at me and cut me off. That is when I screamed and he hit me."

Dickens recoiled as if he had absorbed the blow. It was really quite fascinating to observe him in her presence. I have never seen a man so seized and rendered helpless by a woman's spirit.

"He knocked me down and then he caught me by the hair and tried to drag me to my feet. 'Get up, you whining little slut! You are going into the meadow with me whether you like it or not.' That is exactly what he said. I think he was going to rape me."

She stopped in her telling of this unsavory tale.

"That's wot 'ee said, all right. I 'eard 'im," Thompson broke the awkward silence, "right before I tapped 'im on the 'ead."

"Thank God for Tally Ho," Ellen recovered herself. "He came just in time."

Thompson grinned for all of our benefit.

"Thank God you made him let go of my hair." Ellen actually laughed. "Lord, did that hurt."

What had been a threatening ghost story was turning into a rollicking adventure tale. Field abruptly brought us back to reality.

"Thompson. Wot 'appened next? 'Ow did 'ee get away?"

"I 'it 'im on the side 'o the 'ead from behind, but 'ee

didn't even blink. 'Ee let go of 'er and turned on me. Cursin', 'ee was, but I don't know wot 'ee was sayin'. Like Ellen said, it was all goin' very fast. We fought. 'Ee got me around the middle and was squeezin' and I wos 'ittin' 'im in the ribs, but 'ee wouldn't let go, then everythin' got more strange."

We all stared at Thompson in suspense.

"Well? For God's sake, man, what!" Field's voice echoed our exasperation.

"There wos another man there, that's wot," and Thompson's maddening grin signalled his delight at being the centre of our attention. " 'Ee knocked us both to the ground from behind. That's when I 'urt me leg. I couldn't get up."

"So then what happened?" Dickens took over the role of prompter.

Young Morse's eyes were getting progressively larger as this story continued to unfold.

"The first man, the bigger one who had attacked me, ran off." Ellen Ternan took up the narration once again. "The other man ran after him. I was on the ground and all turned around, and did not know where they went at first, but when Charles came up, Tally Ho said that they ran into the college."

"Did you see two men?" Inspector Field turned to Dickens.

"No. I did not see the men at all. When I arrived, Ellen was helping Thompson on the ground."

"You didn't see where they went?"

"No."

Field turned back to Thompson and Ellen Ternan.

"Were these men together? Confederates?"

"No. I do not think so." Ellen thought for a brief second and added, "I think the first man was alone and trying to . . . well, to . . ."

"To attack her," Dickens finished that unsavory sentence for her.

"All I know is they ran off together." Thompson threw in his tuppence.

Confusion was beginning to drive this narrative. Field attempted to rein it in.

"Did not anyone see 'is face?"

Thompson and Ellen looked at each other first, then said, "No," in unison.

"He had a dark knit hat, the sort that seamen wear, pulled down over his forehead," Ellen slowly remembered, "and a scarf wrapped around his mouth."

"Yes, I remember the seaman's 'at now," Thompson chimed in. " 'Ee wos all muffled up."

"Wot about the second man?" Field pressed.

"Never saw 'im," Thompson was quite certain. " 'It me from behind."

"But you said 'ee was smaller than the first?" Field tried to wring every bit of information out of them.

"Maybe because the first was so thick and so strong." Thompson threw up his hands helplessly. "I didn't see 'im."

"That seems to be the theme of all of this," Dickens addressed Inspector Field, attempting, I felt, to head off any more interrogation of his Ellen.

"Yes, that's right, trying to see more clearly is wot we are most definitely up to," Field petulantly desisted.

"I'm sorry," Ellen was sincere, "it was so dark you could hardly see at all."

A heavy silence fell over the whole group. The saints bleeding from their wounds, pierced with arrows, stabbed with knives, gazed down in painful silence from the walls. The Christ, hanged above the altar, stared silently down. The gargoyles on the pillars bared their fangs. The silence was oppressive in that gloomy place.

"Well, it is over, and you are safe." Field's gaze moved slowly from Ellen to Thompson to Dickens. "There is really not a thing we can do about this attack, is there, Morse?" and he turned to that worthy as if he actually had an interest in his opinion. "They seem to have gotten clean away."

"No, sir, there isn't."

"Then perhaps we shall just keep quiet about it, eh? No need drawing undue attention to Miss Ternan. The only ones who will know about it are her attackers, and perhaps they will betray themselves."

"Yes, sir," young Morse, of course, agreed. What else was he to do?

"Good," Field rubbed his hands together in satisfaction, "then we shall 'ang back on this. That is settled." Field reestablished control over his detective world. "So, on to our business 'ere this night, afore this unseemly affair intruded."

"And that would be?" I ventured to enter our midnight colloquy.

"Why, information, Wilkie. Information. The lifeblood of any detective investigation. That is why we have gathered here in this safe, quiet, holy place."

I looked around, wondering if Field and I were looking at the world with the same eyes. A fanged gargoyle atop the baptismal fount was eyeing my throat. The gloom seemed to wrap us in a shroud.

"W-w-what information?" Dodgson stammered.

"We all 'ave information to share, I'll wager," Field rallied us. "Miss Ternan from the public 'ouse. Constable Morse from 'is inquiries. Each of us from what we 'ave observed the last few days since this investigation came to Oxford."

There was a moment's hesitation as to who should begin, but Miss Ternan stepped almost eagerly into the breach as if she wished to put behind her the attempted rape that had so darkly coloured the prior proceedings of this evening.

"I have noticed some things in the pub," she began rather timidly. "I do not know if they are important," she turned to Field. "That shall be for you to judge."

Field nodded at her in acknowledgment of his willingness to accept that responsibility, and she continued on.

"Every night, the same ones meet at that same round table in the far back of the pub. Mike has promised to save it until one of them arrives to claim it, but no later than half seven. Someone is always there and most of them arrive by eight."

"Every night?" Dickens interrupted her.

"They do not come on Saturdays, Mike told me. They do not like the week's end crowd. The students out on a lark, you know."

"Right." Field tried to move her along to his valuable information.

"They tend to stop talking when I serve them," Ellen became quite focused, as if she had thought at some length about this part of it, "as if they had something to hide and did not want me to hear. But, as the evening goes on and I keep serving them pints, they forget to stop, or they get careless and do not notice me as much, or they get drunk and just cease to care. I've heard many things. I've taken to lighting their cigars for them, carrying lucifers in my smock pocket. They seem to like a woman attending to them like that. Some of them wait for me to do it."

Again, I could see the discomfort rising in Dickens's face. The idea of Ellen acting as a servant to these other, most of them younger, men was utterly repellent to him.

"The cigars," Field pressed her, "what about the cigars?"

"Two of them smoke the thin, twisted ones that you described to me," Ellen answered him directly. "The little vulgar one."

"Squonce of Balliol," Dodgson supplied the identification.

"And the one who advises the rowing," Ellen turned again to Dodgson for the name.

"That is Barnet, of Queen's," Dodgson promptly supplied it.

"But they trade cigars with each other as a matter of course," Ellen added, "so they all might be smoking those little, twisted, foul-smelling ones at one time or another. Stadler rarely does, though. He likes the fat round ones."

Ellen's discourse on the Dons' cigars seemed altogether inconclusive to me, but Inspector Field seemed quite

126

pleased with it and had Serjeant Rogers taking notes the whole time.

"Wot do they talk about? That is, when their guard is down and you can 'ear them," Field moved her in a new direction.

"Politics, I would say," Ellen replied, after thinking for a moment. "They are always talking about what is going on in Parliament, how the country is in the hands of the Lords and the rich merchants. 'Imperialist pigs,' I heard the little vulgar one call them. They seem great admirers of Queen Victoria. They always seem to be talking about her. Fact is, the most inflamed argument I have observed was about her. They stopped talking when I came around, though, so I do not really know what it was about."

She paused to think, to remember.

"It sounds to me as if they're plotting something," Field speculated.

"Politics. Parliament. Imperial pigs. The Queen. Vehement arguments. Is that all they talk about?" Dickens gently pressed her.

"This evening they were talking about you." Ellen smiled radiantly, the first light to pierce the gloom of that infernal church. "When Stadler came back from the front room, he was boasting about having met you, about 'consulting'—that is the word he used—with you on your next story. Oh, they were all very much impressed. Walrus-face made it seem as if you had come all the way from London just to talk to him."

"Were they at all suspicious of my motives?" Dickens inquired.

"No, they did not seem to be," and a mischievous glint crept into Ellen's eye. "The Walrus described you as a 'queer duck,' tall and thin, with 'a neck like an ostrich,' his exact words. They all had a good laugh at that."

Dickens did not find that description the least bit humorous.

"But when they talk of politics," Field pointed her back

to the main road, "wot do they say or 'ow do they say it? Do they argue? Do they all agree?"

"I just catch snatches as I walk close to them. Yes, they argue. They stare and point at others across the table when they disagree. One time when I brought a tray of pints to the table, I think they were talking about their friend who was murdered, but they stopped as soon as I put the first one down. They seem very confused in their discussions, as if nobody knows what to do."

" 'Ave any of them approached you?" Field asked. "In a, um, ahem, social way, I mean?"

"Actually, in a joking way, almost half of them have. Of course, it is clear that some of them do not like women at all," and this time she glanced mischievously at Tally Ho Thompson. "In fact, I think that little vulgar one spent half the night looking across the room at you." Ellen actually seemed to be enjoying her role as spy.

"The tall one that Irish Mike told me directs the Oxford Crew, the fast rowers on the river, that one is the most insistent. He likes me. Once he even came away from the table to talk to me, asked me if I would like to see the boathouses some evening when I did not have to work all night in the bar."

Dickens looked as if he might choke on his effort to suppress his strong emotions. Whether of jealousy, or anger, or concern for her safety, I cannot say, but they were strong emotions indeed. Ellen seemed oblivious to the effect her revelations were having upon him, though I think she was quite happy to feed his insecurity as a means of strengthening his devotion. When it came to Dickens, who it was so abundantly clear was utterly in her thrall, she had become a powerfully agitating little minx.

Inspector Field, sensing that his interrogation of Ellen Ternan had gone about as far as it could go and that it was going to take more time for her to build the confidences that would prove fruitful for his investigation, turned to the rest of us at last.

"Miss Ternan 'as only been in the public 'ouse for three days and nights," he began his own report. "She 'as done well, but it is going to take some time. I say we leave 'er to 'er work."

"How about this?" Dodgson spoke up quite unexpectedly. "It is not unusual for a c-c-common p-p-person without name or wealth, t-t-to approach a Don for p-p-private t-t-tutoring, often in return for some work or favor," and Dodgson almost blushed at the illicit suggestion he knew was implicit in his suggestion. "A letter that one has been t-t-tutored by an Oxford Don c-c-carries great weight in p-p-provincial circles. There are many p-p-people of the t-t-town of Oxford who have c-c-come here for just that p-p-purpose. Though ineligible for entrance into any of the c-c-colleges, nonetheless they c-c-come here seeking an education and attempt t-t-to g-g-get it any way that they c-c-can. P-p-perhaps Miss T-T-Ternan c-c-could p-p-profess herself such a p-p-poor scholar."

Dickens looked as if he wished to strangle Dodgson for his suggestion.

Field was delighted with it and expressed his approval to Ellen on the spot.

All that kept running through my brain was that warning, "Beware the boathouses!" which Dickens had coined from our earlier conversation on the courting habits of the Oxford Dons. Ironically, Dickens's half-serious warning portended to become reality, at least in the case of the most pressing of Ellen Ternan's suitors, Barnet of Queen's College and the Oxford Crew.

"Well, all well and good," Dickens finally blustered, "but I am sure Ellen is hearing enough information being passed amongst these men during her working hours in the public house that it is unnecessary for her to court any further danger of the sort that brought her under attack tonight." His brows knitted tightly together in seriousness as he spoke. "I do not think that private tutoring sessions are a good idea at all."

"Yes, Miss Ternan," Field spoke more for Dickens's benefit than to her, "you must use your own best judgment in these affairs. Do not place yourself into a situation where Thompson cannot guard you," and with that, Field turned abruptly to young Morse. "Reggie 'as been quite busy these last few days," he announced. "There is something going on with these men, there is, and 'ee 'as been checking into their 'abits."

"I 'ave been lookin' into the opium angle," young Morse reported. "The dead Don, Ackroyd, was sorely addicted. I talked to some of 'is students, who I gathered were themselves not unacquainted with the pleasures of the drug, and, to a man, they gave evidence that Ackroyd was a slave to the evil smoke. 'Is weekends in London were notorious and absolutely regular. Opium can certainly be 'ad in Oxford, as can every other sensual vice, but this Ackroyd would not risk the indiscretion of being regularly seen frequenting those places, mainly 'ouses of 'ores, where the drug is readily available. 'Ee must 'ave gotten the drug 'ere somewhere, but 'ee kept it private 'ere in town. 'Ee preferred to take the train to London on Saturdays to pursue his pleasure in the public 'ouses." His report dutifully presented, young Morse blinked his eyes and waited for Inspector Field's reaction.

"Did any of these other Dons favour the drug? Did any of them accompany Ackroyd to London, share his pipes at the Chinaman's in Lime'ouse 'Ole?"

"Yes," young Morse was just as quick to answer. "A number of them smoke opium, and a number of them seem inclined to the vices of London: women, boys, opium dens. The most frequent companions were Stadler, Bathgate from Balliol, Squonce, who seems to like young boys, and Barnet of Queen's College. I learned this from the ticket clerk at the train platform."

"Stadler again," Dickens signalled his prime suspect.

"Yes, 'ee seems to be everywhere in this affair, don't 'ee," Field agreed.

"I'll wager he's our man," Dickens spoke with a grim conviction, "even though he seems to be the dead man's closest colleague."

"He certainly is not acting like a guilty murderer on the surface of things," I ventured.

Dickens frowned at me.

"Yes, quite true," Field agreed. "If 'ee murdered 'is friend, 'ee certainly is puttin' 'is best face on it."

Dickens sulked.

Serjeant Rogers nodded in sycophantic agreement with his master.

Young Morse just looked around at us, not really knowing what to think.

Ellen yawned. She suddenly looked exhausted and rightly so, considering her adventure of the evening.

Thompson was sitting in the pew rubbing his ankle that looked as if it were beginning to swell.

"That is enough for this night," Field finally took charge of the moment. "Miss Ternan needs to rest. Rogers will escort 'er 'ome. The rest of us will disperse singly or in pairs from this place. Who knows, 'er assailant may still be lurkin' about. It is best that we all not be seen together." With those unassailable instructions to the full assembly, he turned to Dickens: "Charles, you must let Miss Ternan play her role unobstructed, else it will be to no avail. She will be found out and that will place 'er in much greater danger."

I understand, Dickens silently signified with an acquiescent bow of his head.

Everyone arose and turned to leave, but I could not help but notice how Dickens and his Ellen did not move. Their gazes seemed locked in longing, in a terrible need to speak to each other with their eyes, in a look of wanting that could not be spoken in words in the company of all these others, these invaders of their private island of intimacy.

"Wait. Just a moment, please," Dickens throwing discretion to the wind, stopped us in our attempt to escape this place of gloom. "Can we have but a moment, please?" he petitioned Field even as he was taking Ellen by the hand and drawing her into the private darkness behind a thick stone pillar. "Only a moment," he said again as they disappeared into a gloomy side chapel.

It all had the feeling of some Gothic novel, of *The Castle of Otranto*.[17]

Outside the church, Field dismissed Thompson, who limped off into the darkness.

As Dodgson and I left, Field and Rogers were still cooling their heels in the vestibule waiting for Dickens and Miss Ternan to reappear.

It was more than an hour later that Dickens let himself in at Dodgson's door. Dodo had already retired for the night and I was dozing over my brandy when Dickens sneaked softly in.

"Ah, Wilkie, I went for one of my night walks," Dickens apologized by way of explanation in lieu of the lateness of the hour. "By the river. Quite pleasant, actually. Stars and moon and all. Though not many. Suddenly clouds. I am sure Ellen will be safe. I have decided to return to London on Sunday."

And with that, he took himself off to bed, leaving me sitting on the loveseat with my mouth agape. I tossed off my brandy in one long gulp, a toast to the quicksilver emotions of my friend. I honestly do not think I will ever understand Dickens, no matter how long I shall live.

[17] *The Castle of Otranto* (1764) by Horace Walpole is generally considered the first major work to signal the romantic subgenre of the "Gothic novel."

GOTHIC DEATH

❧

(December 2, 1853 — After Midnight)

T he Meadow Buildings of Christ Church College. The scientist's rooms in the dead of a winter's night. The moon full and bright through the leaded casement, but disappearing in and out of the scudding clouds. Bright moonlight chased by utter blackness across Christ Church meadows and over the dark waters of the wintry Thames.

The laboratory. Beakers and jars and burners and tubes. Vials and powders and liquids and crystals. A rough bookcase with the secrets of chemistry handy to the reach between the covers of its tattered tenants. Strange racks of wood and hammocked rope for the storage in slings of fragile containers. A laboratory out of Mrs. Shelley's Gothic tale.[18]

A large worktable just below the fickle light of the high casement. That table cluttered with books and strewn papers (the scientist's notes on his latest experiment?) and glass slides and glass beakers. That table's centre

---

[18]This could only be a reference to Mary Wollstonecraft Shelley's novel *Frankenstein, or the New Prometheus*, published in 1818.

commanded by the familiar angularity of a microscope and the familiar bulk of a large metal water pitcher.

The scientist sitting at the table consulting his copious notes.

A dark figure moving silently through the low doorway. A mere shadow. A trick of light passing through the membrane of the clouds.

Hours later, the scientist still seated at his laboratory worktable. His head down. Has he fallen asleep at his work? The midnight oil has guttered out. Moonlight and hopeless blackness take turns intruding through the high casement. The shadowy light plays over the sleeping form at the laboratory table. But, as the moonlight comes and the darkness goes, that figure never moves, and the light catches something very much out of place. The scientist sleeps without his hands beneath his head on the rough table. The scientist's head is turned to the side as if he were looking up out of the casement at the fickle moon. The scientist sleeps with his eyes wide open. His bushy downturned mustachios give the impression that he is frowning. The microscope and the metal water pitcher are both overturned on the table before him. The thin water from the pitcher mingles with the much thicker dark liquid leaking slowly from its much more fragile vessel.

And, as the bright moonlight through the high window suddenly plays across the sleeping form, either God or the Devil looking down from the dark clouds could not help but notice the thick hasp of a butcher's knife protruding from the broad back just below the neck and directly between the shoulder blades of the murdered man.

At least that is how I imagine it must have looked in the dark of the night at the time of our chemist friend Stadler's Gothic death. We, Dickens and I and Charlie Dodgson, saw it all just as it has been described, utterly undisturbed (by Inspector Field's order), but in the bright light of day. After the rigours of our long night before, we were all sleeping late when Serjeant Rogers came violently knocking on poor Dodgson's door at just before ten of the clock. I answered since I was bivouacked on the loveseat in the parlour, closest to the door.

"The Chemistry Don, Stadler, 'as been stabbed!" Rogers announced with no preamble whatsoever as I was still rubbing the sleep from my eyes. Dickens, ever alert, joined me as I ushered our blunt Serjeant into the room. It was good that Dickens, always clearheaded, was there to deal with this situation.

"Stadler dead!" Dickens exclaimed. "Why, he was our prime suspect." Dickens said it as if he felt betrayed by the murdered man, who was showing exceptional bad taste in being dead at this particular stage of our investigation.

But Dickens quickly recovered himself, sat Rogers down on the loveseat, which still had the imprint of my sleeping form, and commenced to interrogate that worthy as to the details of the case.

"Found by the wooman 'oo cleans 'is rooms," Rogers officiously began his narrative. " 'Is door was open on the corridor when the wooman reported for work. She thought 'ee'd just forgot to close it tight when 'ee went out, so she went in to start 'er cleanin'. Found 'im at the worktable in 'is laboratory stabbed in the back. Porter says she let out a scream so loud you could 'ear it all through the buildin': Sounded like a train whistle, 'ee said. Police called in. Morse sent for us when 'ee found out 'oo it was. Inspector Field sent me to fetch you two." He said the last as if something distasteful had flown into his mouth.

We wasted no time in washing, dressing, and making our way the short distance across the quadrangle to the crime scene. The blood lust was upon Dickens. When it came to crime, he was like one of those mythical vampires. An excitement stirred his soul that could only be sated by a close examination of the corpse, a personal inventory of the room, the stage where the murder played itself out. Field and young Morse were waiting for us in Stadler's rooms. An Oxford constable, guarding the door, waved us in. Morse escorted us through the sitting room to the laboratory. The body of the murdered man had not been moved. It was little more than half ten on that morbid morning.

Little seemed out of place in Stadler's laboratory, except of course that large form slumped over the worktable with what looked like a garden stake protruding from the middle of its back. The microscope which the Chemistry Don might well have been consulting when he was stabbed was tipped over just to the side of his wide-open eyes. A large metal water pitcher, of the sort employed in hospitals, lay overturned as well, which accounted for one of the two very different pools of liquid on the floor beneath the feet of the corpse. The water from the overturned pitcher had run off the edge of the table, splashed to the floor, and finally settled into a small clear puddle next to the legs of the high wooden stool upon which the wide-eyed corpse sat. But those stool legs themselves sat in the middle of a much larger, darker, thicker, more sinister pool that had formed beneath the body of the dead man. The sweet smell of death rose out of this horrible pool of lifeblood. It made me shudder to think of it dripping steadily all night long from that wound where the knife protruded from the corpse's back. It made me think of sap running out of a spigot driven into a tree to be collected to make sweet syrup. But there was nothing sweet about this black pool.

Inspector Field moved around the corpse, the worktable, the laboratory, in concentric circles as if creating ripples outward from that dark pool of blood. His eyes raked the room. Suddenly, like a bird of prey descending upon its victim, he glided swiftly to where a waist-high wooden smoking table mounted on a single heavy iron leg supported by three curled black iron feet sat guarding the doorway. This sentinel, placed at the doorway for visitors or the resident scientist himself to extinguish their cigars upon entering the volatile chemical atmosphere of the laboratory, looked as if it were a refugee from some Pall Mall gentleman's club fallen upon hard times. Its lucifer case holder rose like an abandoned stump out of the wooden tabletop while the large round brass ashtray in its center was filled to overflowing with discarded cigars. Burn marks stained the wood over every inch of the smoking table's top and a dirty ring of ashes stained the floor around the black wrought-iron feet. Out of the round brass ashtray filled to brimming with the butt ends of cigars, Field extracted one thin, twisted cigar stub and held it up to us.

" 'Ee's been 'ere," Field growled. "This one's right on top of the 'eap. 'Ee's been 'ere all right and I'll wager 'ee smoked while 'ee did this bit of business," and he nodded at the knife buried in the corpse's back. "But 'ee only smoked it 'alfways down." Field was talking to himself now, utterly unaware that any of the rest of us were even in that room. He held that cigar end up in front of his face. " 'Ee was smokin' it when 'ee came in, but then 'ee put it out before 'ee left. It only took 'im a minute to come up behind Stadler and stab 'im in the back, but 'ee didn't just leave, 'ee stayed, and 'ee put 'is cigar out. Why did 'ee do that?"

We had all formed a close circle around Field—Dickens and Dodgson and I on one side, Morse and Rogers on the other. Field delivered this soliloquy while holding the twisted cigar end before him like Hamlet with his skull. After he arrived at that question and posed it to the room, it was as if he suddenly realized that the rest of us were there with him, that he hadn't been just holding a private conversation with his detective's mind.

"Because 'ee needed both 'ands," Field answered his own question while tossing off a look of triumph that instantly encompassed all of us ranged in the circle around him. " 'Ee needed both 'ands to carry somethin' away, 'ee did. But wot somethin'?" and he began to prowl the room once again.

"Wot isn't 'ere?" He moved slowly around the worktable and the dead man.

"Wot should be 'ere, and isn't?" He stopped and stared over the dead man's shoulder as if trying to visualize Stadler, alive, at work.

"Wot?"

We had all followed him to the worktable like a pack of rats under the spell of a piper.

" 'Allo, wot's this?" Field broke the heavy silence and reached down over the corpse, over the toppled microscope and the overturned water pitcher, to pick up what looked like a Lilliputian hammock, a small rack made of wooden legs and sides and hung with braided string. It looked like a tiny version of a rack for explosive cannon balls on one of Her Majesty's warships.

"Wot's this?" Field repeated himself, holding up this undersized rope hammock for all of us to see.

None of us had the slightest idea and our confused silence clearly attested to that fact.

Field's lips suddenly pursed and a slow, satisfied grin spread itself across his face as he set his mysterious artifact down on the dead scientist's table.

"Nitroglycerine," he snapped in little more than a whisper, but startlingly enough to make the whole pack of us take one step backwards.

"Nitroglycerine. That is wot you said 'ee was workin' with when you talked to 'im in the pub t'other night. Nitroglycerine cannot be shaken or bumped or dropped, remember? Or it will blow up in yer face, 'ee said. It 'as to be treated gently, 'ung in a soft sling, suspended on air," and he paused for dramatic effect, ". . . in this!"

All our eyes fixed on that little hammocklike rack.

"And the nitroglycerine is gone." Dickens was the first to catch Field's drift.

"Yes, that is wot the murderer took away with 'im"—Field spoke quickly and directly, no longer caught in the birth throes of deduction—"carrying it carefully, with both 'ands, knowing that if 'ee dropped it, 'ee would be blown to bits."

"Very good, Inspector Field," a quiet voice from the door-way diverted attention from Field's triumph of deduction to its corpulent, dark-suited, cravatted source. It was our avuncular friend from the Home Office, Mycroft Holmes Esquire, who evidently had been eavesdropping upon us since near the beginning of Field's soliloquy upon a cigar stub.

"Yes, very good indeed," Field glared at that intruder. " 'Olmes of the 'Ome Office, ain't it?"

"Yes, quite right, Inspector Field," he answered jovially. "I stopped around at Bow Street to inquire about our case of the murdered Don in Limehouse and . . ."

"Our case?" Field cut him off.

"Your case, of course. I misspoke," Holmes apologized.

Field glowered at him in silent indignation.

"I went round to Bow Street," young Holmes broke the awkward silence, "and they told me that you had decamped to Oxford to pursue the case."

"They told you, eh? 'Oo told you?" Field thumped the worktable with his angry forefinger as if he would like to bury it in the skull of his betrayer.

"Why, your desk constable, sir." Holmes held his ground against Field's virulent displeasure. Field looked as if he would like to hang anyone involved with Mr. Mycroft Holmes of the Home Office's presence in that room. "I identified myself as Home Office before he would tell me anything."

"Damn 'im and damn the 'Ome Office." Field made no attempt whatsoever to hide his anger at Holmes's meddling.

"Wot are you doin 'ere? Wot does any of this 'ave to do with you?"

"Perhaps it has nothing to do with the Home Office," young Holmes answered with complete equanimity, "or perhaps it has a great deal to do with us. I do not know. But I have been ordered by my superiors to pursue this murder in Limehouse Hole and I am trying to do just that. As I told you at our previous meeting, I will not interfere in any way with your investigation. It would be stupid for me to do so. You are the best detective in London. Everyone says so. I have an eccentric younger brother who thinks that you are a genius, though I must admit I had never heard your name until that night in Limehouse Hole. I simply wish to follow the progress of your case." His explanation (laced with rather transparent flattery) done, Holmes did a strange thing. Placing his two hands together in front of his chest, he made a Chinaman's bow to Field and moved one step back as if to say, "I am your servant."

Field seemed momentarily confused by young Holmes's rapid-fire speech of explanation and flattery. He scowled, but decided not to vent his dislike for this personage and his masters any further. "Stay if you must," he grudgingly consented, "but stay out of my way."

Holmes of the Home Office veritably beamed at this concession that his obvious powers of diplomacy had extracted. "Might I ask," the round young man pressed his advantage, "is this another Don murdered, or is it a robbery of nitroglycerine?"

"Both, wouldn't you say?" Field muttered dryly, underscoring the obviousness of the question.

"But why?" Dickens entered into the debate between these two thinly disguised antagonists. "Why kill Stadler? And why steal his nitroglycerine?"

Dickens's questions seemed to bring all the confrontations in the room to a silent, sudden halt. Nobody seemed to have an answer. Field looked at Holmes, Holmes looked at Dickens, and I looked at the three of them.

"Look at this," Serjeant Rogers broke our awkward silence from across the room. "It's a writing book of some kind," he advanced towards us holding the found object out for Field's inspection, "with some of its pages torn out. See, the whole second 'alf 'as been ripped out."

"It's a notebook of 'is experiments," Field announced, after taking a long look at Rogers's find, "and it is dated. The last date is July 26, late summer, more than three months ago. All the rest 'as been torn away."

"It is like the appointments book in Ackroyd's room," Dickens speculated aloud. "Someone does not want us to read the full texts of these books. Someone is systematically destroying the historical records of what these dead Dons were working on, don't you think?" And he turned to Field for affirmation.

But Field had fallen silent. He had sat himself down on a wooden stool directly across from the slumped-over corpse. The torn experiment book was still in his hands, but he was no longer looking through it. It was as if he had withdrawn into some detective's world of his own and was carrying on a dialogue with himself, perusing the clues in search of an answer. We all watched him as he tried to read all the torn texts he had collected in his mind's eye.

"They were goin' to blow somethin' up," Field finally said quietly in a voice tinged with the wonder of discovery. "They were buildin' an explosive bomb to blow somethin' up!" and he suddenly bolted out of his deductive trance, sprang to his feet, and thumped the table decisively with his triumphant forefinger. "That's what those two was up to—a bomb!"

"A bomb?" Dickens repeated, the idea obviously never having occurred to him.

"A bomb, of course." Holmes feasted upon Field's conclusion as if it were a succulent rack of roast lamb.

"It all fits." Field paced back and forth in the excitement of his discovery. "The chemist, expert in explosives, experimenting with this nitroglycerine. The 'istorian, expert in

the Gunpowder Plot, planning the tactics, knowing everything that could go wrong."

"But why then were they murdered?" Dickens brought
Field back to the reality of the present.

Field pondered that question.

Serjeant Rogers stroked his chin, pondering in concert
with his master.

I had not a clue why these bombmakers had been killed,
and when I looked at Dickens, who had posed the question,
it was clear that he was as bereft of an answer as was I.

"Because someone else wanted their bomb," a quiet voice
from behind us broke the silence. It was Holmes, and this
time Field did not growl at him.

"Yes, of course, that's good, that is." Field actually was
complimenting the intruder, much to the amazement of all
of us who knew well Field's absolute inability to tolerate
interference. "They built it and made the plans 'ow to use
it, and then some'un took it away from 'em."

Our eyes all darted to Holmes, who had the good sense
not to say a word, but simply stood benignly nodding his
assent to Field's genius.

"Some'un was usin' 'em." Field sat back down on his stool
at the dead chemist's worktable and stared hard at the torn
book as if he were reading the missing pages. "Lettin' 'em
plan it and build it, and then 'ee killed 'em for it."

Now all of us were nodding in assent along with Holmes
as Field drew us in the wake of his deduction.

"But who killed 'em and what does 'ee want the bomb
for?" Field posed the question softly to himself, the common
man carrying on a dialogue with the detective. Field was
both, and he pondered his own question for a long moment, then gave it up because he knew that neither part of
him had the answer.

"Who knows? I don't," and his frustrated forefinger
gouged at the corner of his right eye. "Do you know, Mister
Home Office?" and his mocking forefinger pointed accus-
ingly at Holmes. "Or you Charles, or Wilkie, or any of you?"

and his waving forefinger took us all in with a single sweep. "Some 'uns got this nitroglycerine and a plan to use it, and we better find it afore 'ee gits the chance, eh?"

We all looked at one another.

"Well, yes, very good." Holmes of the Home Office stepped forward and extended his hand to Field. "Thank you, Inspector Field, for letting me eavesdrop on your deliberations. Most informative, most informative indeed."

Field shook his hand as if it were a rock that had been held out to him to be crushed.

Holmes winced, withdrew his crumpled hand, and took leave of the rest of us with a general bow of his head.

After he had left, Field turned to the rest of us with his suspicions in full display on his sleeve.

"That 'uns up to somethin' and knows more than 'ee lets on," Field declared. "I don't like this. Wot's the bloody 'Ome Office got to do with two dead Dons?"

Since no one seemed inclined to offer an immediate answer, we all filed out like mourners, leaving the corpse slumped over his microscope as if he were still at work.

Two dead Dons, indeed! We all sensed that life in this supposedly peaceful University town of Oxford had been turned completely upside down, but as yet we did not know how to right it.

"We must bide our time," Field cautioned us as we emerged onto the grey, frozen grass of the Christ Church quadrangle. "We must wait and watch in 'opes that whoever is doin' these murders will give 'imself away."

WAITING AND WATCHING
༨๛

(December 4, 1853–December 8, 1853)

Dickens, true to his word, left the next morning, Sunday it was, on the railway for London. Much to all of our surprise, Inspector Field went with him, leaving Serjeant Rogers alone in Oxford to monitor the proceedings.

Perhaps it was a good thing for all, this brief break in the detecting. Thompson, of course, stayed on as Ellen's bodyguard as she played her barmaid's role in the Bulldog. Rogers was left to follow young Morse about and try to tie up some of the loose ends of the investigation. And Dodgson and I were left to our own devices in his tower aerie with its telescope poised for spying. We speculated that Dickens and Field must have had a great deal to talk about on their railway journey back to the city. We were sure that they minutely sifted every shred of the evidence, reconstructed every movement of our murderer, examined every motive of every person connected to the case. We were very sure that our young acquaintance, Holmes of the Home Office, came in for a good bit of their detective scrutiny.

Before he departed, Charles left me with a clear assignment. "Wilkie, I must attend to my business in London," he began, by way, I think, of an apology for leaving me with all of the responsibility in Oxford, "but you must keep a close eye on Ellen. I know that Thompson never lets her out of his sight, but you too can watch out for her. You and Dodgson can go to the pub in the evenings. It will reassure her to see you there. She will know that a good friend is close by."

Perhaps Ellen was grateful for my presence in Oxford, my nightly attendance at the pub, but if she was, she never showed it. Like a stage actress a week or two into her play's run, she seemed to be becoming quite comfortable in her role. She made friends, it seemed, with everyone who frequented the establishment, smiled her way into their confidences.

Time passed, two days, three, four, but that time was good for her role, her access, her credibility with the Dons. As I watched her every night, it became clear that she was becoming more and more a part of the pub's scenery, like the faded flowers on the wallpaper or the river scenes in the student paintings on the walls. And her ease in her role fortified my courage in our game as well. One evening, as she was serving us our pints and stopped to chat, I asked her straightaway in a friendly, unobtrusive manner and a low voice not susceptible to eavesdropping how her precious Dons were taking the news of Stadler's murder.

"Not very well," she said with a false smile as she waited for Dodgson and me to find the coins to pay for our pints. "It's put them in a panic," she assured us, making it seem like she was discussing the weather. "They're terrified. I think because they don't know who is doing it and they might be next." With that, she took our money and flounced off to tend to her next customer. *How interesting*, I thought. *They are afraid, yet none of them has gone to the police. Why? Because they too are guilty of something.*

When I was not spying on her from a table in the pub, I was watching her from long range through Dodgson's conveniently adjusted telescope. Dickens's assignment as his personal spy was a pernicious contract. It turned me into a voyeur; no, worse, a Peeping Tom. I found myself sitting at that spyglass, waiting for her to appear in the doorway to take the air. She knew I was watching her, I think. I half expected her to wave up at me as she stood smoking on the doorstep. I fell in love with the spying. I watched her day and night, coming to and leaving the pub. I watched her watering the plantings in the window boxes and sweeping the cobblestones in front of the door. I watched her the way that a rapist stalks his prey or a cuckold watches the window behind which his unfaithful wife has disappeared. As I watched her, my imagination concocted full scenarios around her daily routines of coming and going and working at the pub, elaborate scenes of romance and intrigue, rescue and lust, secret fantasies of my perverse imagination, the spy's stories, the voyeur's vagaries, the Peeping Tom's dirty little tales.

But that time passing with Dickens gone back up to the city also gave Dodgson and me, old school chums, the chance to grow comfortable with each other once again. We talked of poetry and of novel writing. He was infinitely curious about my and Dickens's London life. I never mentioned Irish Meg because I did not think she would be of interest to Old Dodo. I did not want to have to explain our rather Bohemian living arrangements to one whom I quickly realized had become a rather fervent devotee of the Church of England. We also talked about the case, the murders, in all their baffling reality.

"Whoever the murderer is, he had to k-k-kill them because they were some sort of a threat to him, or they had d-d-done what he wanted them to d-d-do for him and he was finished with them, or they were g-g-going to d-d-do something that he d-d-did not want them to d-d-do with those explosives." I wasn't sure that Dodo would ever fight his way through all of the hard consonants in his deductive speculation.

"It does not seem that he needed to kill them unless they were making him nervous in some way. These murders come too close together in time to have been carefully planned. The murderer is someone who is protecting himself by killing off those who are threats to him."

"B-b-but a historian and a c-c-chemist?" Dodgson simply could not accept that academics could be a threat to anyone.

"If it is some sort of political plot they are all hatching, then maybe this murderer was afraid that these two would give it all away, whatever it was that they were planning?" I argued for my theory of a conspiracy.

"Or," Dodgson was beginning to like my little intrigue scenario, "p-p-perhaps he was afraid of having his whole p-p-plot in the rather unsteady hands of an opium addict and a d-d-drunkard. I mean, that is what Ackroyd and Stadler were in truth, notwithstanding their being D-D-Dons."

"Or," I countered, "in the best tradition of academics, perhaps they had done all the research and experimentation that he needed and so he stole their work and murdered them so they couldn't complain. The murder of Stadler in his lab and the missing nitroglycerin certainly points to robbery." I rested my case.

"That is ridiculous," Dodgson took my mockery of his beloved Academia seriously. "Was something stolen from Ackroyd as well? His research on the G-G-Gunpowder P-P-Plot? Really!" he scoffed.

"Perhaps each was killed for a different reason? Perhaps each posed a different sort of threat to our murderer?" I backslid upon my argument.

"P-p-perhaps each was k-k-killed by a d-d-different person with a very d-d-different weapon for a very d-d-different reason," now Dodgson was openly mocking me, "and it was p-p-pure c-c-coincidence that they were academic c-c-collaborators at the same Oxford c-c-college and c-c-close friends who met nightly as charter members of the same d-d-drinking c-c-club. Really!"

"What ho! What's this? Who is this one, Dodo? I can't keep your fellow Dons straight." I had suddenly been distracted from our speculations on the motives of our murderer by putting my eye back to the eyepiece of the telescope and seeing Ellen emerge from the front door of the pub with a tall, slender man.

Dodgson crossed the room and looked through the glass: "That is B-B-Barnet of Queen's," he identified the Don who was chatting Ellen up down below in the street. What was unusual about this scene was that it was only half past two by the afternoon clock and the political Dons did not usually make their appearance at the Bulldog until after dark.

"Barnet of the boathouses?" I made the connection.

"Quite the same," Dodo nodded, his eye still pressed to the spyglass. "He seems quite t-t-taken with Miss T-T-Ternan, he d-d-does."

"Here, let me see," and I relieved him in our spying.

Ellen and this Barnet stood conversing in front of the pub. Ellen evidently asked him for a cigarette. He rolled one for her, then one for himself. As he lit her cigarette, she steadied his hand holding the lucifer, and he smiled down at her like a cat preparing to pounce on an unsuspecting mouse. Except, in this case, I was absolutely certain that it was the mouse who was seductively baiting the trap. The Don leaned close to her, perhaps to whisper something, and as he spoke, rubbed his hand up the length of her arm to her bare shoulder. Ellen stepped back as if she had been burned, raised her forefinger to him in a gesture of asking him to wait, and disappeared back into the pub.

I observed Barnet the Don as he waited for her to return. He primped, smoothing his hair, glancing at himself in the reflective window of the pub. Ellen danced out the door with her coat on, her bare shoulders covered, still holding the cigarette that Barnet had made for her. Smiling, tossing her head as she smoked, then tossing away the butt end of her cigarette, she took his arm and the two of them strolled away from the pub down St. Aldate's in the direction of the river. Tally Ho Thompson was nowhere to be seen, at least not within the circular ken of the magnifying telescope's eyepiece.

"Dodo, quickly! We must follow them." I leapt up from the telescope and started for the door.

"He's t-t-taking her t-t-to the b-b-boathouses, isn't he?" Dodgson speculated calmly from his seat in his overstuffed easy chair.

"Perhaps. I don't know!" I was barking at him in exasperation at his slowness, his equanimity. "Come quickly. I promised Charles I would keep her in my sight."

"Well, then, in that c-c-case we will need these," Dodgson said, getting up and reaching towards his desk, but I did not hear or see the rest of what he said or did as I was already out the door in hot pursuit of our two boathouse lovers.

When I reached the street at the base of Tom Tower, the strolling couple was still in sight at the bottom of the hill, passing the police station and heading for Folly Bridge. Much to my surprise, Dodgson was right behind me, had caught up before I had taken my first step out of the stone gateway.

"Well then, shall we g-g-go?" he said brightly, as if we were setting off to shop for cheese or watch for birds over the meadow or go punting on the river.

We pursued our two subjects down the cobblestoned way, keeping our distance, but keeping them in sight. It was an unusual December day, sunny and windless, more like English spring than the Christmas season.

At the very base of St. Aldate's hill, before they reached the bridge, our strolling couple turned off to the left and disappeared into a woodland path through a copse of trees that ran right up to the river's edge.

"He's t-t-taking her t-t-to the b-b-boathouses," Dodgson crowed in that voice which announces that he knew it all the time.

"And she is going willingly," I muttered, "despite all of our warnings."

"She certainly does not seem overly c-c-concerned," Dodgson gloated, "and after all, Wilkie, it is midday. I d-d-don't think they c-c-can g-g-get up t-t-to much mischief in b-b-bright sunlight now, d-d-do you?"

"Only if she is reckless enough to go inside with him," I replied sourly, knowing that he was right and that my anxiety was probably somewhat exaggerated, overwrought perhaps. "Come on, Dodo, we must not lose them in that wood." I spoke with a calm restraint that belied the urgency I truly felt.

"We should not follow them through there." Dodgson spoke in the purely analytical voice of the mathematician and scholar. "The d-d-docks and b-b-boathouses are d-d-directly on the far edge of these t-t-trees. We will not b-b-be able t-t-to emerge from the wood without b-b-being observed. We will not b-b-be able t-t-to see them or where they are g-g-going from inside the wood because the b-b-boathouses will b-b-block our view."

He stopped speaking and we stared at each other, both of us turning the troubling situation over in our minds.

"But I must follow them, keep them in sight," I said, starting for the path through the wood.

"No," Dodgson stopped me. "The b-b-bridge. We c-c-can see them from there and they will not b-b-be able to observe us watching them."

They were well out of our sight down that woodland path. I was torn. Upon reflection, I realized that his was the better part of valour. If I followed them and this Barnet observed me, he could take it back to the other Dons and they would become suspicious and all of the groundwork we had laid for the penetration of their cabal and the divining of their secrets could be exposed.

"There, up on the b-b-bridge," Dodgson pointed, "we c-c-can see the d-d-docks and the b-b-boathouses from there."

"But it is so far away," I protested. "What if she is in danger? What if he tries to . . . ?" and I left the unthinkable unsaid.

"If we see things g-g-getting out of hand, we c-c-can run t-t-to her aid," he assured me. "We c-c-can see them from the b-b-bridge," he started towards it. "It is the b-b-best p-p-place."

In the end, I acquiesced and followed him up onto Folly Bridge, and he proved right. We did, indeed, have a clear view of the riverside stage upon which this scene of Field's drama was going to be played.

As we reached our point of vantage on the crest of the bridge, the two lovers were just emerging from the wood onto the low docks in front of the four boathouses in the distance.

"Here, t-t-try these," Dodgson handed me a square leather case. "They are an experiment that I am working on with a c-c-colleague at B-B-Balliol. We call them b-b-bi-oculars. They are a sort of d-d-double spyglass with focusing lenses. Two eyes are b-b-better than one, eh?" and he laughed as if this was all just some scientific proving ground for his fanciful inventions. I must admit though that he seemed to be supplied with a new machine for every occasion.

I unpacked his strange instrument and looked through its twin tubes. What nonsense! They only blurred my vision. I pushed them back at him in disgust. "These are no good."

"You need t-t-to focus the lenses t-t-to your eye," he patiently instructed me, placing the oversized spyglasses to his eyes and adjusting their tubular shafts with the thumb and forefinger of each hand. "See, here, the sighting t-t-tubes t-t-turn. Look through them and t-t-turn the t-t-tubes until you c-c-can see c-c-clearly."

I did what he told me, and, lo and behold, suddenly Ellen and her amorous Don seemed as if they were only mere inches away from my eye. I could see their lips move. I could see every move they made, as they circled each other, him reaching out to touch her, she flirtatiously drawing back. They walked back and forth on the docks in front of the boathouse, conversing earnestly.

Ellen would tell us later what they were conversing about, but from our point of vantage on the Folly Bridge all I could see through Dodgson's marvellous little spying engines was their physical presence on that dock across the water. Barnet was persistently, but not violently, moving in on her, and Ellen was flirtatiously and playfully moving away from him. It was like a dance viewed from a private box high up in a balconied theatre.

But finally Barnet the Don triumphed in their circling dance. His relentless boring in had manoeuvered her up against the wooden wall of one of the boathouses. His two arms extended beside her shoulders, his hands flattened against the wooden boards of the boathouse wall, imprisoned her in his lover's cage as he leaned in to achieve the object of all his pursuit, a kiss.

But Ellen outflanked him by going on the offensive herself. As he leeringly leaned in to claim her lips, she threw her arms around his neck, kissed him full on the lips, and spun him around all in the same motion so that his back was now to the boathouse wall.

She held for the kiss for a rather long moment, I thought, then, breaking free from his arms, retreated laughing towards the water's edge. And the whole dance of seduction began again, the circling, the touching, the pressing in, until another kiss was won and Ellen was once again imprisoned in his arms. All the while, it seemed to me, spying from afar, Barnet was attempting to lead her to the doorway of the boathouse against which he had manoeuvered her for the kiss. But Ellen would not follow him there, and, in fact, after the second kiss, she broke away from his more pressing embrace and looked as if she were shouting at him, protesting perhaps, scolding him for his impertinence.

Who knows, we could not hear a word from the bridge. I could only interpret the movements of her body, the language of her hands, the defiance of her back-thrown head. I thought that she was refusing him in no uncertain terms, but then, to my surprise, she moved close and kissed him gently on the cheek.

At that moment, a drunken tramp emerged from behind one of the other boathouses, and with his hat pulled down hard over his face and his clothes in utter disrepair, came shambling along the docks towards the two negotiating lovers.

They were not aware of this intruder at first as they spoke quietly, close together, after Ellen had bestowed her gentling kiss upon him. But, as the tramp drew abreast of them, the movement, or perhaps he made some vulgar sound, startled them away from each other. The tramp never even acknowledged their existence as he moved in a drunken sideways stumble past them along the dock and finally into the wood towards us on our spying pedestal above on the bridge.

It was, of course, Thompson. Once again, he appeared out of nowhere in one of his chameleon disguises. He never spoke to the two startled lovers. They never saw his face. But his mere migration across the plane of their supposedly private world utterly destroyed the mood and provided Ellen with an avenue for escape.

I watched their lips move through Dodgson's bi-oculars. She was obviously making excuses as to why she must go. He was obviously protesting why she must stay. Finally, she just turned and began walking away towards the path through the woods in the same direction that Thompson's drunkenly shambling tramp had taken. Barnet the boathouse Don followed her, pleading his case to no avail. The sexual spell was broken. Ellen had escaped the threat of the boathouses this time.

From my perch on the bridge, I waited breathlessly for them to emerge from the green cover of the woods back into my spying eyes. I feared that under the cover of the trees, Barnet would attempt to molest her in unspeakable ways. Just as I was about to race down off the bridge and into the trees, the two of them emerged back out onto the cobblestones of St. Aldate's Street. None of the perverse things I had imagined ever happened as they came along the wooded path because as they returned to the street they seemed quite congenial, quite at ease with one another. Ellen had clearly said or done something which had assuaged our amorous Don's disappointment.

They strolled back up the hill towards Christ Church and the Bulldog, with her bodyguards strung out behind like pull-toys. First Thompson slouching along the way, then Dodgson and I following at a distance. Dickens really had nothing to fear. His love was well protected by watchful eyes.

The only irony of the whole episode, however, was the small teasing sense I had that Ellen Ternan was rather enjoying her role as seductress and spy, was not put off in the least by the crude advances and liberties taken by the Dons whom she was spying upon. I did not feel that was a perception that Dickens would want me to share with him when he returned.

THE SPIES REPORT

(December 8, 1853–Evening)

Dickens and Field returned on the afternoon railway on Thursday of that week. Naturally, the first thing they demanded was a full report on all that had transpired in their absence. I held nothing back in describing the amorous walking out of Ellen and Barnet the boathouse Don. Field was delighted—"She's got 'er 'ooks into 'im," he exclaimed (we were gathered in Dodgson's rooms)—while Dickens almost visibly winced.

Since it was well past six of the clock when this reunion of our detecting party took place, and none of us had yet eaten our evening meal, Inspector Field proposed that we procure some victuals and then proceed to the Bulldog to view the evening's performance. We repaired to the High Street Hotel and dined on roast lamb and Yorkshire pudding.

"It is time to stir the pot a bit with our murderous little group of Dons," Field declared over dinner. "Besides, they would certainly expect someone from the police to interview them now that two of their group 'ave been murdered. Morse"—and he caught that young fellow with a forkful of tasty lamb just entering his maw—"you and I will approach them in the pub tonight. You can introduce me as a detective down from London looking into it. We will see what they say to that."

Young Morse nodded wide-eyed as he tried to chew his substantial mouthful of meat and answer Field at the same time. I was afraid he was going to choke, so eager was he to accommodate his detective idol.

"Per'aps stirrin' things up a bit will make one of 'em break cover," Field went on, unmindful of poor Morse's inability to reply. "Per'aps we can find out wot they are up to. If they are afeerd of us detectives findin' them out," and he tipped a conspiratorial wink to young Morse, who was still chewing violently, "per'aps they'll forget that Miss Ternan is listenin' in, too. They might let somethin' drop to 'er just because they think we are the foremost threat."

"Yessir," Morse finally was able to swallow and speak, but that was all that he could think of to say.

"Also, this Barnet, who is so taken with Miss Ternan," Field measured a thick slice of lamb on the end of his fork, then shook it deliberately at all of us around the table— Dickens, Dodgson, myself, Morse, and Serjeant Rogers—as if it was a pointer and he was some blunt teacher in a Ragged School, " 'ee is their weakest link. We can exploit 'im, we can," and Field punctuated his certainty by biting off about half of the strip of meat he was brandishing. "I'd like to get 'im alone and work on 'im, I would." Field chewed speculatively, then lapsed into a long contemplative silence that made all of us believe he was hatching some new plan for the accomplishment of that task.

"But there is other news from London," Dickens cut through the silence which Field's departure into his detective's reverie had cast over our dining table. "Both the Queen and the P.M. are coming to Oxford in the next ten days."

"Something our fat little friend from the Home Office,

Holmes, neglected to tell us," Field sarcastically reentered the conversation.

"Yes," Dickens nodded in assent to Field's emphasis upon Holmes's impenetrability, "supposedly they are coming here separately, the Queen to Blenheim Palace for a brief respite from the city before all of the Christmas festivities begin, and the P.M. to speak to the Christ Church student body. But the speculation in the city is that they are here to hold a secret meeting on the problems with the Dardanelles."

"I can't imagine that the Home Office didn't know about that!" Field barked.

"Nor I," Dickens agreed.

Then something that I am sure Dickens and Field had been discussing in the growler on the railway all the way from Victoria Station that afternoon suddenly came clear to all of us: a conspiracy of Dons, the Gunpowder Plot, nitroglycerine. Was the Queen (or the P.M.) the target of all this conspiring? Surely not. It was unimaginable. The supposed conspirators were Oxford Dons. Who would wish to harm Queen Victoria? She was England's mum.

"Do you really think that they're goin' to blow up the Queen?" Serjeant Rogers finally blurted out (in the crudest possible manner) that which all of us were thinking.

"Not if I 'ave anything to do with it," Field growled. "That is why we 'ave to find out wot this is all about, and find out quickly."

We finished dinner in near silence, broken only by the amenities of the table and the requests of the waiter. It was as if all of us suddenly realized that perhaps we were involved in something much bigger than simply the murders of two members of the Oxford community of scholars. For the first time in weeks, our thoughts on the case were wrested away from the hallowed halls of Academia and forced to look at things in the context of the wider world.

We arrived at the Bulldog at half nine. Morse and Field, acting professional, marched in after Dickens, Dodgson, and I had been seated. Evidently, Rogers had been told to lay low, Field not wanting to give up the identity of all his associates in the case. Thompson was in residence at the tap, sipping noncommittally on a pint of dark Irish stout. The public house was not crowded, and when Morse and Field entered they gave no evidence of any acquaintance with us, but proceeded directly to the back room to beard the Dons in their den. No one paid much attention to them as they passed through. Ellen was collecting a tray of drinks at the tap from Irish Mike.

I can only report from hearsay what conversation was exchanged when Morse and Field joined the Dons in the back room, but their *tête-à-tête* went on for some forty-five minutes as Dickens, Dodgson, and I amused ourselves over our pints discussing various subjects in which none of us had a great deal of interest. Dickens could not keep his eyes off of his Ellen as she moved about the room serving the pub's sparse clientele. We had been directed by Field to surreptitiously direct Ellen to meet us in the church after closing to report on her progress. I could see that Dickens waited eagerly for the opportunity to speak to her, to impart that message certainly, but also just to hear her voice, to look into her face in close proximity.

After the aforementioned time, their business evidently concluded, Morse and Field emerged from the rear room and passed out through the street doors of the establishment. Heads did not turn. No one seemed to notice, much less care about either their coming or going. We stayed on until closing time at Field's direction to observe any reaction that the accosted Dons might have to the London detective's visit. But, if anything, as they left the public house at closing time with the rest of us, which had shrunken to a rather small number, they did not seem excited or in confusion. Rather, they seemed more subdued than their usual drunken, arrogant selves. The Dons dispersed in different directions, heading for residences in their respective colleges as Dodgson and I crossed the street towards his rooms in Tom Tower. Out of the corner of my eye I caught sight of Thompson sauntering up the hill. A man in a brown Mackintosh was following a few paces behind him going in the same direction.

Dodgson and I entered the tower gate, greeted the porter, but did not go up. We waited until all of the Dons had dispersed, and then, checking the street to see that it was deserted, we made our way up St. Aldate's to the High Street, then halfway down to the dark bulk of St. Mary's Church.

PLOTTING A DON'S DOWNFALL

(December 8, 1853 — Midnight)

St. Mary's Church at midnight was no more inviting than it had been that night almost a week before when we had met there for the first time. Gloomy from its blackened pillars, mouldy with winter damp to its scenes of martyred saints staring down in pain from the stained-glass windows, it was an unwelcoming place. God may have been present in that church, but I got the feeling that at night He chose to frequent some cheerier places.

Field, Rogers, and young Morse were waiting for us when we arrived.

"Well, that was an interestin' evenin'," Field opened congenially as our two groups came together directly in front of the main altar. We commandeered two pews and ranged ourselves facing each other for the purpose of discussion.

"For you perhaps!" Dickens growled. "At least you had the entertainment of talking about the case. We had to sit there drinking that awful treacle that Irish Mike serves and looking as if we were having just a splendid time."

We were just finishing this petulant exchange when Ellen

Ternan arrived, followed in due course by her faithful shadow, Tally Ho Thompson.

"Aha, we are all 'ere," Inspector Field convened us as if we were the church choir come to rehearse. "Our exploratory foray into the lion's den produced little of value," he began his report of how he and young Morse had accosted our Dons in their pub. "But now they know that we are lookin' at them."

He looked around at all of us as if he expected questions. None forthcoming, he asked one himself. "Wot do you think, Reggie?" he addressed young Morse. "Did we capture their attention?"

"Oh yes, sir, we did, sir," that worthy eagerly supported Field. "I think we made summat of 'em quite nervous, sir. In fact, when you announced who you was, sir, I thought that little Squonce one of Balliol was goin' to choke on 'is bitter."

"They gave up almost nothing," Field turned back to the rest of us, "which means that they 'ave a great deal to 'ide. When I asked about Ackroyd and then Stadler, they fell all over themselves expressing their grief, their loss, and their total lack of even the slightest idea why anyone would want to kill their colleagues. Oh, that's the way it went all right, and it was enough to make you want to cuff them 'ard about the ears. Oh, they're a smug lot, they are. It's goin' to give me real joy to bring some of them down a peg or two, it is."

"Some of 'em, especially that little Squonce of Balliol, the Literature Don, and Carroll of All Souls, spoke quite a lot," young Morse consulted his small notebook. "Some of the others 'ardly spoke at all. They seemed 'appy to let that little ponce, Squonce, be their spokesman."

"Our friend Barnet of the boat'ouses said very little." Inspector Field shot a quick glance Miss Ternan's way.

Ellen flinched, as if she would have preferred to keep the representation of her fledgling relationship with that man for her own report, even though it was all part of the play that Inspector Field was directing.

It was Dickens who broke the awkward silence. He reaffirmed his support for his Ellen. "Ellen, Wilkie tells me that you have been successful in gaining the confidence of this Barnet."

Now it was my turn to flinch under Ellen Ternan's sharp glance. Dickens had thrown me to her as the spy, the Peeping Tom.

"I asked Wilkie to keep you in his sight, Ellen," Dickens leapt to my defense when he observed the momentary awkwardness between us, "sort of a backup for friend Thompson here, in case Tally Ho would get overpowered or deceived. For your protection."

"Well, then," and there was a mischievousness in her voice, "perhaps I should just let Wilkie or Tally Ho give my report of the last few days."

She was teasing Dickens, and it was obvious to everyone. Her sarcasm actually lightened the gloomy atmosphere of that infernal church. Field certainly was right about picking St. Mary's at night as our meeting place. Nobody in their right mind would ever disturb us there.

"No, I think you can tell us yourself," Field played along. "From what I 'ear, things are moving along quite nicely, eh?"

"They seem to like me," Ellen Ternan began. "They do not stop talking right away any more when I come to serve their pints. I have heard all sorts of things. I do not think they know who killed the other two because they all seem affrighted by it. If it is one of them, he is alone in the killings, because all of them could not be acting their panic and fear that well. One of them could be an actor, but not all. And they are all terrified, afraid that they will be the next. Beyond their fears, they are hiding something, or planning something. I do not know what. I have heard them say: 'Should we go on with it? Should we see it through?' Things like that make me think that these murders were not part of their plan." She paused for a brief moment to catch her breath.

"And then there is Barnet, out boat'ouse Don, wot of 'im?" Field prompted.

"Ah yes, John Barnet; a real man about town, he thinks he is. Unlike the others, he drinks absinthe in the pub. It gives him his courage and makes him think he is God's gift to womankind. He has promised to tutor me in the sciences. He likes the idea of me walking out with him, especially to his beloved boathouses. I have already survived their evil reputation once, though Tally Ho was stumbling around us playing drunk while John was trying to seduce me."

"Oh, it's John, is it?" Tally Ho Thompson taunted her.

"Yes, we went for a walk to the boathouses at the height of the day and, and," she faltered, "and I just let him kiss me, but it went no farther."

"Go on, go on," Field prompted her eagerly.

"That is all of it. He tried to get me into the boathouse. To do more perhaps. Oh, I do not know." This was proving difficult for Ellen because she had to tell it all right under the silent gaze of Dickens, her lover. "I got away from him. I told him I had enjoyed the walk, but I had to get back to the pub. He tried to argue me out of it and into the boathouse, but I would not go. But he is going to want me to go back there. I know he is."

"Good," Field pounced. "That is exactly what I want you to do."

"What!" Dickens leapt to his feet. "You cannot be serious! It is too dangerous. No! I will not allow it. My God, man, anything could happen to her once he gets her inside and out of sight."

"Oh Charles, calm yourself." Field treated him like some minor annoyance, a persistent fly, or a loud noise in the street. "We will already be inside the boat'ouse watching 'is every move, 'earing 'is every word. In fact, once Ellen gets as much out of 'im as she can, I might 'ave a little talk with 'im myself."

Now Field took the stage, getting to his feet and walking

out in front of the pews in which we were all sitting, dismissing Ellen Ternan as just one of his minions, and taking over all the attention for himself.

" 'Ere is 'ow we will do it. Early this evenin', I sent young Morse 'ere to reconnoitre the boat'ouse that friend Barnet seems to favour. 'Ee reports that it is well appointed for our purposes, and this Barnet's. We can set up surveillance behind the rowing shells, which are rather tightly stacked on racks. It seems that friend Barnet 'as a small space in the front of the boat'ouse furnished for 'is purposes. A sofa, a table, a rug on the floor, nothin' fancy at all, you see, but good enough for a seduction. That is where 'ee will take 'er. We will be able to see and 'ear all that goes on. Per'aps we may need to intervene if things get out of 'and or finally to obtain the information that we need. But first we will let Ellen try 'er best with 'im."

I could see on his face that Dickens did not like Field's plan, but he chose not to speak out.

"This Barnet is the weak link in this little conspiracy," Field forged on. "If we can break 'im, then we will 'ave them."

"But why must Ellen be the bait for the trap?" Dickens finally made his weak protest. "It is her, her"—he seemed to struggle for the fitting word—"her virtue which is at risk." He intoned that word "virtue" somewhat sheepishly, as if, in light of Ellen's own past and his relationship with her, he was himself skeptical about just how fitting it might be. Or perhaps it was just a sense of himself sounding pretentious or prudish that made him hesitate on that word.

"Come, Charles, she is an actress," Field's voice was all pacification and assurance, "and a damn good one, I would say. Why, she 'as the gigolo of a Don eatin' out of 'er 'and, she does. And 'ee 'olds all the information we need, the answer to our questions. We needs to turn 'im, one way or another, to doing our bidding, not theirs."

"He thinks that I want an education, Charles." Ellen turned to him to try to explain. "Since Oxford is all men, he thinks that I'll do anything to get him to teach me the secrets of his science. He thinks he owns me because of his knowledge. It will give me great pleasure to turn the tables on him, to unmask him as the Parson Square that he is."[19]

Everyone laughed at her allusion. Even Dickens could not help but see the situation as it really was. Ellen was doing the acting job that Inspector Field had sent her to do (and Dickens had pledged to support), and she was doing it quite well. This was no time for Dickens to balk or become faint-hearted simply because that acting role involved the ostensible proffering of sexual favours for knowledge. Ellen was simply playing Faust to Barnet's Mephistopheles.[20]

Dickens acquiesced, subsiding into a somewhat sullen silence.

That settled, Inspector Field proceeded to set out his plan. Ellen Ternan would accept Barnet's next invitation to walk out and would tip Thompson as to the time and place. Prior to the appointed time, we—Field, Dickens, Dodgson, and myself—would secrete ourselves in the boathouse. Ellen would lure her Don to the place of assignation, and as he attempted to seduce her, she would try to catch him off guard concerning the plots of his fellow Dons.

"Fine. Wonderful. Now let's git out of this infernal dark cellar," Thompson suggested none too shyly. "I'm freezin' and my teeth are chatterin'."

No one raised any objection. I think we all felt oppressed by the gloominess of that church.

As we filed out of St. Mary's Church into the moon-lit courtyard of the Radcliffe Camera, Dodgson fell back to have a brief word with Field. I overheard him say, "Inspector Field, I have an idea about this surveillance at the b-b-boathouse," but the rest was lost in the clatter of all of our feet on the cobblestones of the courtyard.

[19]The allusion is to a prominent character in Henry Fielding's novel, *Tom Jones* (1749).
[20]The allusion is to Christopher Marlowe's *Dr. Faustus.*

PARSON SQUARE EXPOSED

☙

(December 10, 1853 — After Closing)

I t was two nights later, Saturday night in the Bulldog tavern, when our opportunity arose. The Dons were not in attendance, as was usual, since they did not frequent the pub on the weekends. The public house was crowded with people out celebrating their temporary freedom from labour and study and the sheer dreariness of winter. We had eaten supper at the Bulldog, mutton pie and Irish stout followed by apples and cheese. Then, with no Dons in sight, we had retired to Dodgson's rooms to smoke cigars, drink a brandy, and otherwise amuse ourselves as we waited for something to happen. Dickens and Dodgson soon entangled themselves in a discussion of the London publishing scene and how it might receive a rather elaborate children's story complete with illustrations which Dodgson was proposing to both write and draw.

I soon grew bored by their conversation and took to entertaining myself with the telescope, watching the people crowding into the pub and moving through the street down below. It was almost ten of the clock when a familiar face caught my attention. Stopping in the centre of my eyeglass to light his cigar, he shouldered his way into the pub.

"It's Barnet!" I cut Dodgson off in mid-sentence and brought Dickens to his feet with a bound. "He's going in."

"By himself, is he?" Dickens stood at my side staring down at the dimly lit street. Dodgson too joined us at the window.

"Yes. Alone. He just went in."

"He has come to get her when the pub closes." Dickens sounded convinced in the way a man who knows he is going to be hanged in the morning sounds. "Else why would he be arriving so late?"

"Should we notify Field and Rogers?" I suggested.

"Field probably knows he is in there already." Dickens laughed. "Field is always on the watch. Never fear. Field will come to us with this news as soon as Tally Ho confirms it."

Dickens was most assuredly right in that regard. A half hour passed. We took turns at the telescope. At half ten, Tally Ho Thompson, smoking a cigar, made his way out of the pub and disappeared into the darkness. What seemed like only moments later, Field and Rogers were knocking on Dodgson's door.

Field did not step in.

"Come now. We are off," he ordered us.

We scrambled for our greatcoats and hats.

As we were wrestling ourselves into our coats, Dodgson was distributing two bundles wrapped in canvas, one long and thin to Serjeant Rogers, one square and as big as a man's head to Field. As for himself, he carried two objects, a small canister and a square flat package that looked like a wrapped-up picture frame. These transactions completed, Field turned and plunged down the stone steps of the tower. He barely gave us time to button our coats or wrap our scarves around our necks, but we hurried after him.

We stopped just inside the shadows of the Tom Tower gateway. It was a strange mob: five gentlemen in greatcoats lurking in the darkness. Young Constable Morse was nowhere in evidence.

"It is ten minutes yet until closing," Field consulted his repeater. "Rogers, you stay 'ere. As soon as you see them come out of the pub, you run through the meadow to the boat'ouse to warn us. Thompson will stay back and follow them just to make sure that nothing is amiss, that 'ee does not get too amorous on the way," and Field cast a quick sidelong glance at Dickens. "She will not be able to leave until at least a 'alf 'our after closing. That gives us an abundance of time. Come to us when you see them, Rogers; we will be ready."

With that, he marched us off down St. Aldate's to the boathouses.

Led by Field, who seemed to know his way rather well, we passed through that small dark wood at the bottom of the hill and came out upon the river and the boathouses. The moon was shrouded by clouds and brooded down upon us like a ghost hiding in a hedge. Smoke was rising off the river in a thin mist that only added to the eerie gloom of the night.

Beware the boathouses indeed! Emerging from the wood into that ghostly scene made me want to flee this ill-fated adventure before it even began. Really! Hiding out in some damp boathouse to spy on two illicit lovers, one of whom is attempting to entice the other into revealing murderous secrets, suddenly seemed just a bit too Gothic for my blood.

"Is this really a good idea?" I stopped Dickens and Field who were unconcernedly strolling towards the dark boathouses. "Do you really think that he will bring her to this godforsaken place in the middle of the night?"

"No fear," Inspector Field turned to me with an amused chuckle, " 'ee'll bring 'er. Ellen will make sure of that."

There were four boathouses ranged in a row along the docks. The docks were but a thick wooden slab extending right out over the river precisely at water level, and painted white, which added even more to the ghostly aura of the place.

Young Morse was waiting by the door of the first boathouse. He had already picked the lock for us. He greeted us, smiling. He did not seem the least bit concerned that what we might be doing could possibly be dangerous. Thoughts such as "what if friend Barnet carries a revolver?" or "what if he brings harm to Miss Ternan?" never seemed to have entered these gentlemen's minds.

"Once we're inside," Field directed young Morse, "lock us in. Make everything look undisturbed. Retire to the side of the boat'ouse there, out of sight, and wait for Serjeant Rogers to appear. When 'ee comes, knock 'ard on the boat'ouse wall where I showed you. That will alert us. Then you and Rogers stand guard out 'ere, close and out of sight. If anybody 'appens along, escort them out of our way. Only rush in if we shout for your assistance or witness."

"Yes, sir. Right, sir."

It was black as pitch inside that boathouse. When the door closed behind us and the dark enveloped us, I once again felt the unmistakable urge to flee. But Inspector Field was prepared for every eventuality. In the flutter of an eye, he had got his bull's-eye lit and its piercing light sent the shadows scurrying up and over the walls. His light played over Barnet the Don's secret little *pied-à-terre:* the couch upon which he would surely attempt his seduction of Miss Ternan, the table which held the candle that would shed fluttering deceitful light upon their romantic encounter, the tattered Persian rug upon which he might well consummate his perverse designs on Dickens's love.

"Over 'ere is where we will 'ide." Field led us behind a rack of rowing shells stacked to the ceiling. We could stand behind these long thin boats, and looking through the narrow apertures between them, see everything that transpired.

"And 'ere is where your contraption will be set up." Field stood at the very end of the rack of rowing boats. "You can operate it from be'ind the boats. In the darkness of the place, 'ee should not notice that anything is amiss."

With that, Dodgson set to work. Dickens and I had ended up carrying his two mysterious packages, what with Rogers being dismissed to watch for the lovers, and then Field needing both hands to light his bull's-eye. Out of the long, thin package Dodgson unwrapped a wooden tripod of about four and a half feet in height. Out of the small square package he produced a black box with what in the dim light looked like holes in its front and back, which he mounted atop the tripod.

We recognized Dodgson's camera, the same with which he took the charming portraits of the little girls and their dog that decorated the mantelpiece of his Christ Church sitting room. He poured flash powder from the canister he had brought along into a shallow tray along the top rear edge of the black body of the machine, and then inserted the flat photographic plate into a slot in the centre of the top of the black box. We realized that Dodgson and Field were going to take a picture of the whole proceedings: catch our amorous Don in the act. Blackmail was their game, and this new toy of Dodgson's was their witness.

Of course. If they could get a picture of the Don cavorting licentiously on sanctified college ground, they could ruin him, or they could ensure that he would bear witness against his fellow Dons in a court of law if it ever came to that. It was really quite brilliant, and Dodgson had given Field the opportunity to experiment with a valuable new weapon to add to his already formidable detectiving arsenal.

"There. It is ready," Dodgson announced.

"Good. Let's 'ope it works," Field skeptically replied, consulting his repeater under the light of the bull's-eye. "Fifteen after the 'our," he pronounced. "Now all we 'ave to do is wait."

The stage was set. The audience was in place. All that was lacking was the actors.

We did not have to wait long.

Knock. Knock. Knock—the signal, hard against the wall right next to our hiding place. Field's bull's-eye was doused immediately. The darkness encompassed us.

"They are on their way," Field whispered. "Ellen must 'ave gotten away early. All's mum now. Not another sound. Stay still. No rustling of clothing or bumping into anything. We must give Miss Ternan a chance to pry the man's secrets loose, then we shall 'ave some fun with 'im."

We waited in the dark.

The rasp of the key being inserted in the lock seemed so loud that it startled all of us. The sound of the door opening, and the dingy light of the cloud-tossed moon seeping in through the open door, served as an overture for the human intrusion upon our settled silent dark.

"It is so-o-o dark in here," Ellen Ternan cooed as she came through the open door. I remember thinking how in character she sounded, like a half-literate minx of a barmaid, not the rather sophisticated actress and mistress to one of the most famous men in England that she was. "You'll surely have to light a lamp or a candle or something—if we are going to talk, that is." She said it coyly, as if she and Barnet were in on some secret joke.

"Of course, come through here." Barnet the boathouse Don led her by the hand through the hanging sculls and the stacked shells. "This is a little secret place of mine where I come to be alone, to read and think, that sort of thing." Barnet began to construct his tapestry of seductive lies as he lit the candle on the small table in front of the couch.

"And to bring girls who catch your fancy, eh?" Ellen said it with a light playfulness which rang with invitation.

Who is seducing whom here? I thought.

"To bring girls whom I am drawn to because they are beautiful and intelligent and they want to learn from me," Barnet picked up, immediately, the tenor of Ellen's playful tone, "and I from them," and his arms were snaking around her waist, "the joys and pleasures of love." And as soon as that word "love" reared its ugly head, Barnet kissed Dickens's Ellen hard on the mouth.

In the fluttering candlelight, we could all see that Ellen

Ternan was passionately kissing him back, her mouth oscu-
lating intensely against his, her hands rising up around his
neck as she clung to his kiss.

I glanced quickly at Dickens. He stood staring straight
ahead at the scene, a look of horrified resignation upon his
face. And yet, he could not avert his eyes from this horror
of his beloved being molested by another man.

She held Barnet's mouth for a long moment as his arms
about her waist pressed her body hard against his own. But
then, she broke away from his embrace as if frightened by
her own passion. It was all quite convincing.

"Oh my God, what am I doing?" Ellen murmured breathlessly as if thrown from her horse by the intensity of her
own passion.

"You liked it, did you not?" Barnet moved in close to her
again. She had turned away from him and his hands went
to her shoulder blades just at the side of her long, thin neck
and pulled her to him. "You liked kissing me. You liked my
body against yours." He was kissing her neck, his tongue
licking like a serpent at the tiny wisps of golden brown hair
that hung to her naked shoulders.

"Oh God yes." she seemed to slowly slide backwards into
his arms, which enveloped her from behind and pulled her
close to the treacherous arguments of his lips, pressing their
advantage in slow kiss after slow kiss all over the back of her
neck and shoulders. "Oh God yes," and this time it was she
who spun in his arms and possessed his mouth like a hungry
animal, her tongue darting hard between his startled lips,
her hands to the back of his head pressing his mouth to
hers in brutal urgency, her body pressing against him as if
she wanted to climb inside the warmth of his waistcoat.

She kissed him long and passionately, and he kissed her
back, pressing her to him, pressing what he perceived as his
clear advantage.

But once again she broke out of his grasp, fled from his
intentions.

"It is too fast. What are we doing? You press me too hard."

In anguish at her own indecision, she backed away from him, staring into his face wide-eyed in confusion. "I can't do this. I cannot." But in complete contradiction to her own words, she rushed back into his arms and took his mouth once again in another long and passionate kiss, her arms flung around his neck.

This time, he pressed his advantage more forcibly. He locked his arms around her so that she could not escape his kiss, then moving his randy hands down over her hips to possess her *derrière*, he caressed her buttocks and pressed them hard into confluence with his own aroused sexual quarter.

Dickens must have been going mad as the four of us crouched in our place of concealment behind the stacked rowing shells and voyeuristically spied upon the lubricious antics of the two alleged lovers.

Barnet moved relentlessly forward with his molestation of his conquest. His hands wandered lasciviously over Ellen Ternan's body, drew her long peasant's shirt up by handfuls and tried to get beneath it to the skin. And all the while they were kissing passionately, breathlessly, to the point that it had to end or both lovers would suffocate.

Wresting herself from his perverted grasp, Ellen suddenly whirled away, overcome, gasping for air, her hands pressed to the sides of her feverish face.

Oh, it was all extremely convincing. So much so that I think Dickens was about to burst out of his skin at the torment of it.

"Oh, my, my, you have gotten me in such a heat! Please leave me be, leave me be for a moment," she begged. But he was loath to leave her alone.

He advanced, reaching for her.

She retreated, attempting to cool his ardour.

It was like a dance.

"You 'ave brought other girls 'ere, 'aven't you?" Ellen teased him, in an exaggerated Cockney accent.

He did not answer, but moved closer, reaching out to

touch her, to once again take possession of her hips with his hands, to pull her to him.

She pirouetted away from him: "Do you just use this one boathouse with its couch and candle? Or do you use the others as well? Are they all provisioned like this, as places for you to bring your girls?"

"No, they are not," his voice was irritated. "These are not *my* places. This is but a waiting place, for the rowing crews to rest and wait out the rain, storms, that sort of thing, interruptions to their rowing exercises."

"Then I am the first that you have brought here for . . . for . . ." she coyly hesitated, then decided not to finish, changed the subject. "Are all the boathouses like this, with their little parlour?"

"No, they are filled with shells and oars, quite boring really; the one on the other end is abandoned, actually." He was growing impatient, his voice stretched taut by the confluence of his own arousal and her delaying tactics. "Its bloody roof leaks," and he lunged at her, attempting to reassert his mastery over her body and lips.

But she backed away, leading him.

He was not to be denied, however. He stopped and stared at her, for he was done talking about boathouses and rowing crews.

"I must have you, and I will." He spoke in a low, menacing voice, like a wolf growling as he advanced.

His words stopped Ellen Ternan in her tracks. The dance of flirtation and seduction was over. The sexual match was mounted.

"Have me? What do you mean?" Ellen feigned innocence, but it was not convincing, as her earlier flirting had been.

"Do not play innocent," his voice was frightening. "You are here with me. We have kissed. You are a public house serving girl. I am an Oxford Don. I must have you."

This time, she was not able to escape his lunge. He caught her in his arms about the waist and held her clasped against his body, his mouth tight against her ear:

"I want you to take off your clothes. I want to see you completely naked. If you do not, I will tear them off you, and when we are done, I will leave you here naked to make your way home."

"Good God, man, stop this," Dickens pulled at Inspector Field's sleeve and whispered desperately, almost audibly, in his ear.

Field's forefinger leapt instantly to his pursed lips in commanding gesture of silence even as his eyes were shifting from the contrived scene that we were viewing through the cracks in the stacked boats to Dodgson, who stood poised next to his ungainly tripod.

Dodgson shook his head in the negative and raised his open hand, palm outward, in a gesture that we must wait. Field snapped his withering gaze back to Dickens and once again, even more sharply, thumped his forefinger against his tight lips, ordering Dickens to be silent.

Sensing by her silence that he now was in complete control, Barnet stepped back from her and changed his tone from menace to the most transparent flattery of seduction: "You are so beautiful. Your kisses have inflamed my desire for you. I must have you. Will you do what I ask? Let us be like Adam and Eve, naked before each other."

Ellen regained control of her emotions. I think that she was genuinely frightened of him for a moment when he was threatening her. "If I am to take off all of my things," she teased him, no longer moving away from him but standing and facing him, realizing that any further flight from his rapacious attentions might only inflame him to violence once again, "then you must take off yours as well. Fair is fair."

"I knew you were a gay and jolly slut," he laughed hungrily. "Fair is fair, indeed," and he eagerly began to unbutton his breeches.

Field pointed his commanding forefinger at Dodgson and held it rigidly in the air like the blade of the guillotine waiting to drop.

Ellen watched Barnet, unmoving, mesmerized, as if by a snake.

He dropped his trousers to the floor, exposing his aroused red member.

Field's forefinger dropped decisively.

A bright white light suddenly exploded upon the whole scene.

THE NEW GUNPOWDER PLOT

❧

(December 11, 1853 — After Midnight)

The flash powder from Dodgson's camera burned brightly for a brief moment and then hissed out.

The photograph was taken.

The Oxford Don was caught with his trousers down and his rather small member standing at shocked attention.

Ellen's virtue, such as it was, was saved.

"What the devil!" Barnet cursed.

"Inspector Field of the London Protectives 'ere," that worthy answered. "We 'ave just taken your likeness in a photograph. You remember me, do you not?"

Ellen Ternan had both hands over her mouth, trying to suppress the laughter that was rolling out of her as the naked Don first attempted to cover himself, then attempted to pull up his trousers, then tripped over his desperate efforts and sprawled across the ratty couch while all the while his previously arrogant member proceeded to shrink up to the size of a modest mushroom.

Almost before the flash had subsided, Field was out from behind the boats and standing over our boathouse Don. When Dickens and I emerged from our place of concealment and came around the corner of the stacked shells, Barnet was sitting up straight with Field's murderous-looking knobbed stick poked into his chest. His trousers were still bunched around his ankles and his two hands were cupped protectively over his pitiful little member. It was abundantly clear that Field was quite comfortable carrying on his interrogation of his subject in this semi-naked state. Even Dickens, horrified as he had been only moments before, had to laugh.

Our Don, Barnet, did not find it at all humorous.

"What is this?" he protested.

"You cannot do this!" he harrumphed.

"How dare you!" he cursed.

"Who are you?" He looked at Dickens and Dodgson and me as we all materialized out of our hiding place and stood staring at him.

"Remember me? Inspector Field of the London Protectives," and Field poked the naked Don once again in the middle of the chest with his stick, "investigating the murder of your friends, Ackroyd and Stadler. I think you know more than you are telling me, and if you do not tell me all, I shall display this photo all over Oxford. I shall nail it to the chapel door of every college in Oxford. I will drop it right on the desk of the Dean of Queen's College, and you will be expelled for gross immorality before the fortnight is out."

Barnet actually began to shake and shiver, whether from the cold assaulting his nakedness or from simple terror of Field, I cannot say.

" 'Ere, you sniveling weasel," Field withdrew his stick. "Pull up your breeches and we shall talk."

Our chastized boathouse Don did exactly what he was told, then proceeded to answer Field's questions without a single grumble and with an economy equal to the extreme vulnerability of his humiliated condition.

"Who killed Ackroyd and Stadler?"

"We do not know. None of us do. Everyone is fearful. We

do not know who or why, and all are afraid that he may be the next."

"Then why were they murdered?"

"Because of the plot to frighten the Queen. It is all over this Turkish war with Russia. The New Gunpowder Plot is what Ackroyd used to call it before, before—" his voice trailed impotently off.[21]

"*Frighten* the Queen?"

"It was to be a prank, nothing more. We felt the Queen would be coming here sometime during the Christmas season. She almost always does. Set off a nice explosion somewhere along the Queen's route, to Blenheim perhaps. Not to ever hurt anyone, mind you. Just to send a message was all. 'Blow up all her bloody complacency!' Wherry Squonce would say. 'Show her she cannot simply wage war in the name of Empire.' "

"Were you all in on it, all of the group in the Bulldog?"

"We all knew about it. Some were deeper in than others. It was Ackroyd's idea and he planned it all. Stadler was in charge of the explosion because that was what he did in his chemistry researches. He could get the explosives and he knew how to set them off clean and safe so that no one would get hurt."

"And the others?"

"Norman, from Trinity, he is a political theorist. He has friends in London who are out with this P.M. in. He is the one who found out about the Queen's plans to rest at Blenheim.

[21]This reference is to what would eventually become known as the Crimean War. Turkey had declared war on Russia in October 1853 over a dispute about the rights to control the Palestinian Holy Places, which Russia claimed and France felt that it had secured in 1852. England was concerned that this war would cut off its trade routes through the Dardanelles. In fact, in December 1853, at the time of the events of this case, the decision was being made to send an English fleet to the Black Sea. By March 1854, when England and France also declared war on Russia, that fleet was already in place. England's motives in this war were perceived as economic and necessary to support the trade routes of Empire.

The plot was really only in the talking stages until he heard that she might visit. Then he focused all his efforts on finding out when exactly and where exactly she would be."

"Others?"

"Wherry Squonce and Bathgate—the Balliol boys, we call them—were in charge of writing the literature for afterwards, making the statements that explain why someone would want to blow up our beloved Queen Victoria, 'that petulant little bulldog of a woman,' Squonce calls her. He hates the Queen, the monarchy, the whole system."

"And you?"

"Because I am in Engineering, I was to help Stadler set up his explosion so that it would go off at the right time in the right place and not hurt anyone."

"So, this was never a plot to assassinate the Queen?"

"No, never. It was simply an attempt to make a political statement."

"Then why are Ackroyd and Stadler dead?"

"We do not know. That is why we have abandoned the whole thing."

"You 'ave given it all up?"

"Yes. We could not do it anyway without Stadler and his explosive chemicals."

Field looked at Morse and Rogers, who had joined us from outside at Field's signal. Tally Ho Thompson had also made his way in. He stood off to the side, listening, next to his private charge, Ellen Ternan, whose performance this evening was over. Field's look signalled that Barnet did not know that Stadler's nitroglycerine had disappeared the night of the murder. The realization that the explosives were still out there, even though, if we were to believe Barnet, the plot against the Queen had been abandoned, dawned upon all of us in the mere moment of Field's silent look.

"Who proposed that you give it up?" Field mercilessly pounded his questions at the cowering Don.

"I do not know. Norman of Trinity perhaps. He was totally

shaken when Ackroyd was murdered. He wanted to give it up then."

"Did all agree?"

"No. Not at all. Not when Stadler was killed. Squonce and Bathgate wanted to go on even after that. Wherry Squonce, that evil little Sodomite, wanted to break in and steal the chemicals from Stadler's laboratory."

The irony of this rake's morally righteous tone was not lost on Inspector Field, who turned and rolled his eyes at Dickens and the rest of us before resuming his relentless questioning.

"Did 'ee steal them?"

"No. I do not think so. He would not know what to steal. He is a Literature Don, for God's sake!" Barnet clearly held Squonce in the highest degree of contempt.

"Could this Squonce 'ave killed them?" Field was standing over Barnet and growling down at him like a mastiff. Barnet was terrified of him; that was clear. He was shaking, hugging himself around his shoulders with his arms crossed over his chest, and rocking back and forth as if caught in the clutches of a palsy.

"Answer me, you snivelling little twit!" Field screamed right into his terror-stricken face. "Answer me or that picture will be 'anded out on broadsheets on the 'Eye Street in the morning. Your John Thomas will be more famous around 'ere than the Oxford spires."

"Wherry Squonce is queer, a woman," Barnet leapt to answer. "I do not think he could kill them."

"What about 'is friend Bathgate?"

"He is a quiet one. I think he is Squonce's man. They are both Balliol. They are always together. Perhaps. I do not know. Please. Please." The broken Don was begging Field to leave him alone.

"Where was the bomb to be set?"

Barnet was an empty shell. His eyes darted left then right like a cornered animal. His eyes moved from one of us to the next, pleading, hopeless.

"Answer me," Field slapped him across the face with his open hand. "Where? Where?"

"I don't know. I don't," Barnet utterly broke down, bursting into tears.

"Do not lie to me!" Field raised his hand, threatening to strike him again. "Tell me where."

"I don't know, dear God, I don't know," he wailed. "We did not know her path yet when Stadler was killed. Norman had not got her path yet, I swear. None of us knew where the bomb would be; then we gave it all up. Please. Please leave me be." He was slobbering from the mouth in fear.

"Morse," and Field turned to that worthy, "take this snivelling piece of dung away. Put him under lock and key. Keep him close somewhere until this affair is over."

Young Morse led Barnet away. Field blew out the flickering candle which had provided the light for this brutal contretemps and led us out of the boathouse. Outside, on the docks, Field waved for Morse to take our docile prisoner on ahead. The rest of us milled around him waiting. Clearly, he was thinking through his next move in this dangerous game of "Button, Button, Who's got the Button," except it was "Bomb, Bomb, Who's got the Bomb?"

"Ellen," Field finally broke the silence, his voice low and thoughtful, "go about your business at the pub as though nothing at all 'as 'appened. Keep a close watch on this Squonce and Bathgate pair. It will take a day or so for them to figure out that this Barnet 'as gone missin'. That should put a scarer on them. If they are our killers. They'll wonder who is cuttin' in on their game. If they are not, they'll fear that another member of their little plot to blow up the Queen 'as been done. Watch them close. They'll give themselves away. Thompson," and he turned to Tally Ho, "take 'er 'ome," he ordered, turning back to Dickens's Ellen for one last word. "You 'ave done good work this night, Miss Ternan, as fine an actin' job as I 'ave ever seen. Go on 'ome and get to sleep. You 'ave earned it."

Escorted by her faithful bodyguard, Ellen departed, leaving the rest of us there on the riverside by those ghostly boathouses. Field watched her go and then turned back to us.

"Charles," Field addressed Dickens speculatively, "this Squonce and Bathgate are literary Dons. These ponces would probably muddy their britches if a literary man down from London saw fit to call on them. Find some pretence, fashion some story, it is what you do best, and see if you can get into their digs. Dodgson 'ere can introduce you, I'd wager. See what you can find out. Don't do anything reckless," Field cautioned. "Do only what is possible, only observe."

He always gave us this same "only observe" speech when he sent us out to consort with dangerous criminals, and Dickens never heeded it.

"Rogers will stay 'ere, but I must go up to London. I will be back as soon as I can. Who knows, per'aps the nitroglycerine will turn up in their rooms."

With that, he turned on his heel and led us on a forced march through the grove of trees and back out to St. Aldate's. He bid us goodnight at the Tom Tower gate, and that was the last we would see of him for three days (but we did not know that at the time). The whole situation did not inspire a great deal of confidence in me. Dickens, however, was downright exuberant. "Wilkie," he said with a bounce in his voice as we walked up to Dodgson's rooms, "we are off once again!"

THE BALLIOL BOYS

❧

(December 12, 1853 — Afternoon)

Inspector Field left for London on the next morning's railway.

It seemed rather strange to me that just as this Oxford investigation appeared to be reaching a critical point, he should dash off to London for no immediately discernible reason.

"He is going up to report to Holmes of the Home Office," Dickens speculated. "All of this talk of bombing the Queen is quite troubling. He must warn Holmes and his frock-coat gang. One must not tarry when it is a question of endangering the life of Queen Victoria."

Dickens was so smugly certain that I prayed that he was wrong. But he was not, as we shall see.

Field left on the morning train, and Dickens was eager to get on with our part of the bargain. He was after Dodgson right away, as soon as that poor fellow was up trying to cook our tea and roast our morning toast at the hearth.

"Do you know this Wherry Squonce or this Bathgate, Dodo?" Dickens had taken to calling him by our college name as if they had sat for exams together. Dodgson did not seem to mind in the least, but I found it rather presumptuous and familiar. Dickens an Oxford man? Really!

"I have met them at University do's, mostly p-p-poetry g-g-gatherings. They are somewhat notorious. Always together. A queer c-c-couple. Everyone around Oxford accepts it. No one thinks much of it. They do not p-p-parade their p-p-perversion."

"What shall we tell them that will make them let us in?"

"T-t-tell them the t-t-truth"—he paused and held up the toasting fork with two thick pieces of bread steaming on it—"or something like it," he grinned, "something they will want to b-b-believe."

"How about the theatre?" Dickens suggested. "We are getting up a play and we are looking for a place to stage it."

"Oh yes, that's it." Dodgson brandished his toasting fork as if he were directing an orchestra. "Squonce is very b-b-big on theatre. They have front-row seats for every Shakespeare that shows its d-d-doublet in Oxford. Oh yes, theatre is a sure t-t-tack."

"Then theatre it is," Dickens decided. "Can you send a note around to their rooms requesting an audience to talk about theatre? You know: 'Remember me. Famous friends down from London. Can we meet? Your rooms? When?' That sort of thing." Dickens was actually writing Dodgson's missive for him, but again, Dodgson did not seem to mind. He delivered us our toast and tea, and set right about the task that Dickens had given him.

The note written, Dodgson rang for the porter, gave him a shilling and asked him to dispatch it to Balliol by one of the street urchins who hung about the Tom Tower gate hoping for just such work.

We idled away that day. We went for a pub lunch at the Bulldog so that Dickens could get his required afternoon dosage of his beloved Ellen. The reply, in the form of a hand-delivered note, arrived from the Balliol boys at about half past five. "By all means," it read, "I would love to meet with the eminent Mr. Charles Dickens to discuss Oxford theatre." It was signed "Wherry Squonce Esquire, Balliol College." It proposed Squonce's college rooms the next day at one in the afternoon.

That evening also passed uneventfully. At about nine, Dickens proposed that we all go out for a brisk walk. Dodgson begged off, something that I was not allowed to do. If I had tried to beg off going out in the bitter December wind to hike at forced-march pace through the streets of Oxford, Dickens would have sulked over it for days on end. And so, I tried to keep up with Dickens's long strides as we traversed the High Street, crossed Magdalen Bridge, and struck off along the river towards the Queen's Deer Park. It was a rather gloomy walk, even though the signs of Christmas were beginning to make their appearance. We crossed back over the river at the cattle ford and came back into the town through the University Parks. It was not like our night walks in London at all. We saw very few people out, and those we saw were either scurrying to get indoors out of the wind or bundled up so closely that it was almost impossible to tell if they were man, woman, sheep, or cow.

Dickens finally gave up on encountering anything of interest, and as we came through the park, suggested: "Let us stop at the first pub we hit, Wilkie, and have a hot gin. It will be a pleasant change. I am sick to death of that bloody Bulldog every night."

I could not have been happier. That first pub could not be encountered soon enough for my taste. It was the King's Arms, one of the oldest pubs in Oxford, dating back to the billeting of the troops of King William, that took us in out of the cold. It was all decorated for Christmas with greens and mistletoe, a welcome refuge that offered light, warmth, soft couches, and burned gin. It did not take long for the ambiance and the gin to warm us through and through. Dickens was right. It was a pleasant break from the pressures of the case and the tension of constant surveillance that marked our nocturnal visits to the Bulldog.

The next day at half noon we set out under Dodgson's

escort to invade the fortress of the Balliol Dons, Squonce and Bathgate. Balliol is the second oldest of Oxford's colleges after University College. It was founded in the thirteenth century and sits on St. Giles behind massive wood and iron gates as tall as the tallest windmill in *Don Quixote*. The porter sent his lackey to inform Squonce of our arrival. After a short wait, the porter directed us to go up.

Wherry Squonce was waiting in the hallway two storeys up, while his friend Bathgate stood behind him lounging in the doorway. Attired in a purple smoking jacket and a flowered silk ascot cravat and smoking an ostentatious Meerschaum pipe, Wherry Squonce, fluttering towards us with arms outstretched, looked as if he were a peacock somehow escaped from the palace grounds.

"Oh Dodgson," he squealed as we breasted the landing to his floor and our heads rose up out of the stairwell, "it is so good to see you again, old fellow, and so good of you to bring Mr. Dickens along to meet us. Oh dear boy," and he ran his hand lasciviously over Dodgson's shoulder and upper arm, "we really cannot thank you enough for thinking of us and introducing us to your friends."

Through this whole display, Bathgate, in the darkest of suits, stood utterly taciturn, looking at us hard as if trying to see right through us.

"Come in. Come in," little Squonce flounced all around us like some old neglected mum whose children have finally come to visit, "we've got tea and cakes, a regular tea party, I'd say. Come right in."

Bathgate retreated, still silent and suspicious, as we were escorted through the door and into an extremely elaborate sitting room that looked as if it would be more at home amongst the orientalist extravagances of the Prince Regent's Pavilion in Brighton. That room was truly something out of the *Arabian Nights* or the *Tale of the Genji*. The floors were bathed in Oriental rugs, the walls flowing with bright silks and exquisitely woven tapestries. The furniture was all brightly colored pillows and oddly shaped divans. Carvings in ivory and wood—Chinese, Indian, Malaysian—of naked men posed on every table and mantle and shelf in the room. It was the most indulgent exercise in interior decoration that I had ever encountered, and when we first entered that room and it all descended upon us like some Oriental dream, both Dickens and I were struck momentarily speechless. How does one react to something so out of the ordinary, so reckless, so shockingly sensual and unnerving?

Dickens saved the day. Dodgson and I were too stunned to even speak.

"My, what wonderful colours for a room," Dickens exclaimed after his initial shock. "Is the strongest influence Chinese or Indian?" he asked ingenuously.

Squonce was delighted.

God knows what dour Bathgate was thinking.

"Oh yes, yes, both, both," Squonce gushed. "Aren't the colours amusing and amazing? This is Jack Bathgate, by the way. My neighbour here in this thirteenth-century monastery. He tends to darken any room no matter how bright it may be."

"Gentlemen," glum Bathgate greeted us with a bow, utterly ignoring Squonce's demeaning raillery.

"Sit down. Sit down," little Squonce insisted. "We have read all of your novels, have we not, Jack? But then, who hasn't? Mr. Dickens is the most read man in England after friend Shakespeare perhaps. Sit down. Sit down. The tea is hot. The cakes are sweet. We have so much to discuss."

We did as we were directed, ranging ourselves rather self-consciously about the room on pillows and hassocks and stuffed shapes of all sorts.

"Please. Please. Help yourself to the cakes. Can I pour you a cup of hot tea? Or would you like something a bit stronger?" this Squonce just seemed to be nattering on while his dour companion, Bathgate, sat and stared at us from the sofa. "We've got a nice Anjou pink that you might enjoy, or perhaps something a bit more adventurous for your London tastes, an absinthe liqueur?"

"No, no," Dickens raised his hand to Squonce's out-of-control rambling. "Tea is fine, excellent, especially this early in the afternoon."

"Excellent, then. Tea it shall be." Little Squonce seemed delighted at our choice. "Can I sweeten it for you? Lemon perhaps? Milk?"

"Yes, please, lemon." Dickens affably let him play the compleat hostess.

Our tea delivered, the cakes passed and politely sampled, our host collapsed into a wildly flowered jungle chair that looked as if it had just been canoed out of the interior of Sumatra, and resumed his gushing over Dickens's eminent presence. "What an unutterable surprise and happy event to have you here in our house," Wherry Squonce went on. "I have always wanted to entertain a great writer like yourself, isn't that right, Jack?" and he turned to his gloomy companion, who nodded his assent and, to all of our surprise, spoke.

"Yes, you have said that," dour Bathgate glared at us, "even if they do come here as spies of the Queen!"

For a moment, I did not think I had heard him right. Dickens's head snapped up towards him as soon as he said it. Dodgson looked at me and I at him in utter confusion.

"I beg your pardon?" Dickens was the first of the three of us to recover. "What did you say?"

"Oh, and it was such a nice tea party," little Squonce mourned this turn.

"I said," and glum Bathgate scowled levelly at us as he repeated himself, "that we know that you are here as spies of the Queen."

As he said it, he reached beneath one of the pillows on the sofa on which he sat and his hand emerged holding a large black revolver, which he proceeded to level at Dickens, Dodgson, and myself. We sat staring at him, mouths agape, the taste of the tea turning bitter in our throats.

"Oh, don't fret at all," rabbitty little Squonce smiled reassuringly at us. "We knew you weren't all the way down from London just to talk about putting on an amateur play. Jack, put that ugly thing down. You'll frighten our guests." He waved his hand at his dark co-conspirator. "And our guests you are going to be, for at least a couple of days. Then, we will be off to the Continent and away from this terrible hell-hole of pretension and overrated intellectual narcissism."

I almost choked on his metaphor, considering the way he was dressed and the preponderance of mirrors that nearly outnumbered the paintings on the walls of his parlour. It was all so civilized yet inexplicable. How could they know why we were here? Not thinking, I jumped to my feet to protest the absurdity of it, but Bathgate slowly levelled his pistol right at my face.

"Do you think that we are so stupid that we did not notice your poking around Oxford?" Bathgate growled like a mastiff.

But my leaping to my feet had occasioned an even more inexplicable effect. As I stood looking at that pistol pointed right at me and then turned to look at Dickens and Dodgson, who were still sitting on the sofa in shock, my eyes began to blur, my knees began to buckle, and the room began to float and waver as if I was in a dream. I tried to steady myself and staggered sideways, knocking one of those ridiculous pieces of sensual sculpture off its fragile pedestal table and sending it crashing to the floor. I reached out to Dickens and Dodgson, who were just sitting there on the sofa as if they were asleep, but they offered no help. I toppled sideways to the welcoming softness of the Oriental rug on the floor, and everything went dim and dark as I sank into a furry bed of blackness.

THE COTTAGE IN THE WOOD

(December 13, 1853 — Night into Day)

I awoke on a rustic bed on the floor of a pitch black room with a terrible ringing in my head and my greatcoat wrapped around me like a blanket. I sat bolt upright and must have muttered something because Dickens's voice answered me out of the darkness.

"I am here, Wilkie," Charles attempted to reassure me, "and Dodo is still sleeping, there, next to you on the floor. Do not step on him."

"But what? Where?" It seemed that all I could muster through the throbbing in my brain and the deepness of the dark were a few disconnected words.

"I do not know where we are," Dickens answered my incoherence as if we were conducting a perfectly intelligible conversation. It never ceased to amaze me how utterly unflappable, no matter what the circumstances, that man could be. "I have just awakened myself, only moments ago. It appears we have been drugged. In the tea those scoundrels poured us, I presume. I have already expended one of my lucifers looking about. Some sort of country cottage or rough hunting lodge. There is only one door and it is bolted fast from the outside. Somehow they have transported us here and locked us in. They evidently want us out of the way."

"Oh my head," I groaned.

"That could be the effect of the drug, or perhaps you fell and hit your head when the drug overcame you. The last I remember, Bathgate was threatening you with his pistol, then everything went dark."

"Ohhh," a long moan came from the darkness to my side.

"Dodgson, we are here." Dickens turned his attention to our painfully awakening friend and apprised him of our circumstances.

Dickens struck a light, another of his lucifers. Thank God we smoked cigars.

The three of us huddled in the centre of this small room like cavemen around the first fire. Rough straw pallets covered the floor and had provided our only comfort. The walls were of heavy stone. The door looked to be of stout wood. Only one window was set in a side wall, and it seemed to be tightly shuttered on the outside because no light or movement could be discerned upon looking through it. Then Dickens's lucifer flickered out and the darkness encompassed us once again.

We decided that it was the better part of valour to conserve our remaining lucifers and to wait until day broke before trying to escape our rustic prison.

"It is unthinkable that t-t-two Oxford D-D-Dons would k-k-kidnap gentlemen at g-g-gunpoint," Dodgson took up our midnight colloquy.

"For some reason, they have grown quite desperate," I offered.

"Field's visit to their ring of conspirators in the pub the other night must have thrown quite a scare into them," Dickens speculated.

"Or they murdered Ackroyd and Stadler," Dodgson pursued the logical path, "and they feel they have nothing t-t-to lose by k-k-kidnapping us."

"If that is the case," Dickens's voice was cold, "why did they not just kill us?

"In Balliol C-C-College? In the centre of Oxford? I think not!" Dodgson scoffed. "The b-b-blood. The b-b-bodies. It would never do."

"It must have been some trick to carry us out of there in our state." Dickens pictured the awkwardness of it.

"They must have sent the g-g-gate porter off on some errand while they t-t-took us out," Dodgson speculated.

"They must have had help." Dickens was certain. "If that is the case, then they have brought us out here to keep us out of the way so that no one will find us until long after they have fled to the Continent."

"But why are they planning to leave?" I posed the next question. "They spoke about leaving as if it was a planned thing, something they were going to do anyway, before we ever entered the picture."

"Precisely, because it was already part of their plan," Dickens pounced upon my puzzled question. "You have hit on it, Wilkie. Something is afoot. Some larger plan that they are going to carry out before they flee to wherever they are going."

"The Queen?"

"The Queen!"

Dodgson and I, in the pitch darkness, simultaneously saw the light.

"That may be it," Dickens sounded much more calculating. "They are going to set off their bomb and kill the Queen, then flee to the Continent."

"And we suspected it," Dodgson was thinking aloud, "and, and, they need t-t-to k-k-keep us out of the way until all is d-d-done."

"Precisely!" Dickens snapped his fingers in the void of darkness. "Until they bring their bloody Gunpowder Plot to fruition."

How did they know that we were on to them?

How did they know that we were Field's spies?

Were they really out to assassinate the Queen?

Why did they murder Ackroyd and Stadler, two of their own?

What were we to do? How were we going to escape?

These were but some of the questions that entertained our conversation over the ensuing hours until small chinks of grey daylight began to poke through the ancient stone walls of our makeshift prison.

Daylight's coming did not give us much light inside our musty hovel, but it gave us enough to move about and see what we had at our disposal for making our escape if an opportunity presented itself.

The door was immovable. It was dead-bolted from the outside. The window was tightly shuttered and also seemed to have a heavy iron bar across it. The inside furnishings offered little more encouragement. Besides the rough pallets of straw on the floor, there was a chamberpot and a wooden bucket filled with water. A wooden armchair, sitting lopsided and useless with one of its legs rotted off, completed the interior furnishings of the place.

Dickens prowled the room in the dim light looking for some means of escape. He picked up the chair with the rotted leg and swung it as hard as he could against the shuttered window, to no effect. The heavy wooden shutters did not move and, upon two more applications of the chair, would not break.

Dickens gave up on that avenue of escape and went back to prowling the room, thinking, searching for something, anything.

"Aha!" he exclaimed, as if he had just come upon some buried treasure. "What have we here?"

He emerged from the mould and spiderwebs of one of the hovel's dark corners holding a tattered and rotting coil of rope in his right hand. "We ought to be able to use this for something." He held it out encouragingly to Dodgson and me.

Nobody said a word for a long moment.

"We c-c-could b-b-build a mant-t-trap," Dodgson tentatively suggested. "I have read about them in a b-b-book. It is how the p-p-pygmies and c-c-cannibals hunt in Africa."

Dickens and I just stared at him, attempting to visualize what he was seeing in his esoteric academic brain.

"Something that swings on this rope that will take down a man." Dickens's powers of visualization were much stronger than mine.

"Yes, yes," Dodgson nodded avidly, "that was how it was described in the b-b-books."

"Here," Dickens darted across the room, "we can hang it here on this roof beam and aim it at the doorway."

"And when someone comes in, we push it at him and it knocks him down," I finished Dickens's thought, envisioning this contraption.

"Exactly, Wilkie," Dickens beamed, already testing the rope in his hands.

"I think that it will work." Dodgson the mathematician stood directly under the roof beam, first looking up, then swivelling his head towards the door, "b-b-but we must c-c-calculate exactly the height of the p-p-projectile, the length of the swing, the angle at which we t-t-tie the rope, and the weight of the p-p-push that b-b-begins its momentum."

I looked at Dickens and Dickens looked at me. We both burst out laughing at our mathematical Don. Dodgson's academic seriousness, his inventor's curiosity, in this absurd and desperate situation seemed both so out of place and so genuine that we could not help but laugh. It broke the tension, made us forget for a moment our forced imprisonment.

We chose the broken chair as our projectile. Dickens, standing on Dodgson's and my shoulders, fastened the rope securely around the roof beam. Dodgson actually calculated the length of the rope and the distance of the swing, and even indulged himself with calculating the velocity that the flying chair would reach before hitting the man coming through the doorway square in the face and chest (depending, of course, upon the height of the man, which he also calculated).

We worked upon our creation the better part of the morning and tested it twice, making adjustments to Dodgson's satisfaction. "No matter if it is Squonce or B-B-Bathgate," Dodgson explained, "the chair is large enough that it will knock either of them d-d-down. Besides, they are b-b-both really the same height because B-B-Bathgate will have t-t-to stoop t-t-to g-g-get through the d-d-door."

The engineering completed, and our mantrap ready to spring, we set about planning how we would lure our captors into the doorway when they arrived to deal with us, which they would surely do.

"What if they have just left us here to starve? What if they have no intention of coming back?" Dickens finally voiced the one dread that had haunted all of our minds during the preparation of our wonderful machine.

We waited what seemed an eternity but was only a matter of hours for someone to come. Dodgson was in charge of the mantrap. When the door opened, he would set it in motion with a strong push towards its target. I was stationed to the side of the doorway to leap upon the man entering and seize his pistol when the mantrap knocked him down. Dickens was to be the voice of the operation, presenting the arguments to lure our captors into the opened doorway.

We waited. Noon passed, then one on my gold repeater. We all dreaded the prospect of spending another damp and freezing night in this godforsaken place. Finally, a little after two, we heard a horse's hoofs approaching up what must have been a path to the cottage door.

SPRINGING THE TRAP

❦

(December 14, 1853 — Afternoon)

The rider took a moment to tether his horse. We could hear footfalls through the chinks in the stone walls.

"You three in there!" His voice boomed in our eagerly listening ears from just on the other side of the door. It was Bathgate, unmistakably.

"Yes, we are here," Dickens answered him calmly, though rather overstating the obvious.

"I have brought you some food, bread, and a skin of wine. It will hold you until you are released."

That answered a number of our questions. They were not out to kill us or leave us imprisoned to starve.

"Why have you locked us in here?" Dickens asked, still as calm as an infant playing in the line of fire.

"That is none of your concern," Bathgate answered, as if he and Dickens were sitting in a pub over a pint of Irish stout rather than conversing through a bolted prison door. "Now move away from the door. I will slide these things in. My pistol is primed and cocked in my hand."

"But Dodgson is quite sick. The cold, the damp of last

night. He has been quite delirious all morning. His health is quite fragile. You must get him to a physician or into hospital. We are afraid he might die."

Dickens was really quite cunning in his argument. He had decided that Bathgate's reason for coming back and bringing food was that he and Squonce, his co-conspirator, did not want us to die.

"Damn ye all!" Bathgate cursed us from outside the door. He seemed confused, hesitant. "I never should have come back," he lamented.

"No, do not go. We need the food. Dodgson will surely die if he gets no sustenance. Please do not leave us here to starve."

"Stand back from the door!" Bathgate ordered again. "I will shoot any man that I see!"

"Yes, yes, we will," Dickens shouted through the door and immediately went to his knees on the floor against the wall on the side away from which the door would swing.

"Are you back and away?" Bathgate shouted again. "Stand clear."

We could hear the heavy bolt being lifted from the other side of the door.

Dickens raised a finger to me behind the door, and then to Dodgson poised across the room with his mantrap, cautioning us to wait.

The door slid open a crack, then stopped. A line of November sunlight traversed the rough dirt floor of the dim cottage.

Dickens, on his knees low, pressed himself against the cottage wall.

"Stand clear!" Bathgate barked once again.

Dickens's finger was still raised to us in the low light. We held our collective breaths in silence, waiting.

The door slowly opened, a bit wider, then wider still. Well above Dickens's head as he crouched low against the wall, the iron barrel of a pistol poked through the crack in the door, then quickly withdrew.

Dickens's finger was still upraised.

We waited.

A long silent moment passed.

The door opened, just a bit wider.

A hand pushed a loaf of bread through the aperture at about knee level and dropped it to the floor inside the door.

As the hand holding the skin of wine came through the narrow opening between the door and the wall, Dickens pounced.

Reaching swiftly up, he fastened upon the wrist holding the wine skin and pulled hard.

Bathgate lurched forward against the partially opened door and sprawled into the room.

The door slammed forward as well, swinging full into my face where I was poised too close behind, and pinning me hard against the wall. I was temporarily incapacitated, both stunned by the blow to my face and wedged tightly between the wall and the door, thus unable to help Dickens and equally unable to see what was going on in the room.

The pistol fired off with a huge frightening boom which, inside that small closed space, sounded to me like a ship's cannon.

A heavy, dull thud.

A deep grunt.

A yowl as from a wounded animal.

The sound of a scuffle on the floor.

A shout of triumph: "Yes! I've got it."

A critical comment: "I say. Well d-d-done!"

And finally I managed to extricate myself from behind the door and stagger, disoriented, holding my bloodied nose, out into the now brightly sunlit room.

Dickens was sitting atop what seemed to be a semi-conscious Jack Bathgate on the floor. He had Bathgate's pistol in his hand. Dodgson was standing over the two of them, beaming.

Our improvised mantrap swung to and fro in the air above the fallen man.

"Oh Wilkie, it worked perfectly." Dodgson could not hold back his excitement at the triumph of mathematics over criminality.

"What happened?" I asked through the blood streaming from my poor nose.

Bathgate, insensate, stared wide-eyed up at me from the floor.

"I pulled him through the doorway," Dickens voice was somewhat subdued, as if even he was temporarily shocked at the audacity of what he had just done. "He tried to right himself and fire the pistol at me, but the chair hit him, knocked him sideways, and he missed"—and Dickens looked first at me and then at Dodgson in a curious sort of disbelief—"Thank God."

Dodgson actually laughed. "Thank G-G-God, indeed!"

I pressed my thumb and forefinger hard together against the bridge of my nose to stop the blood and stared in disbelief at the two of them. Dickens had joined Dodgson in a volley of cathartic laughter. They both seemed to think it was all very funny, but I was the one with the bloodied nose.

MURDER IN HIS EYES

୭ତ

(December 14, 1853 — Mid-Afternoon)

Bathgate just lay there on the floor, knocked senseless by Dodgson's, I must admit, ingenious and precisely calculated device. We dismantled that lethal contraption and bound Bathgate hand and foot with the rope that had served us so well. He began to come around as we were doing this, and by the time we were finished rather thoroughly tying him up, he was sitting up and glaring evilly at Dickens.

"Why did you and Squonce drug us and bring us here?" Dickens asked in an utterly flat voice, unthreatening, as if he were ordering a muffin in a baker's shop.

Bathgate never uttered a word. He just glared hatefully up at Dickens with murder in his eyes.

"Why did you want us out of the way? Why did you lock us in here? What is going on?" Dickens politely rephrased his question.

Utter silence. No answer. Bathgate remained obstinate. It was clear that he was going to be of no aid to us. Then Dickens did something the likes of which I have never seen him do before or since. He looked down at the sulking, glowering Bathgate and slowly shook his head. Then Dickens raised his hand and smashed him brutally hard right in the face with his open palm.

The trussed-up man howled at the shock and pain of this sudden act of violence. But Dickens did not stop at that. When Bathgate howled, Dickens swung his heavy hand again and slapped him hard on the side of his face. But Dickens still did not stop. Taking one step back, he thudded a sharp kick right into the tied-up legs of our murderous Don. The defiance drained from Bathgate's face. His initial howl of surprise and anger at Dickens's unforeseen attack gave way to a low moan of pain from the savage blows that Dickens rained down upon him. Never uttering a word, Dickens hit him again and then again, kicked him twice more, once hard in the buttocks, once sharp and cutting in the stomach. The man was sobbing, begging for his life when Dickens finally stopped.

Dodgson and I stared, eyes wide, mouths agape. We were witness to a sudden eruption of brutal, uncivilized violence and cruelty from a man whom we both thought we knew and understood.

"Oh please, please," Bathgate moaned pitifully. "Please don't. No more."

Now it was Dickens who had murder in his eyes. He stood over Bathgate, glaring down at him. He raised Bathgate's pistol, which had been in his other hand the whole time he had been beating and kicking the poor helpless man, and leveled it right at Bathgate's red and stinging face.

Murder glared hard and cold out of Dickens's eyes, as cold as the steel of the pistol. Terror bloomed in Bathgate's tortured eyes.

"Now," Dickens paused as he moved the gun so that the barrel was no more than an inch from Bathgate's battered face.

"Charles, don't!" I heard myself involuntarily cry at the horror of what he was doing.

"Be quiet, Wilkie," Dickens cut me off in a sharp, curt whisper. "Stay out of this."

"Please don't kill me," the cowering Don begged.

"Now," Dickens began again, "what is happening in Oxford that made you lock us up here to keep us out of the way?"

Now Bathgate could not wait to answer. He was in love with Dickens's question. He leapt to embrace it.

"They are going to send an explosive message to the Queen," the words came in a rush, trying to stave off any further blows from Dickens's hand or foot, trying to outrace the bullet that was aimed right at his head.

"Oh my God." Dodgson exhaled beside me as if he had just been kicked in the solar plexus.

"How?" Dickens poked him in the forehead with the revolver. "Where? When?"

"Today it is," Bathgate's voice trembled. "This evening when she tours the boathouses. The explosion will not hurt her. They're going to blow up one of the boathouses near her, to catch her attention, so the people and the Parliament will listen to our denunciation of this madness of Empire, this Turkish war."

Again, Dickens poked the snivelling Don in the face with the barrel of the pistol: "Who?"

"Wherry, the others—we've been planning it for months. Our statements are all written and ready to distribute."

"You fool," Dickens snapped at him, while at the same time throwing that ugly revolver across the room as if it were some distasteful piece of dung that had somehow materialized in his hand, "you do not threaten the Queen. The people love her more than anything English. She is England. No one would ever listen to you if you threaten the Queen."

With that, Dickens turned and walked away from his victim, his hand shaking, his anger subsiding, I feel, into a shocked disbelief at his own behaviour.

"My God, I am getting to be just like Field," I heard

Dickens whisper more to himself than to anyone else in the room.

Dodgson ministered to the wounded Bathgate, gave him a long squeeze of wine from the skin.

"We must get into Oxford and warn them," Dickens turned back to Dodgson and me.

"What about him?" Dodgson queried, a nurse inquiring about a patient.

"We will lock him in here as he locked us in," Dickens's voice hardened once again. "Morse can send someone for him once all this is resolved."

"I will stay with him until he is recovered," Dodgson asserted to Dickens in a voice that brooked no objection. "You t-t-two are much more experienced at this d-d-derring-d-d-do than I. You g-g-go ahead. T-t-take his horse. I will make my way on foot into Oxford when I am assured that this man is c-c-comfortable."

"Do not untie him," Dickens voice was grim with warning. "He is not hurt. If you untie him, he will overpower you, perhaps kill you. Do not untie him."

Dodgson assured Dickens that he realized the danger of the situation: "I will lock him in and follow after you. G-g-go, you must warn them."

"Come, Wilkie," Dickens was already out the door and I hastened to follow. Outside, I got my first view of our place of imprisonment. The stone cottage with its thatched roof seemed to be deep in a very thick, grey wood. The sky was dim and muddy through the sparse winter foliage, but I got the sense that we were up rather high. It was an altogether desolate locale that greeted me, but I did not have more than a moment to contemplate it. Dickens was already mounting Bathgate's horse.

"Here, Wilkie," and he extended his hand, "climb up behind and we shall see if we can find our way out of here."

I just stared at him. I had never liked horses. They were too big and unwieldy (though this particular one seemed one of the smaller of the breeds).

"Good God, Wilkie, climb up," Dickens barked in exasperation. "We don't have all day. There is a plot against the Queen!"

Against all my better judgment, I took his hand and scrambled up behind.

MODERN VERSUS CLASSICAL TRANSPORTATION

৵

(December 14, 1853 — Late Afternoon)

The beast that Dickens forced me to mount was balky. Bathgate's horse was clearly unaccustomed to carrying two rather well-fed Victorian gentlemen as compared to one lean Anarchist. I fell off the rearward end of the horse before the cottage where we had been imprisoned was even out of sight. A squirrel or some other small woodland creature darted across the path and the horse shied to the right, causing me to be jettisoned to the left, where I landed with a thud on the, I must admit, rather soft forest floor.

"Charles, this is ridiculous," I protested from the ground. "The animal is not big enough for two of us."

"Nonsense, Wilkie. You just have to hold on to me. Arms around my waist. Now climb back on. We do not have time for this."

"I could be seriously hurt falling off that brute," I pressed my complaint as I struggled to my feet.

But Dickens would hear none of it: "Climb back on Wilkie, for God's sake. We must hurry back to Oxford. For Queen and Country."

Put in those terms, I really had no choice.

"It is a pity, though," Dickens joked after I had climbed up behind him once again, "that we cannot just put out our little red flag and have Rob gallop up in his growler to transport us."

A pity indeed, I thought, but did not say.

I managed not to fall off again until we reached civilization. As the horse became more accustomed to carrying the two of us, Dickens gradually gave him his head, and soon we were racing through that forest at what I felt was a breakneck pace, but which Dickens dismissed as just "a steady canter."

In my desperation to hold on, I had no idea how far we had galloped when we crested a small rise in the forest lane and emerged out of the trees into a fairly wide country road. With the trees behind us, I realized that we were up at the top of the Cumner Hills. And when Dickens reined in the horse and pointed, I could see the spires of Oxford rising out of the trees in the distance.

"There it is, Wilkie, and this road must take us to it."

With a wider passage, Dickens felt he could go even faster. It seemed to me as if we were racing down that road completely out of control. I held on to Dickens for dear life. We galloped on for what seemed an eternity until we came around a sharp turning and a large stone manor house loomed up directly in front of us.

Startled perhaps by this sudden sign of civilization, Dickens reined in a bit abruptly. This brought our horse to a sudden stop, which caused that worthy to rear up on its hind legs. The result of our horse's gambit was to cause me to slide inelegantly down off its lathered rump and land, with an indecorous thump, on my own posterior in the roadway.

"Oh, sorry, Wilkie," Dickens apologized, walking the horse around me in a tight circle. "I should not have pulled him in so hard. Are you hurt?"

"No, I am not hurt," I scrambled to my feet and brushed myself off, "but I am not getting back on that horse. Twice is quite enough for me. You go on without me and save the precious Queen."

Dickens heard me out and was about to press his arguments as to why I should climb back up behind him yet again when something else caught his eye.

"There, Wilkie," he pointed. "There is the solution to our dilemma."

My eyes followed his outstretched forefinger, but he was simply pointing to the high stone house across the road whose presence in the first place had caused him to rein in and throw me off.

"Here, this will do." Dickens rode over to the front door of the house and dismounted.

I followed and, for the first time, noticed that one of those high-wheeled contraptions, that I later learned was called a penny-farthing, was leaning against the wall of the stone building.

"It is a bicycle," I stupidly stated the obvious.

"Yes, and you can ride it while I ride the horse," it all seemed so simple to Dickens.

I, of course, protested, but to no avail. Dickens would have none of it. He saw this gangly machine of wheels and gears and chains and pedals as the heaven-sent answer to our dilemma. He goaded me into mounting it and gave me my initiatory push down the road before remounting his horse.

"It is not far into Oxford, Wilkie," he shouted as I tottered away from him, trying to balance the two mismatched wheels and steer the contraption along the ruts in the road. "Just keep it upright and follow me."

That was all he needed to say. I immediately tipped that bicycle over sideways and fell off it into the dirt.

Showing considerable patience (for him), Dickens dismounted again and helped me to my feet, all the time coaxing me back onto that rolling machine. "You can do this, Wilkie. It is merely a matter of balance." Then he paused for a moment as if getting a spark of inspiration. "Or would you rather ride the horse and let me try my hand at this thing?"

I would rather have been cut up in little pieces by the mad barber of Fleet Street and cooked in a pie! There was not the slightest chance in the world that I was going to climb back on that creature. Dickens's sly suggestion, for all intents and purposes, ended the discussion. This time I stayed on that contraption longer. In fact, I rode that bicycle without incident all the way to the high road.

When we came out onto that wide thoroughfare, Dickens shouted, "Stop, Wilkie!" That was quite easy for him to say, but much more complicated for me to do. I had no idea either where it was located or how to operate the bicycle's braking mechanism. By the time I realized that it somehow involved a metal rod mounted near the central point of the high front wheel to be operated by the rider's foot, it was too late. I had already sailed past Dickens, and was headed straight for a thick wooden post at the side of the high road. I managed to avoid crashing head-on into that post, but my alternative was a bushy hedge that divided the high road from a partially cleared farmer's field.

"Oh Wilkie, you *are* getting the worst of it." Dickens was all sympathy and concern as he leapt off his horse and helped to extricate me from that prickly hedge. "But we are getting close now. Look here."

He pointed to the signpost planted next to the high road that I had so narrowly missed. The post had three cross-pieces roughly nailed to its top. The uppermost slat, pointing back in the direction whence we had come, had "LONDON" scrawled upon it in some hardy black paint. The other two slats, pointing in our direction, read first "HEAD-INGTON," then "OXFORD."

"I do not know what Headington is," Dickens studied the signs, "but this is the way to Oxford and we shall be there soon."

With that, he leapt back onto his horse and exhorted me: "Climb back on it, Wilkie. I think you have mastered it now.

There will be no more mishaps. We will be in Oxford to warn the Queen in no time. What a story this will be back in London, eh Wilkie? Riding to the rescue of the Queen, Her Majesty herself."

Unenthusiastically, I remounted my iron steed and pedalled assiduously after the captain of my malleable fate. The town of Headington was four buildings decaying at the side of the high road. Two local bumpkins sipping pints at a garden table at a public house watched us go by, then returned to their beer without the slightest glimmer of curiosity. *Just two silly London gentlemen,* they must have thought, if they were capable of thought.

Just outside this Headington hamlet, the high road suddenly dropped off as if we had gone over a cliff. Without warning, we crested a low hump in the road and began to pick up speed at an alarming rate going down. After only seconds, the wheels on my bicycle were racing and I felt as if I was flying into thin air.

Terror was the first emotion to flash in my mind. *My God,* I thought, *if I fall off this thing at this speed, I shall be killed or maimed!*

But then a strange thing happened.

The bicycle sped faster.

I bent forward over the handlebar, clutching on for dear life, trying to hold the huge front wheel to a steady line on the high road.

Then, suddenly, an overwhelming feeling of exhilaration washed over me, cleansing me of all my fear, infusing me with a curious confidence. Dickens was right. I had, indeed, mastered the machine.

I was riding on the wind.

I was free and alive and controlling my destiny at a speed I had never even imagined approaching before.

I looked to my left and Dickens on his horse and I on my wonderful machine were neck and neck racing down that high hill. Leaning hard into the wind, the cold air rushing over me as the wheels whirled and picked up more and yet more speed, I felt what a bird must feel, a feeling of soaring liberation cut loose from the earth, racing on the wind. I never wanted that downhill plummet to end. I felt like Daedalus, finally understanding the power of his wings, and glorying in their speed. I no longer feared my fall.[22] The sheer speed and joy of that downhill flight took over my being as I sped past Dickens. In triumph, I dashed away from him towards the bottom of that steep hill, which I could see racing up to meet me.

I never thought of braking until it was too late.

At the foot of the hill the high road curved and entered a low stone bridge over the Cherwell, a lazy tributary of the Thames. It was called Magdalen Bridge because of its proximity to Magdalen College, the southernmost of the Oxford quadrangles.

I entered the bend in the high road under full control, but I did not see the narrow bridge until it was too late. I tried to apply the stick brake, but I kicked it too hard, and the stick broke off its fragile mount on the bicycle frame and became caught in the spokes of the high front wheel. The result was a lurching, bobbling, side-twisting motion that turned the bicycle into the low stone wall that made up the side of the bridge. This, of course, brought a sudden stop to my downhill flight, which occasioned—as the simple physics of such an event would predict—the launching of my body up and over the handlebar and front wheel of the bicycle, and out and over the side of Magdalen Bridge. I became a projectile. Fortunately, I landed in water deep enough to cushion my fall, and save my back from breaking.

The cold winter water certainly dashed my excitement.

---

[22]In Greek mythology, Daedalus builds wings of feathers and wax for him and his son Icarus to fly out of imprisonment. But, caught up in the freedom and exhilaration of flight, Icarus flies too near the sun, which melts the wax and sends him plummeting to his death. Collins has evidently mistaken the names in this reference or else has conflated Daedalus and Icarus into one.

Two fishermen on the bank bundled in heavy coats barely gave notice to my airborne intrusion into their millpond world. Finally, one of them, who turned out to be a woman, prodded her husband, who had on high Wellingtons, to wade into the water and help me out. By the time this silent river salvage was accomplished and I was dragged, dripping, up onto the bank, Dickens had dismounted and somehow made his way down off the bridge to meet me on the riverbank.

I was soaked to the skin, frozen and bruised, and what does Dickens do? He runs up, smiling like a baboon, tosses a coin and a "thank you" to the muffled fisherman who had helped me out, grabs me by the arm, and without so much as a by-your-leave, starts dragging me up the slippery bank of the roadway.

"Wilkie, I've never seen anything like it," he says. "You were thrown out into the water as if launched from a catapult. Amazing!"

Amazing indeed! I thought. *Amazing that I'm not dead following your lead, you . . . you . . .* even my thoughts were left speechless.

But Dickens, of course, babbled on: "It is getting late in the day, Wilkie. The Queen's cavalcade will be starting soon. We must get you into some dry clothes and warn them of the danger."

"I am not getting back on that mechanical contraption."

"No, no," Dickens reassured me. "I have hailed a passing hansom. It will deliver us to Dodgson's rooms and we will have you in dry clothes in a trice."

I was beginning to shake and shudder from the cold. My coat was actually beginning to freeze in the late afternoon wind. I feared I would catch ague and die. And Dickens? All he could think of was getting on with his bloody detective game, which he was convinced was destined to be the saviour of Queen and Country.

So, as ever, I followed him. I changed into dry clothes as quickly as I could. I tried to suppress the violent chattering of my teeth. I wrapped myself in an old greatcoat of Dodg-son's that we found in his rooms. And, as ever, totally against any judgment I may ever have possessed, I followed Dickens out in pursuit of Field and some resolution to this whole out-of-control affair.

QUEEN VICTORIA'S CAVALCADE

(December 14, 1853 — Early Evening)

We found Field and Morse in the makeshift field headquarters set up in the Oxford Police Station. "We must stop the Queen's cavalcade!" Dickens (with me in tow) burst in upon them just as they were putting on their coats.

"Where 'ave you been?" Field growled. "We 'ave been lookin' for you two the whole day. And Dodgson 'as disappeared as well."

"We were kidnapped to the forest," I offered, then felt very stupid as they just stared at me in disbelief, as if Dickens and I were Hansel and Gretel.

"Kidnapped?" Field gaped.

"Forest?" Morse blinked.

"Yes, yes, it is a long story," Dickens tossed it away, "but we must warn the Queen."

"The Queen's tour of the city 'as already begun 'alf an 'our ago," Field informed us. "We were just going out to see 'er pass up St. Aldate's from the Folly Bridge. 'Olmes gave us 'er route."

"She will never get to here." Dickens protested. "They are

going to blow up one of the boathouses as she passes in front of it."

"Good God!" Field grasped the urgency in Dickens's voice. "We must warn 'Olmes. The Queen will be approaching the boathouses at any moment."

Wrestling themselves into their greatcoats, Field and Morse led us out through the police station and into the street. It was only now that I noticed that lower St. Aldate's was beginning to fill up with people. A line of gawkers stood on the curbstones, with more arriving every moment. The word had spread through the town, and the mob was forming in expectation of the Queen passing.

"She's in an open carriage, she is," a street vendor held forth.

"She's wavin' to everyone as she goes along," another man, speaking with authority, announced. "I saw 'er in the 'Eye Street as she passed by."

"This way," Morse urged us, and sprinted off to the left down St. Aldate's towards Folly Bridge.

We ran after him, and in what seemed only about ten strides, he took a sharp turning to the left into a copse of trees. I recognized the area from my earlier spying on Ellen Ternan from the bridge. The path Morse led us down was narrow and treacherous, its floor man-trapped with roots and ruts. Merciless branches whipped at our faces.

Thank God that it was a narrow copse of trees. We emerged from its gloom fairly quickly onto the wide expanse of wooden boat docks which fronted the boathouses of the Oxford crews.

The docks were lined with people. Each of the college boat crews had mustered in the full regalia of white jerseys, flannel trousers, and peaked wool caps in their school colours. They had ranged their rowing shells on trestles in front of each boathouse for the Queen to view as she passed. In the fading light of day, all of these young men standing to attention by their fragile boats with their oars planted on the ground in straight rows pointing to the sky were quite impressive. Indeed, they resembled small companies of soldiers waiting in formation to be reviewed. It was a colourful wintertime salute to the rowing joys of summer.

This view of pomp and pageantry momentarily stopped us in our tracks. At just that moment, as we stood staring at the ranged legions of oarsmen, the royal procession turned the corner off the stone bridge over the canal at the opposite end of the docks and began its stately progress in our direction.

The high front doors of all the boathouses were open for the purpose of displaying the shells. A single shuttered boathouse was located in the middle of that row of whitewashed buildings. It was the very one that Barnet had indicated was abandoned.

"There," Dickens pointed, "that is the one they are going to blow up."

"We must stop this blasted procession before the Queen gets too near," Field shouted, even as he took off running for the carriages that were just turning on to the docks and proceeding towards us.

The white horses drawing the carriages pranced and tossed their heads to the music as if they were a hurdy-gurdy come to life. The four musicians, huddled in the lead carriage against the wind, played their brass trumpets with all the gusto they could muster. The Queen was in the third carriage, waving graciously at the gawkers and the rowers lined up in front of the boathouses. The route of the procession took her straight across the docks and around the front of the copse of trees on the river side, then up onto Folly Bridge, from whence she and her entourage would proceed on up St. Aldate's and back into the city of Oxford proper.

The four of us, Field in the lead, Dickens close behind, Morse and I bringing up the rear, raced across the docks. About halfway there, following Field's lead, we started waving our arms frantically in the air and shouting for the carriages to stop.

But the procession was too far away to hear us or heed us. Just then, however, a singular apparition in velvet lapels, bowler hat, and dark ebony walking stick stepped out of a group of jerseyed rower boys and, waving his stick, motioned for us to stop, directed us out of the thoroughfare.

"Field, what on earth is it?" Holmes of the Home Office confronted our leader. "Why are you making such a fuss?"

"They are going to blow up the boat'ouse! That closed one there! As the Queen is passing." Field shouted into his face with the strained urgency of a man fearful that a member of his own family was about to perish.

"Inspector, Inspector, it is quite safe here," Holmes reassured Field in a patronizing voice that brought a glare into Field's eye and anger into his voice.

"Safe? You fool!" Field spat at the little man with the walking stick. "They are going to blow up that whole building. Can't you see? They are trying to murder the Queen!"

Field wrenched himself away desperately. The carriages were drawing closer. In but a few moments they would be abreast of the abandoned boathouse.

"There is no need to stop the procession," Holmes shouted in Field's wake. But Field never heard him. He had taken off running once again, straight towards the Queen's carriage. However, Field did not reach the Queen to warn her of her danger.

Holmes of the Home Office waved his walking stick once in a sweeping circle in the air. It was clearly some sort of signal. In answer, three burly men, dressed as college rowers, intercepted Field's headlong dash before he had come close enough to the carriages to capture anyone's attention. They blocked him, tackled him viciously, wrestled him to the ground, and dragged him into the crowd behind a range of shells. They were still fighting to subdue him when we, now following Holmes's lead, came up to them.

"Inspector Field, Inspector Field, calm yourself," Holmes shouted as Field angrily writhed in the clutches of Holmes's three thugs. "The Queen is quite safe."

Field, still clasped tight by the three men, stopped his struggling, stared disbelieving at Holmes.

"We have searched all of the boathouses, including that one," Holmes, smiling annoyingly, explained. "We found no explosives."

"But, but," Dickens stammered, "we have new information that they are trying to blow up the Queen." All of our eyes followed the Queen's carriage as it moved slowly past, the Queen waving to everyone as she went.

Field stopped struggling. Dickens and I watched in horror as the Queen's carriage glided slowly along the docks and passed in front of the abandoned boathouse.

And nothing happened.

The abandoned boathouse did not explode, sending its substance like lethal shrapnel slashing across the docks. The Queen's carriage was not tossed into the air by the concussion. The Queen was not injured or killed. The carriage simply rolled slowly past and away, with the Queen waving to her subjects all the while.

"Let him go," Holmes ordered his three henchmen, who stepped warily away from Field.

Field brushed himself off and seemed none the worse for wear. In fact, he seemed more relieved than angry at the indignities that had been inflicted upon his person.

"Thank God the Queen is safe." Field voiced all of our relief.

"The Queen has always been safe, and always will be," Holmes smugly declared. "If I have anything to say about it. And that is not the Queen," Holmes said the last rather quietly, darting a quick look over his shoulder to ensure that no outsider would hear what he said.

"Not the Queen?" Dickens stared at Holmes in disbelief. "Not the Queen?"

"Do you think I would risk the life of Her Majesty in an open carriage when we know that there are assassins about?" Holmes did not say it unkindly; rather, he said it as if it were a simple fact, easily understood, indisputable. "That is not the Queen. It is an actress who sometimes doubles for the Queen, a counterfeit Queen, if you will. The real Queen Victoria is well guarded and resting in the warm confines of Blenheim Palace."

"Not the Queen." Field was still having trouble fixing this concept as we all watched the counterfeit Queen's carriage disappear around the corner of the woods in the direction of Folly Bridge.

"You 'ave known all along, then, that the Queen is in danger, and that is why you employed this actress?" Field was trying to justify this whole turn of events in his mind.

"Inspector Field," Holmes was making his best effort not to sound patronizing to this older, more experienced hand, "the Queen is always in danger. It is my duty to provide for her security. To seek out threats to her person and stop them before they ever occur. It is my decision whether the Queen or our actress friend there shall be the one to appear in public. Mind you, most often it is the Queen. But sometimes, when circumstances . . . Well, you understand."

"Yes, yes, of course." Field shook his head slowly, doubtfully, as if his firm confidence in reality had been shaken.

'EE'S THE ONE

(December 14, 1853—Evening)

Dusk had fallen. As we made our way back towards the police station it had become quite dark indeed, one of those winter nightfalls where even the gas lamps on the street corners find themselves startled by its suddenness.

"But how was Bathgate so certain that the boathouse would blow up?" Dickens posed that question to the whole group—Field, Morse, Dickens, me, and Holmes—as we proceeded up St. Aldate's in the plummeting darkness.

No one ever got the chance to answer it.

Out of the dark from the direction of Christ Church and the Bulldog rushed Tally Ho Thompson, an uncharacteristic look of panic on his face.

"They 'ave taken Miss Ternan," he rushed up to us. "I went to 'er rooms and she is gone. The door was open and there were signs of a toss-up. I went to the Bulldog and no one was there. I fear she 'as been taken by someone."

It was Dickens's turn to panic then. He turned so white that even in the darkness he looked like one of Scrooge's ghosts.

"They are on to 'er," Inspector Field spoke grimly. "They know she is a spy and they 'ave kidnapped 'er just as they kidnapped you."

"Who has?" Dickens voice was as thin as paper.

"This conspiracy of Dons," Holmes of the Home Office honoured us with his pronounced opinion.

"But there are none of them left," Morse piped in.

"What do you mean?" Holmes said it in a voice that clearly indicated his impatience with anyone who dared to challenge one of his pronouncements.

"Well," it was clear that Morse was carefully thinking this out as he went, "two are dead. Barnet is taken up. Bathgate is tied up in the hills. And that only leaves . . ."

"Squonce. It leaves Squonce." Dickens's voice was desperate.

"Yes. Squonce is at the bottom of this," Field agreed somewhat tentatively, his confidence still a bit shaken, perhaps, in view of Holmes's cavalier tampering with Queen Victoria's identity.

"We must go back to their rooms at Balliol," Dickens proposed. "Perhaps he has her there," his voice could not hide his vain hope, "or perhaps he has left some clue as to where he has taken her," and his voice grew even thinner with despair.

"Yes, it is worth a try," Field humoured him.

Dickens set off at a run up St. Aldate's and the rest of us had no choice but to follow. Up the hill and then down through the Haymarket to St. Giles we went at forced march, no mean feat in the heavy winter dark without all of the gas lamps yet lit. In a trice, we arrived at Wherry Squonce's rooms and found his door standing wide open. Squonce was lying flat on his back on his parlour floor with his eyes wide open and a carving knife driven deep into the centre of his chest.

"Blimey, 'ee's murdered too." Tally Ho Thompson stated the painfully obvious for all of us.

We were gathered in a shocked mob just inside the

doorway to his parlour. All of us, even Field, were getting too large a dose of death in this case.

We all circled the body, looking down at the wide-eyed corpse.

"There is no sign of a struggle in this room." Field's voice was low and grim. He went to one knee beside the body, felt the corpse's face, bent the corpse's arms at the elbow. "This 'as just been done." Field was in a world of his own. " 'Ee is still warm and 'ee 'as not yet begun to stiffen."

"But who killed him?" Holmes of the Home Office posed the question that was on all of our tongues.

"Someone 'ee knew and trusted," Field obliged with a partial, less than satisfactory, answer. "Someone who surprised 'im with this knife, who was very close to 'im when 'ee plunged it into 'is 'art."

"But who?" Dickens's voice was little more than a desperate howl. "And where is Ellen? Oh God!"

"One of the other Dons?" Holmes asked Field.

"Which one?" Morse asked Field.

"Where have they taken Ellen?" Dickens asked Field.

It was as if Field, all of a sudden, was the all-knowing, the omniscient, the god of this fallen world.

"And where is the nitroglycerine?" Field asked himself.

"What do you mean?" Holmes interjected, all of his attention suddenly drawn to Field's line of reasoning. "What about the explosive?" But Holmes did not wait for Inspector Field to answer. His own reasoning overran his own question. "Oh my God!" he exclaimed. "The explosive has not been found, could still be used. But how and where?"

Again, Holmes did not give Field a chance to answer. "Not the Queen. They had their chance to blow her up. Good Lord!" and he turned to Field, who merely nodded. "The P.M.?"

"Yes," Field finally got a word in, "that seems the logical target. All of this fuss about blowing up the Queen was just a diversion to distract us from this terrorist's true intentions."

"It is the P.M. they are after," Holmes tested the idea as if it was too young and inexperienced to trust, "and we don't have a double for him!"

"The Queen was but a decoy," Dickens repeated. "But then, who has the nitroglycerine? And who has kidnapped Ellen?" Dickens's mind and young Holmes's were clearly running in the same direction though towards different destinations: Holmes intent upon saving his country, Dickens upon saving his love.

"If I am seeing it all clearly now," Field said quietly, "there is only one person it can be. My God, I 'ave been such a trusting fool! 'Ee 'as been there all the while, since the very beginning, and we 'ave never noticed 'im, looked right past 'im."

"The P.M. is addressing the college in the Sheldonian Theatre at this very moment," Holmes, utterly preoccupied with the assassination that he foresaw, had not even heard Field's confession. "We must go there at once. They could blow up the P.M.'s carriage. They could throw the nitroglycerine into the crowd around the P.M. My God, they could blow up the stage of the theatre!"

"If I am right about our man," Field led us out of Squonce's parlour at double-time and down the Balliol steps, "we shall find 'im in the crowd at the Sheldonian, and," turning to Dickens, "your Ellen will be with 'im."

Suddenly Dickens stopped in his tracks and whirled in disbelief upon Field. "No!"

"Yes, 'im," Field nodded as if some secret mental message had passed between them.

"For God's sake, who?" I heard myself shouting at the two of them in utter annoyance.

"Yes, who is it?" young Morse echoed me, smashing out his words as if he was about to burst.

"Irish Mike's the one," Inspector Field finally let the cat out of the bag. " 'Ee 'as been lurking around in the middle of this case since the first day we came to Oxford and I never paid any attention to 'im. But 'ee's the one who knew all that was goin' on. 'Ee's the one who knew all of what the Dons were up to. 'Ee's the one who knew that Ellen was the spy and that's why 'ee tried to get 'er out of the way. 'Ee's been the one all along, and we never saw 'im."

"STOP! I AM CHARLES DICKENS!"

(December 14, 1853 — Evening)

All of us in a ragtag group—Field, Dickens, myself, Holmes, young Morse, and Tally Ho Thompson—ran helter-skelter toward the Sheldonian Theatre. The gas lamps were all ablaze as we ran out of Balliol and up St. Giles, then right down the center of Broad Street at full tilt, disregarding the odd carriage or cab, pedestrians dodging out of our way as we bore down upon them and burst past.

The Sheldonian's end of Broad Street was full to brimming with people, a curious crowd gathered in the hopes of catching a glimpse of the Prime Minister. As we reached the outskirts of the mob, first a shout, and then a cheer went up, signalling the Prime Minister's emergence out of the front door of the theatre, where he paused at the top of the high stone steps to wave to the admiring throng.

"He is already out of the theatre," Holmes gasped in panic. "We must find that villain before he attacks the P.M. Go through the crowd, all of you. We must stop him!" And Holmes plunged into the crowd in search of Irish Mike.

All the rest of us were prone to follow his example and search the crowd, but a cooler head prevailed.

"Wait," Field stopped us. "Let 'im go. Thompson, go about the fringes of the crowd that way and look for Ellen and Irish Mike. Do not accost them. Simply stay close to them and observe. If 'ee looks as if 'ee's going to do anything dangerous, jump 'im. Morse, you go that way and do the same."

Those two quickly moved on Field's order and were gone.

Field turned to Dickens and me: "Charles, 'ee 'as the nitroglycerine. 'Ow would 'ee use it to kill the man?"

Dickens thought for a moment: "Well, he probably would not throw it into the crowd. Everyone would see him do it. It would draw too much attention to him. He would try to blow up the P.M. in a way that would allow him to escape."

The Prime Minister was descending the steps of the theatre.

The crowd was cheering and pressing close for a glimpse of power.

Dickens and Field stood in silence for a long moment, lost in thought, searching their minds and imaginations for the answer.

" 'Is coach!"

"His coach!"

They both solved the problem at the same time, Field's voice saying it a mere wisp of a breath before Dickens.

"That's it." Field clapped Dickens on the back. " 'Ee will try to throw the explosive into the P.M.'s coach."

"Or," Dickens grasped a handful of Field's greatcoat, "he has already attached the nitroglycerine to the P.M.'s coach and will blow it up as soon as the man is inside."

"That's it." Field clapped Dickens on the shoulder once again so hard that it knocked Charles backward. "To the wheel. When the coach starts up, it will crush the bottle of explosive and the whole carriage will blow up!"

Our heads turned to the rear of the crowd outside the gate of the Sheldonian courtyard. The stone heads on their pillars frowned down at us. There were three closed carriages pulled up on the far side of Broad Street. Their coachmen, in the Queen's livery, loitered beside their horses. The footmen were two fully kilted Scots Guards who were responsible for the protection of the Prime Minister. The P.M. was slowly descending the steps of the ancient theatre on the way to the security of his coach. The coachmen were taking their seats and picking up their reins in preparation for departure. The Guards came to attention, ready to open the door of the carriage and help the P.M. in.

Field was pushing his way through the cheering crowd with Dickens close behind. Field was actually throwing people out of the way in his progress through the mob. I became separated almost immediately from Dickens and Field as the crowd closed up angrily behind them after they had passed so roughly by. This turned me into little more than an observer of the action.

Field and Dickens broke out of the crowd and onto Broad Street just as the P.M. was clearing the Sheldonian gate. Thank God, the mob, jostling for a view of him, was still holding him up, blocking his way to the carriages.

As Field and Dickens broke through the crowd, they began running directly at the waiting coaches.

The two Scots Guards, vigilant for any possible threat towards their charge, moved to meet these two running men.

"Inspector Field. Metropolitan Protectives," Field was shouting as he bounded towards them. "Police. Police." He was waving his arms in the air like a madman. "The Prime Minister is in danger!"

Dickens was right at Field's shoulder.

Seeing the two Guardsmen advancing militantly upon them, Field stopped dead in the middle of the street, holding up Dickens with an outflung arm, then raising both his hands in the air, palms outstretched towards the advancing soldiers in surrender and appeasement.

"I am Inspector William Field of the Metropolitan Protectives of London," Field explained at the top of his voice, "please hear me out. There is a bomb in the Prime Minister's coach."

Only then did the Guardsmen cease their advance upon these two intruders.

Meanwhile, I was still trapped inside the uncomprehending crowd, whose eyes were on the P.M. and whose backs were turned to the drama being played out in front of the waiting carriages.

All except for one couple. This couple was facing in the opposite direction from all the rest of the crowd.

I caught sight of them out of the corner of my eye as I slowly advanced. They were moving in the same direction as I was, with their eyes riveted upon the confrontation in the street between Dickens and Field and the Guardsmen.

It was Irish Mike, pulling Ellen Ternan by her wrist in his wake. She was clearly a prisoner, under duress, yet unable to resist his superior strength. He dragged her towards the carriages, elbowing people out of his way as he went.

"You must keep the P.M. away and keep the people clear of the carriages," Field was explaining to one of the Guardsmen who had approached him to negotiate.

The P.M., however, had already cleared the crowd and was proceeding at much too fast a pace across the street towards his carriage.

"Get 'oot 'o the street," one Guard ordered, not understanding at all what Field was trying to impress upon him. "I doo na care 'oo yoo har, get 'oot 'o the street." The P.M. was almost to his coach. I think that Dickens and Field simultaneously realized that they could never convince the Scotsman of their good intentions in time. Almost instinctually, as if they could read each other's minds, they darted around him, one to the left, the other to the right. They were past him and the other Guard before those two behemoths could react, and running toward the P.M.'s carriage and the P.M. himself, whom they stopped in his progress toward the coach with a shout.

"Mr. Prime Minister. Your honour. Stop!" Dickens

shouted, running straight at him. "I am Charles Dickens. Please stop. You are in danger!"

I think it was the name more than the warning that stopped the Prime Minister in his tracks. It was probably the only name in the kingdom as famous as his own and the Queen's.

Meanwhile, Field made a beeline for the coaches. He ran up to the P.M.'s coach, and grasping a handful of the coachman's greatcoat, pulled him bodily down off the box.

As the coachman was pulled off, his reins snapped from his hands, and the pair he had been holding in waiting shied and skittishly reared away from their stationary position. The carriage moved only a short distance out into the centre of the street, but it was enough.

I watched in horror from the edge of the crowd. It seemed to happen very slowly, though I know it all took but a whisper of time.

I saw Dickens knocking the P.M. to the ground and covering him with his own body. I saw Field dragging the coachman away from the shying horses. Then the whole scene tore apart. The P.M.'s coach exploded in a hellish fireball. Flames shot straight up in the air and the concussion ripped across the street like a broadside from one of Her Majesty's ships. The gaslit night turned into lurid day. People and horses were knocked to the ground. Flaming debris cartwheeled through the air.

I stared in horror, then covered my head and dived for the ground as everyone else in that crowd was also doing. But I was fascinated by the spectacle of it. I could not take my eyes off the scene. Yet the drama was not yet done. Even as the fragments of the explosion were still falling in the street, I saw Irish Mike with Ellen Ternan still in his tow and a large black revolver in his free hand, advancing upon Dickens and the P.M., who were still lying prone on the ground, stunned perhaps by the concussion of the explosion.

WILKIE ON THE SPOT

❦

(December 14, 1853 — Evening)

I do not remember even thinking about what I was doing. I must have picked myself up off the ground and found my legs rather quickly because I was running full tilt right at Irish Mike's broad back as he dragged Dickens's Ellen across the street. Another man was running at them as well. I caught a glimpse of this one to my right out of the corner of my eye. It was a man in a brown Mackintosh wearing a porkpie hat. Irish Mike must have seen this fellow running towards him because of a sudden he raised his revolver, levelled it at the running man in the Mackintosh, and ordered him to "STAND!"

That running man obeyed. He stopped short and raised his hands in appeasement, palms out, in a gesture that screamed "PLEASE DON'T SHOOT!"

But I was at Irish Mike's back, and, as he levelled his gun at the man in the Mackintosh, he could not see me coming. As I drew near, the sound of my footfall, or the motion of my approach, must have captured his attention, because he suddenly wheeled and the huge black barrel of his gun came swivelling around and levelled off right between my eyes. Looking into that gun barrel was like looking into a dark cave.

But I was already upon him. He had turned too late. I launched myself at the last instant and careened into Irish Mike's chest just as the gun went off and the sound exploded over me.

I was sure that I was dead. I was certain that I had been shot between the eyes and Tally Ho Thompson was picking my body up off the street of either heaven or hell. I facetiously hoped it was the former, but dreaded it was the latter because of the sharp smell of burning wood and gunpowder that seemed all around.

"Well done, Mr. Collins!" Tally Ho Thompson was babbling at me for some incomprehensible reason. "You laid 'im out like 'ee'd been 'it by a beer barrel."

"Bravo, Wilkie!" Inspector Field was also brushing me off for some reason. "On the spot you are."

It took me a long moment to realize that all of this adulation was aimed at me and that I was very much alive and being treated like some sort of hero in the middle of Broad Street, Oxford. In another moment I remembered what I was doing when the gun went off, and I looked around and saw Irish Mike lying on the ground with the two Scots Guardsmen hobbling him. Dickens was there too, with his arms around his Ellen, who was sobbing into his chest. And Holmes of the Home Office was standing with the Prime Minister of England, with the crowd gawking and gaping at the lot of us.

"We've got 'im, Wilkie!" Field seemed to be shouting right into my face. "You knocked 'im right off 'is pins."

And that is when my knees began to buckle and the air seemed to go all furry around me. I looked to Dickens and Field for help, to steady me, but they were dancing like madmen in my vision. Alas, dear reader, I fear I fainted.

AROUND THE WASSAIL BOWL

૭ઌ

(December 15, 1853—Evening)

I t was only later, the evening of the following day, that we finally sorted it all out. It had been a long day for Field and Morse and Holmes of the Home Office, writing it all down, recording and preserving all of the evidence against Irish Mike and the conspiracy of Dons. At half six, we gathered, all the principals in the case—Field, Rogers, young Morse, Dickens, myself, Ellen Ternan, even Tally Ho Thompson and Sleepy Rob—in Dodgson's rooms at his invitation. Holmes sent his regrets, saying that he could not attend because he was called back to London on pressing affairs of state. "More like pressing Prince Albert's trousers," Serjeant Rogers laughed, and we all joined in.

Despite the gravity of the recent events and the discussion of such serious topics as murder, assassination, conspiracy, blackmail, and drug addiction, it was really quite a convivial party. Dodgson felt that it was high time we were given a taste of the Christmas spirit. Of course, no one was more enthusiastic about this little Christmas party than Dickens. He loved Christmas. I think it brought out the child in him that he always seemed to be pursuing.

We gathered around a large wassail bowl warming on Dodgson's hearth. He had even gone to the extravagance of hanging and draping some Christmas greenery about. Pine boughs and sprigs of holly decorated the books and furniture and various machines about his parlour. The pungent smell of the wassail punch, its nutmeg and clove scents, filled the room. A few cups of it brought smiles to our faces and loosened our tongues. Cigars were lit. Cakes were consumed. Many questions were answered.

"What I simply c-c-cannot understand," Dodgson made the opening gambit, "is why Irish Mike d-d-did it all, k-k-killed Ackroyd, Stadler, and Squonce, and attempted to assassinate the P.M. He d-d-did not seem like a p-p-political zealot."

" 'Ee wasn't," Field leapt to the answer. " 'Ee didn't give a 'ang for politics. 'Ee did it all out of love and 'ate and grief and revenge. Seven years ago, by mistake, some English soldiers killed 'is daughter in a skirmish with some Irish rebels in Waterville. The provos ambushed the English boys outside a pub that Mike owned. 'Is little daughter, only eight years old, was sleepin' in an upstairs room and an errant ball killed 'er in 'er bed. It drove Mike's wife mad, and two months later she drowned 'erself in a millpond. After that, Mike sold everything up and skipped out for England with revenge festerin' 'in 'is 'eart. 'Ee bided 'is time and waited on 'is chance, and these political Dons and their scheme to scare the Queen was just what 'ee was waitin' for."

"But why did he kill Ackroyd?" Dodgson, who had missed out on almost everything whilst making his way out of the Cumner Hills on foot, finally had his opportunity to exercise his curiosity.

"Irish Mike was selling drugs, opium, to Ackroyd," Field picked up the story, "and blackmailin' 'im to boot. Most of Ackroyd's money went to Mike. We found a ledger book in Mike's rooms at the Bulldog."

"But Ackroyd would not have much money to pay Irish Mike," Dodgson was puzzled. "An Oxford Don, especially a

233

historian, makes a very small stipend. Believe me, I know, mathematics is not much better."

"The ledger shows that Ackroyd paid a regular sum each month to Irish Mike by cheque. But you are right," Field bowed to Dodgson, "the sums were not large. Morse and I feel that these regular sums were for the opium, to support Ackroyd's addiction. The blackmail was of a very different sort."

"What do you mean?" Dickens interposed. "Blackmail is blackmail, especially in these times."[23]

"Ah," Field raised his formidable forefinger to correct Dickens, "but this was an uncommon sort of blackmail."

"In what way?" Dickens's, and all the rest of our curiosity was piqued.

"Irish Mike was blackmailin' 'im for service, for formin' the conspiracy and plantin' the seeds of violence in 'is fellow Dons."

Field possessed everyone's attention now.

"You see," Field went on, "Mike needed someone to lead this conspiracy against the Queen and the P.M. Mike was in no position to control the plot. Oxford Dons would never follow a mere publican. But they would listen to one of their own. Ackroyd was perfect for 'im. 'Ee was an expert on gunpowder plots."

"So Ackroyd, to keep his drug addiction quiet," Dodgson

[23]Dickens's comment on the phenomenon of blackmail is quite a perceptive one and demonstrates his social acuity. In the Victorian age, anyone in a socially visible position of trust, such as an academic, and especially an Oxford Don, was extremely vulnerable to blackmail. Opium addiction would be an offense against the high public morality of the Victorian age. Ackroyd would surely have lost his position, thus his identity and livelihood, if it had come out. Silence was a valuable commodity in the capitalist economy of the Victorian age, and it was regularly bought and sold as a means of mediating between one's role in that very public and proper society and one's private life.

ruminated aloud, "became Irish Mike's familiar, his Mephistopheles."[24]

" 'Is who?" Rogers forthrightly displayed his ignorance.

"Ackroyd became Irish Mike's voice and created the conspiracy of Dons," Dodgson explained.

"That's it." Field thumped the table.

"But why then did Irish Mike kill Ackroyd?" Dickens followed the logical track of the story. "I presume it was Irish Mike who did it?"

"Yes, of course it was," Field concurred without hesitation. "Mike took the train to London and shot Ackroyd in the street in Lime'ouse 'Ole."

"But why?" Dickens pressed.

"The original plan was not to 'urt the Queen at all, just send an explosive message to 'er. It was the Turkish War and the greed of Empire that Ackroyd used as the 'ook. The Queen visits Oxford at least once a year. Irish Mike 'ad been cultivatin' the political Dons for years, waitin' for 'is chance. When they showed their anti-monarchy stripes, 'ee planted the seeds in their drunken minds that they ought to stage some protest during the Queen's visit. But then 'ee raised the stakes in the game. 'Ee forced Ackroyd to pursue the harmless bomb plan to throw a scare into the Queen and to draw attention to their message about the Turkish-Russian War." Field paused for breath and a sip of Dodgson's pungent punch.

"And the Dons went for it?" Dickens, exhibiting his usual impatience, pressed Field to continue his narrative.

"Yes, they did," Field answered, "as long as no one was goin' to be 'urt and no one would know they did it."

"But that still does not explain why Irish Mike had to go to London and shoot Ackroyd." Dickens's curiosity was brimming over.

"Because Mike, who controlled Ackroyd, changed the

[24]Dodgson is referring to Satan's representative devil, who barters for the soul of Dr. Faustus in Marlowe's famous play.

plan in the late stages. 'Ee wanted Ackroyd and Stadler the chemist to actually blow up the Queen."

As evidenced by the moment of hushed silence all around the room, the very idea of bringing harm to Queen Victoria was still a hard pill for any of us to swallow.

"When Ackroyd balked at assassinating the Queen, and then later the P.M. as well, Irish Mike killed him."

"Why did Irish Mike rifle Ackroyd's rooms in college?" Dodgson's curiosity took its turn.

" 'Ee didn't. 'Ee sent Jack Bathgate to do that one," Field answered. " 'Ee controlled them all. 'Ee was blackmailin' all of them. 'Ee threatened to make an issue of Bathgate and Squonce's Sodomite ways. Barnet for 'is liaisons with all manner of women in the college boat'ouse. Stadler for 'is affection for young boys. Bathgate was the one who smoked the little cigars. 'Ee tossed Ackroyd's rooms. We found the missing pages from the appointments book in Bathgate's rooms and Bathgate confessed to all of it once we got 'is nose repaired from gettin' it in the face with whatever you blokes 'it 'im with," and Field chuckled pleasantly at that last.

"But that's not all we found in Squonce and Bathgate's rooms," Serjeant Rogers added his tuppence to his master's narrative.

"Oh yes," Field continued with a frown at Rogers's unsolicited prompting, "we found all manner of papers. Designs for the bomb, street maps. A complete 'istory of the conspiracy. Manifestoes to appear after the bombing. It was all there. Some of it verging on madness, I'd say."

"If it was madness," Dickens became philosophical, "then Mike always served it up with a smile."

"Yes," Field thumped the table, "that was where I went all wrong in this case. 'Ee was right in front of me all the time and I never saw 'im."

"None of us suspected him," Dodgson commiserated.

"But I should 'ave," Field flagellated himself. " 'Ee knew that Miss Ternan was one of ours. 'Ee knew why Charles and

Wilkie were 'ere in Oxford. 'Ee knew when we started get-tin' close to the Dons' plot."

"So that is why he attacked Ellen in the street that night?" Dickens saw the light for all of us.

"That's it," Field thumped the deal table with his forefin-ger once again, " 'ee felt she was 'earin' too much, that we were gettin' too close, and the visit of the Queen and the P.M. was only a few days away. 'Ee feared it was all goin' to come out before 'ee got a chance for 'is revenge."

"But he killed Stadler, the Chemistry Don, on the same night that Ellen was attacked," I refreshed all of their mem-ories. "Why?"

"Same two reasons," Field leapt to his answer. He was really getting caught up in the telling of his story. "Same reason 'ee attacked Miss Ternan. Same reason 'ee killed Ackroyd. Stadler was talkin' too much, in the pub, to you and Charles that night 'ee sat down with you. And Stadler was also gettin' cold feet just as Ackroyd 'ad. But most im-portant, Stadler 'ad the nitroglycerine and Irish Mike knew 'ee 'ad to 'ave that in order to blow anything up."

"Inspector Field?" Ellen Ternan's soft voice startled all of us. It was so different from all of the contending voices that had so dominated this conversation thus far. "If Mike was my attacker, who was that other man who drove him off?"

"That was 'Olmes's man in the Mackintosh coat and the porkpie hat." Field smiled at her in an almost fatherly way. "When 'ee saw Thompson 'ere gettin' the worst of it from Irish Mike, 'ee stepped in. 'Olmes put 'im on the case right away after Ackroyd was shot to keep an eye on our investi-gation. That devious little sod could 'ave told us about 'im, but 'ee didn't," Field finished indignantly.

"But how did Mike do it?" Ellen's curiosity took over. "He was in the pub when I left that night, but then he was wait-ing for me in the dark of Blue Boar Street."

" 'Ee took a shortcut through the Christ Church quad-rangle. After you left, 'ee popped out the front door of the

Bulldog and got through the Tom Tower gate without being seen."

"I cannot understand how he did that," Dickens interrupted Field. "We were rushing down those steps at that very moment to follow Ellen. We saw her leave the pub through Dodgson's telescope."

"Yes," Field thought on it, "it must 'ave been close timin' and it was the darkest of nights. You could only 'ave seen Miss Ternan in the telescope if she passed under a gas lamp in the street. You were lookin' for 'er in the street lamps as she went up the street. You were payin' no attention to the Bulldog, which was dark as pitch when Irish Mike came out. 'Ee must 'ave gotten through the Tom Tower gate before you three came rushin' down the stairs."

"We d-d-did wake up the p-p-porter when we c-c-came d-d-down," Dodgson offered. "I remember him c-c-coming out, rubbing his eyes."

"After Mike crossed the quadrangle, 'ee took that tunnel through the buildin's," Inspector Field picked up the narrative. "What is it called?" and he turned to Dodgson for verification.

"The P-P-Peckwater P-P-Passage," Dodgson supplied.

"Yes, that's it," Field agreed. "That got 'im around in front of Miss Ternan. 'Ee was waitin' for 'er to walk right into 'is little trap. And she did."

"Thank God for Tally Ho," Ellen beamed at her saviour across the room, causing Thompson to tip her a wink and causing a sour twitch to begin at Dickens's pursed mouth and spread tightly across his face. He wanted to be the only St. George in Ellen Ternan's life.

"Yes, that's right. Thompson stopped the assault, for Mike did not want to rape you. 'Ee was out to strangle you dead. 'Ee did not want you ruinin' 'is plans."

" 'Ee might still 'ave succeeded," Thompson laughed, not really believing his own modesty, "if that bloke of 'Olmes 'adn't come along."

"Oh, that was not chance," Field corrected Thompson.

"That one 'ad you all under surveillance the 'ole time. 'Ee stepped in only when 'ee saw 'ee 'ad to. 'Olmes told us all of that."

"Why was Holmes so involved in this whole affair?" Dickens asked Field.

" 'Is duty is to protect the Queen and the P.M. and whoever else of that lot needs protection. 'Ee is in charge of Whitehall security. 'Ee looks young, but they've given 'im a big job."

"So Irish Mike fails in his attempt to kill Ellen," Dickens prompted Field, "and then he goes straight to Stadler's rooms and murders him?"

"Not right away, we don't think. We think that when Thompson and 'Olmes's man and then you all came chargin' up, that drove 'im off. Then 'ee 'id some place in the quad, waitin' for it all to die down. That's most likely when 'ee decided to solve 'is other problem. You see, 'ee killed Stadler with Stadler's own kitchen knife. 'Ee wasn't plannin' to kill 'im because 'ee didn't bring 'is own weapon along. 'Ee was afraid that Stadler in 'is drunkenness would talk too much and give the 'ole plot away. 'Ee 'ad seen Stadler sittin' at the table with all of you," Field nodded at Dickens, Dodgson and me, "and 'ee didn't like the way it looked."

"Is that why he had Squonce and Bathgate kidnap us?" Dickens was truly caught up in all of this revelation.

"You were gettin' too close, and it was the day before the Queen and the P.M.'s visit, and 'ee was afraid you would ruin it all. 'Ee 'ad already killed two people. 'Ee ad to get you out of the way so that 'ee could explode 'is bombs without interference."

"But why d-d-did he murder Wherry Squonce?" Dodgson's curiosity loosed one more arrow in Field's direction.

"Per'aps out of blind anger, per'aps out of fear of exposure. 'Ee would 'ave killed Miss Ternan too, if 'is plan to blow up the P.M. had succeeded."

"What do you mean, blind anger?" Dickens questioned that curious conclusion.

"We think, 'Olmes and me, that 'ee wanted to blow them both up, but 'ee saw all of us come runnin' up to the Queen's carriage wavin' our arms and 'ee knew that you two," and he cast a quick look at Dickens and me, " 'ad escaped Squonce and Bathgate's custody and were out to ruin 'is plot."

"So he was angry at Squonce and Bathgate for their failure t-t-to k-k-keep us p-p-prisoner?" Dodgson was trying to follow it all.

"Per'aps. Who knows?" Field made it clear that he was only speculating. "We think 'ee was 'idin' in the abandoned boat'ouse waitin' to throw a nitroglycerine bomb at the Queen's carriage when we ruined 'is plan. So 'ee fled the boat'ouse and came back to the Bulldog where 'ee 'ad left Miss Ternan in charge. Then 'ee took 'er," and Field turned to Miss Ternan, who wobbled her head in the affirmative, "and forced 'er to go to Squonce's digs in Balliol College. Miss Ternan was locked in the entrance hall cupboard while Irish Mike talked to—I should say murdered—Squonce. Then 'ee took Miss Ternan with 'im to carry out the second 'alf of 'is plan, against the P.M."

"Why did he not murder Ellen as well?" Dickens asked in a voice that was almost trembling with emotion.

" 'Olmes thought 'ee was using 'er for a sort of disguise; the happy couple, that sort of thing. Per'aps 'ee thought no one would pay attention to 'im if she was 'is companion. Per'aps, per'aps, who knows 'ow 'is mind was racin'?"

"Well, all's well that ends well." Dodgson raised his glass to Inspector Field. "Well d-d-done, sir!" he toasted him.

But Field was determined to have the last word.

"Thank you, but I take no joy in bringin' this one to the gallows. These Irish troubles destroyed 'is 'ole life—first 'is child, then 'is wife—turned 'im mad with grief and 'ate. No, sir, no, I will take no joy in his dance with Jack Ketch."

We were all a bit surprised at this outburst on Field's part. He was never a man of strong feelings on the outside.

One final—call it "historical"—event, put a full stop upon

this strange case of the Oxford Christmas Plot (as we came to call it in ensuing years). Dodgson set up his photographic contraption and took all of our portraits.

Thompson and Sleepy Rob refused his invitation for quite different reasons: Thompson to preserve his mysteriousness, I am sure; Rob out of simple fear of the machine. But young Morse, thinking it all a great lark, and Ellen, smiling sweetly, both sat for Dodgson. Then Dickens forcefully suggested that he, Field, and I all be taken together. Dodgson sat us all down on his loveseat, Dickens in the middle (where else?), and disappeared beneath the black cloth of his spindly machine.

With a hiss, and a flash, and a puff of smoke, Dodgson made us all immortal. Charles's photograph was taken many times in the years that followed this Oxford affair, but to this day I think that this is the only photograph of him and Inspector Field together.

TWO CHRISTMASES

(*December 25, 1871*)

When I went to visit Dickens's Ellen last Christmas, the Christmas after Dickens's death, those brown and faded photographs were sitting in lovely shell frames on her mantelpiece. Ellen's picture showed a smart and smiling young woman, gazing confidently into Dodgson's camera. The other showed the three of us—Field, Dickens in the middle, myself—staring rather stiffly at the camera as if we were poachers stopped in our tracks by some gamekeeper's blunderbuss. The two photographs sitting side by side overlooking our meagre little Christmas celebration made the three of us look like suitors to Ellen Ternan's beauty; made me remember how much in love we all were at the time: Dickens with his Ellen, me with my Meggy, Field with the chase and the mystery and the detective life.

I remembered how, when we all returned from Oxford, Meggy was so glad to see me.

"Oh Wilkie, I missed you." She pressed me to her capacious bosoms. Later, after she had ardently made me feel quite at home again, as we were dressing, she smiled mischievously and announced, "I've got a little surprise for you."

She led me into our darkened parlour, which we had by-passed in our rush to the bedroom, and lit a gas lamp. As the light grew and spread throughout the room, it revealed a quite magical scene. The whole room, from the mantel over the hearth to the velvet wing chair to the tall candle-sticks to the loveseat to the deal table to the sideboard to the very doorway in which we stood, was draped and hung and wound and garnished with all manner of Christmas greenery, pine branches, and holly sprigs, cones and boughs and twists of berried branches. The Christ Child rested in state in his manger on the sideboard as the Three Wise Men peered out of a forest of pine boughs in wonder.

And in the very centre of the room, all green and fresh and innocent, sat a lovely little Christmas tree. All around it on the floor were marshalled brightly coloured orna-ments, most made of paper, some of tin and glass.

"I cut them out myself, Wilkie," my Meggy was so proud of her surprise, "except for a few that I saw in some shop windows and just couldn't resist," and she picked up a silver angel and waved it in front of my awestruck face.

I was truly speechless. Irish Meg had turned our modest rooms into a Christmas wonderland.

"Oh Wilkie, I've always wanted to 'ave a real Christmas. I've never 'ad one, livin' on the streets as I was before you took me up. It's going to be a real Christmas this year, Wilkie, just like a real family. We'll have Charles and Ellen in, and Tally Ho Thompson and Inspector Field and Ser-jeant Rogers, and Sleepy Rob the cabman, and we'll serve a wassail punch and cinnamon buns." She was carried away with her enthusiasm for it all. "Say something, Wilkie," she laughed, with her eyes sparkling. "Isn't it beautiful? Won't it be a great lark?"

One could not help but be carried away by her excite-ment.

"It is truly wonderful and amazing." I clasped her in my arms and swung her around the room. "Yes, yes, we shall do just that. We shall have a Christmas party to end all Christmas parties."

And that is exactly what we did. We all celebrated Christmas together, albeit two days early since Dickens, naturally, had to spend Christmas at Broadstairs with his family. We laughed and sang and my Meggy importuned Ellen Ternan to tell her every detail of her adventure as a barmaid in the employ of a murderer in Oxford. Ellen told it all vividly, and Dickens and Field, magnanimous in the spirit of the season, graciously acquiesced to her lively version of the story.

"Never ever shall you be placed in that sort of jeopardy again." Dickens attempted to usurp the last word when she had brought the whole story of our adventures in Oxford to an end.

"Actually, I rather enjoyed working in that pub," Ellen rebuffed him coquettishly. "The gents were quite attentive," she teased. "It was not at all a bad way to serve Queen and Country."

As I sat in Ellen's tiny parlour that sad Christmas after Charles's death, I remembered that glorious Christmas party so long ago. I thought of mentioning it, but I did not. She has her own memories and I have mine.

Two Christmases. Two very different situations. Two people sharing the kinship of our silent memories. Both of our lives for so long had been entwined in his. Dickens gave us the excitement in our lives. He gave us the gift of his love, his friendship, and his art.